LOTTA SCHMIDT AND OTHER STORIES

ANTHONY TROLLOPE, the fourth of six surviving children, was born on 24 April 1815 in London. As he describes in his *Autobiography*, poverty and debt made his childhood acutely unhappy and disrupted his education: his school fees at Harrow and Winchester were frequently unpaid. His family attempted to restore their fortunes by going to America, leaving the young Anthony alone in England, but it was not until his mother, Frances, began to write that there was any improvement in the family's finances. Her success came too late for her husband, who died in exile in Belgium in 1835. Trollope was unable to afford a university education, and in 1834 he became a junior clerk in the Post Office. He achieved little until he was appointed Surveyor's Clerk in Ireland in 1841. There he worked hard, travelled widely, took up hunting and still found time for his literary career. He married Rose Heseltine, the daughter of a bank manager, in 1844; they had two sons, one of whom emigrated to Australia. Trollope frequently went abroad for the Post Office and did not settle in England again until 1859. He is still remembered as the inventor of the letter-box. In 1867 he resigned from the Post Office and became the editor of *St Paul's Magazine* for the next three years. He failed in his attempt to enter Parliament as a Liberal in 1868. Trollope took his place among London literary society and counted William Thackeray, George Eliot and G. H. Lewes among his friends. He died on 6 December 1882 as the result of a stroke.

Anthony Trollope wrote forty-seven novels and five volumes of short stories as well as travel books, biographies and collections of sketches. The Barsetshire series and the six Palliser or 'political' books were the first novel-sequences to be written in English. His works offer an unsurpassed portrait of the professional and landed classes of Victorian England. In his *Autobiography* (published posthumously in 1883) Trollope describes the self-discipline that enabled his prolific output: he would produce a given number of words per hour in the early morning, before work; he always wrote while travelling by rail or sea, and as soon as he finished one novel he began another. His efforts resulted in his becoming one of England's most successful and popular writers.

Lotta Schmidt and Other Stories (1867) is Trollope's third volume of short stories and, like its predecessors, it draws on the author's travels abroad and within Britain on behalf of the Post Office. All the stories had been previously printed in collections of original work or the magazines *The Argosy* (later to be owned by Mrs Henry Wood) or *Good Words*. It was the editor of *Good Words* who rejected *Rachel Ray* (1863) on the grounds that it contained scenes of dancing.

LOTTA SCHMIDT
AND OTHER STORIES

ANTHONY
TROLLOPE

PENGUIN BOOKS

PENGUIN BOOKS

Published by the Penguin Group
Penguin Books Ltd, 27 Wrights Lane, London W8 5TZ, England
Penguin Books USA Inc., 375 Hudson Street, New York, New York 10014, USA
Penguin Books Australia Ltd, Ringwood, Victoria, Australia
Penguin Books Canada Ltd, 10 Alcorn Avenue, Toronto, Ontario, Canada M4V 3B2
Penguin Books (NZ) Ltd, 182–190 Wairau Road, Auckland 10, New Zealand

Penguin Books Ltd, Registered Offices: Harmondsworth, Middlesex, England

First published 1867
Published in Penguin Books 1993
1 3 5 7 9 10 8 6 4 2

Printed in England by Clays Ltd, St Ives plc

re-sold, hired out, or otherwise circulated without the publisher's
prior consent in any form of binding or cover other than that in
which it is published and without a similar condition including the
condition being imposed on the subsequent purchaser

CONTENTS

LOTTA SCHMIDT.

S all the world knows, the old fortifications of Vienna have been pulled down,—the fortifications which used to surround the centre or kernel of the city; and the vast spaces thus thrown open and forming a broad ring in the middle of the town have not as yet been completely filled up with those new buildings and gardens which are to be there, and which, when there, will join the outside city and the inside city together, so as to make them into one homogeneous whole.

The work, however, is going on, and if the war which has come and passed has not swallowed everything appertaining to Austria into its maw, the ugly remnants of destruction will be soon carted away, and the old glacis will be made bright with broad pavements, and gilded railings, and well-built lofty mansions, and gardens beautiful with shrubs, and beautiful with turf also, if Austrian patience can make turf to grow beneath an Austrian sky.

On an evening of September, when there was still something left of daylight, at eight o'clock, two girls were walking together in the Burgplatz, or large open space which lies between the city palace of the emperor and the gate which passes thence from the old town out to the new town. Here at present stand two bronze equestrian statues, one of the Archduke Charles, and the other of Prince Eugene. And they were standing there also, both of them, when these two girls were walking round them ; but that of the prince had not as yet been uncovered for the public.

There was coming a great gala day in the city, Emperors and empresses, archdukes and grand-dukes, with their archduchesses and grand-duchesses, and princes and ministers, were to be there, and the new statue of Prince Eugene was to be submitted to the art-critics of the world. There was very much thought at Vienna of the statue in those days. Well ; since that, the statue has been submitted to the art-critics, and henceforward it will be thought of as little as any other huge bronze figure of a prince on horseback. A very ponderous prince is poised in an impossible position, on an enormous dray horse. But yet the thing is grand, and Vienna is so far a finer city in that it possesses the new equestrian statue of Prince Eugene.

"There will be such a crowd, Lotta," said the elder of the two girls, "that I will not attempt it. Besides, we shall have plenty of time for seeing it afterwards."

"Oh, yes," said the younger girl, whose name was Lotta Schmidt; "of course we shall all have enough of the old prince for the rest of our lives; but I should like to see the grand people sitting up there on the benches; and there will be something nice in seeing the canopy drawn up. I think I will come. Herr Crippel has said that he would bring me, and get me a place."

"I thought, Lotta, you had determined to have nothing more to say to Herr Crippel."

"I don't know what you mean by that. I like Herr Crippel very much, and he plays beautifully. Surely a girl may know a man old enough to be her father without having him thrown in her teeth as her lover."

"Not when the man old enough to be her father has asked her to be his wife twenty times, as Herr Crippel has asked you. Herr Crippel would not give up his holiday afternoon to you if he thought it was to be for nothing."

"There I think you are wrong, Marie. I believe Herr Crippel likes to have me with him simply because every gentleman likes to have a lady on such a day as that. Of course it is better than being alone. I don't suppose he will say a word to me except to tell me who the people are, and to give me a glass of beer when it is over."

It may be as well to explain at once, before we go any further, that Herr Crippel was a player on the violin, and that he led the musicians in the orchestra of the great beer-hall in the Volksgarten. Let it not be thought that because Herr Crippel exercised his art in a beer-hall therefore he was a musician of no account. No one will think so who has once gone to a Vienna beer-hall, and listened to such music as is there provided for the visitors.

The two girls, Marie Weber and Lotta Schmidt, belonged to an establishment in which gloves were sold in the Graben, and now, having completed their work for the day,—and indeed their work for the week, for it was Saturday evening,—had come out for such recreation as the evening might afford them. And on behalf of these two girls, as to one of whom at least I am much interested, I must beg my English readers to remember that manners and customs differ much in Vienna from those which prevail in London.

Were I to tell of two London shop girls going out into the streets after their day's work, to see what friends and what amusement the fortune of the evening might send to them, I should be supposed to be speaking of young women as to whom it would be better that I should be silent; but these girls in Vienna were doing simply that which all their friends would expect and wish them to do. That they should have some amusement to soften the rigours of long days of work was recognised to be necessary; and music, beer, dancing, with the conversation of young men, are thought in Vienna to be the natural amusements of young women, and in Vienna are believed to be innocent.

The Viennese girls are almost always attractive in their appearance, without often coming up to our English ideas of prettiness. Sometimes they do fully come up to our English idea of beauty. They are generally dark, tall, light in figure, with bright eyes, which are however very unlike the bright eyes of Italy, and which constantly remind the traveller that his feet are carrying him eastward in Europe. But perhaps the peculiar characteristic in their faces which most strikes a stranger is a certain look

of almost fierce independence, as though they had recognised the necessity, and also acquired the power, of
standing alone, and of protecting themselves. I know
no young women by whom the assistance of a man's arm
seems to be so seldom required as the young women of
Vienna. They almost invariably dress well, generally
preferring black, or colours that are very dark ; and they
wear hats that are, I believe, of Hungarian origin, very
graceful in form, but which are peculiarly calculated to
add something to that assumed savageness of independence of which I have spoken.

Both the girls who were walking in the Burgplatz were
of the kind that I have attempted to describe. Marie
Weber was older, and not so tall, and less attractive
than her friend ; but as her position in life was fixed,
and as she was engaged to marry a cutter of diamonds,
I will not endeavour to interest the reader specially in
her personal appearance. Lotta Schmidt was essentially
a Viennese pretty girl of the special Viennese type. She
was tall and slender, but still had none of that appearance of feminine weakness which is so common among
us with girls who are tall and slim. She walked as
though she had plenty both of strength and courage for
all purposes of life without the assistance of any extraneous aid. Her hair was jet-black, and very plentiful,

and was worn in long curls which were brought round from the back of her head over her shoulders. Her eyes were blue,—dark blue,—and were clear and deep rather than bright. Her nose was well formed, but somewhat prominent, and made you think at the first glance of the tribes of Israel. But yet no observer of the physiognomy of races would believe for half a moment that Lotta Schmidt was a Jewess. Indeed, the type of form which I am endeavouring to describe is in truth as far removed from the Jewish type as it is from the Italian ; and it has no connexion whatever with that which we ordinarily conceive to be the German type. But, overriding everything in her personal appearance, in her form, countenance, and gait, was that singular fierceness of independence, as though she were constantly asserting that she would never submit herself to the inconvenience of feminine softness. And yet Lotta Schmidt was a simple girl, with a girl's heart, looking forward to find all that she was to have of human happiness in the love of some man, and expecting and hoping to do her duty as a married woman and the mother of a family. Nor would she have been at all coy in saying as much had the subject of her life's prospects become matter of conversation in any company ; no more than one lad would be coy in saying that he hoped to

be a doctor, or another in declaring a wish for the
army.

When the two girls had walked twice round the
hoarding within which stood all those tons of bronze
which were intended to represent Prince Eugene, they
crossed over the centre of the Burgplatz, passed under
the other equestrian statue, and came to the gate leading
into the Volksgarten. There, just at the entrance, they
were overtaken by a man with a fiddle-case under his
arm, who raised his hat to them, and then shook hands
with both of them.

"Ladies," he said, "are you coming in to hear a little
music? We will do our best."

"Herr Crippel always does well," said Marie Weber.
"There is never any doubt when one comes to hear
him."

"Marie, why do you flatter him?" said Lotta.

"I do not say half to his face that you said just now
behind his back," said Marie.

"And what did she say of me behind my back?" said
Herr Crippel. He smiled as he asked the question, or
attempted to smile, but it was easy to see that he was
too much in earnest. He blushed up to his eyes, and
there was a slight trembling motion in his hands as he
stood with one of them pressed upon the other

As Marie did not answer at the moment, Lotta replied for her.

" I will tell you what I said behind your back. I said that Herr Crippel had the firmest hand upon a bow, and the surest fingers among the strings, in all Vienna— when his mind was not wool-gathering. Marie, is not that true ? "

' I do not remember anything about the wool-gather-ing," said Marie.

" I hope I shall not be wool-gathering to-night; but I shall doubtless ;— I shall doubtless, — for I shall be thinking of your judgment. Shall I get you seats at once ? There; you are just before me. You see I am not coward enough to fly from my critics," and he placed them to sit at a little marble table, not far from the front of the low orchestra in the foremost place in which he would have to take his stand.

" Many thanks, Herr Crippel," said Lotta. " I will make sure of a third chair, as a friend is coming."

" Oh, a friend ! " said he ; and he looked sad, and all his sprightliness was gone.

" Marie's friend," said Lotta, laughing. " Do not you know Carl Stobel ? "

Then the musician became bright and happy again. " I would have got two more chairs if you would have let me; one for the fraulein's sake, and one for his own. And I will come down presently, and you shall present me, if you will be so very kind."

Marie Weber smiled and thanked him, and declared that she should be very proud;—and the leader of the band went up into his place.

"I wish he had not placed us here," said Lotta.

"And why not?"

"Because Fritz is coming."

"No!"

"But he is."

"And why did you not tell me?"

"Because I did not wish to be speaking of him. Of course you understand why I did not tell you. I would rather it should seem that he came of his own account,— with Carl. Ha, ha!" Carl Stobel was the diamond-cutter to whom Marie Weber was betrothed. "I should not have told you now,—only that I am disarranged by what Herr Crippel has done."

"Had we not better go,—or at least move our seats? We can make any excuse afterwards."

"No," said Lotta. "I will not seem to run away from him. I have nothing to be ashamed of. If I choose to keep company with Fritz Planken, that should be nothing to Herr Crippel."

"But you might have told him."

"No; I could not tell him. And I am not sure Fritz is coming either. He said he would come with Carl if he had time. Never mind; let us be happy now. If a bad time comes by-and-by, we must make the best of it."

Then the music began, and, suddenly, as the first note of a fiddle was heard, every voice in the great beer-hall of the Volksgarten became silent. Men sat smoking, with their long beer-glasses before them, and women sat knitting, with their long beer-glasses also before them, but not a word was spoken. The waiters went about with silent feet, but even orders for beer were not given, and money was not received. Herr Crippel did his best, working with his wand as carefully,—and I may say as accurately,—as a leader in a fashionable opera-house in London or Paris. But every now and then, in the course of the piece, he would place his fiddle to his shoulder and join in the performance. There was hardly one there in the hall, man or woman, boy or girl, who did not know, from personal knowledge and judgment, that Herr Crippel was doing his work very well.

"Excellent, was it not?' said Marie.

"Yes; he is a musician. Is it not a pity he should be so bald?" said Lotta.

" He is not so very bald," said Marie.

" I should not mind his being bald so much, if he did not try to cover his old head with the side hairs. If he would cut off those loose straggling locks, and declare himself to be bald at once, he would be ever so much better. He would look to be fifty then. He looks sixty now."

" What matters his age ? He is forty-five, just ; for I know. And he is a good man."

" What has his goodness to do with it ? "

" A great deal. His old mother wants for nothing, and he makes two hundred florins a month. He has two shares in the summer theatre. I know it."

" Bah ! what is all that when he will plaster his hair over his old bald head ? "

" Lotta, I am ashamed of you." But at this moment the further expression of Marie's anger was stopped by the entrance of the diamond-cutter ; and as he was alone, both the girls received him very pleasantly. We must give Lotta her due, and declare that, as things had gone, she would much prefer now that Fritz should stay away, though Fritz Planken was as handsome a young fellow as there was in Vienna, and one who dressed with the best taste, and danced so that no one could surpass him, and could speak French, and was confidential clerk at one of the largest hotels in Vienna, and was a young man acknowledged to be of much general importance,—and had, moreover, in plain language, declared his love for Lotta Schmidt. But Lotta would not willingly give unnecessary pain to Herr Crippel, and she was generously glad when Carl Stobel, the diamond-cutter, came by himself. Then there was a second and third piece played, and after that Herr Crippel came down, according to promise, and was presented to Marie's lover.

"Ladies," said he, "I hope I have not gathered wool."

"You have surpassed yourself," said Lotta.

"At wool-gathering?" said Herr Crippel.

"At sending us out of this world into another," said Lotta.

"Ah! go into no other world but this," said Herr Crippel, "lest I should not be able to follow you." And then he went away again to his post.

Before another piece had been commenced, Lotta saw Fritz Planken enter the door. He stood for a moment gazing round the hall, with his cane in his hand and his hat on his head, looking for the party which he intended to join. Lotta did not say a word, nor would she turn her eyes towards him. She would not recognise him if it were possible to avoid it. But he soon saw her, and came up to the table at which they were sitting. When Lotta was getting the third chair for Marie's lover, Herr Crippel, in his gallantry, had brought a fourth, and now Fritz occupied the chair which the musician had placed there. Lotta, as she perceived this, was sorry that it should be so. She could not even dare to look up to see what effect this new arrival would have upon the leader of the band.

The new comer was certainly a handsome young man, such a one as inflicts unutterable agonies on the hearts of the Herr Crippels of the world. His boots shone like mirrors, and fitted his feet like gloves. There was something in the make and set of his trousers which Herr Crippel, looking at them, as he could not help looking at them, was quite unable to understand. Even twenty years ago, Herr Crippel's trousers, as Herr Crippel very well knew, had never looked like that. And Fritz Planken wore a blue frock coat with silk lining to the breast, which seemed to have come from some tailor among the gods. And he had on primrose gloves, and round his neck a bright pink satin handkerchief joined by a ring, which gave a richness of colouring to the whole thing which nearly killed Herr Crippel, because he could not but acknowledge that the colouring was good. And then the hat! And when the hat was taken off for a moment, then the hair—perfectly black, and silky as a raven's wing, just waving with one curl! And when Fritz put up his hand, and ran his fingers through his locks, their richness and plenty and beauty were conspicuous to all beholders. Herr Crippel, as he saw it, involuntarily dashed his hand up to his own pate, and scratched his straggling, lanky hairs from off his head.

"You are coming to Sperl's to-morrow, of course?" said Fritz to Lotta. Now Sperl's is a great establishment for dancing in the Leopoldstadt, which is always open of a Sunday evening, and which Lotta Schmidt was in the habit of attending with much regularity. It was here she had become acquainted with Fritz. And certainly to dance with Fritz was to dance indeed! Lotta, too, was a beautiful dancer. To a Viennese such as Lotta Schmidt, dancing is a thing of serious importance. It was a misfortune to her to have to dance with a bad dancer, as it is to a great whist-player among us to sit down with a bad partner. Oh, what she had suffered more than once when Herr Crippel had induced her to stand up with him!

"Yes; I shall go. Marie, you will go?"

"I do not know," said Marie.

"You will make her go, Carl; will you not?" said Lotta.

Lotta Schmidt.

"She promised me yesterday, as I understood," said Carl.

"Of course we will all be there," said Fritz, somewhat grandly; "and I will give a supper for four."

Then the music began again, and the eyes of all of them became fixed upon Herr Crippel. It was unfortunate that they should have been placed so fully before him as it was impossible that he should avoid seeing them. As he stood up with his violin to his shoulder, his eyes were fixed on Fritz Planken and Fritz Planken's boots, and coat, and hat, and hair. And as he drew his bow over the strings he was thinking of his own boots and of his own hair. Fritz was sitting, leaning forward in his chair, so that he could look up into Lotta's face, and he was playing with a little amber-headed cane, and every now and then he whispered a word. Herr Crippel could hardly play a note. In very truth he was wool-gathering. His hand became unsteady, and every instrument was more or less astray.

"Your old friend is making a mess of it to-night," said Fritz to Lotta. "I hope he has not taken a glass too much of schnapps."

"He never does anything of the kind," said Lotta, angrily. "He never did such a thing in his life."

"He is playing awfully bad," said Fritz.

"I never heard him play better in my life than he has played to-night," said Lotta.

"His hand is tired. He is getting old," said Fritz. Then Lotta moved her chair and drew herself back, and was determined that Marie and Carl should see that she was angry with her young lover. In the meantime the piece of music had been finished, and the audience had shown their sense of the performer's inferiority by withdrawing those plaudits which they were so ready to give when they were pleased.

After this some other musician led for awhile, and then Herr Crippel had to come forward to play a solo. And on this occasion the violin was not to be his instrument. He was a great favourite among the lovers of music in Vienna, not only because he was good at the fiddle and because with his bow in his hand he could keep a band of musicians together, but also as a player on the zither. It was not often now-a-days that he would take his zither to the music-hall in the Volksgarten; for he would say that he had given up that instrument; that he now played it only in private; that it was not fit for a large hall, as a single voice, the scraping of a foot, would destroy its music. And Herr Crippel was a man who had his fancies and his fantasies, and would not always yield to entreaty. But occasionally he would send his zither down to the public hall; and in the programme for this evening there had been put forth that Herr Crippel's zither would be there and that Herr Crippel would perform. And now the zither was brought forward, and a chair was put for the zitherist, and Herr Crippel stood for a moment behind his chair and bowed. Lotta glanced up at him, and could see that he was very pale. She could even see that the perspiration stood upon his brow. She knew that he was trembling, and that he would have given almost his zither itself to be quit of his promised performance for that night. But she knew also that he would make the attempt.

"What! the zither?" said Fritz. "He will break down as sure as he is a living man."

"Let us hope not," said Carl Stobel.

"I love to hear him play the zither better than anything," said Lotta.

"It used to be very good," said Fritz; "but everybody says he has lost his touch. When a man has the slightest feeling of nervousness he is done for the zither."

"H—sh; let him have his chance at any rate," said Marie.

Reader, did you ever hear the zither? When played, as it is sometimes played in Vienna, it combines all the softest notes of the human voice. It sings to you of love

and then wails to you of disappointed love, till it fills you
with a melancholy from which there is no escaping,—
from which you never wish to escape. It speaks to you
as no other instrument ever speaks, and reveals to you
with wonderful eloquence the sadness in which it delights.
It produces a luxury of anguish, a fulness of the satisfaction of imaginary woe, a realisation of the mysterious
delights of romance, which no words can ever thoroughly
supply. While the notes are living, while the music is
still in the air, the ear comes to covet greedily every atom
of tone which the instrument will produce, so that the
slightest extraneous sound becomes an offence. The
notes sink and sink so low and low, with their soft
sad wail of delicious woe, that the listener dreads that
something will be lost in the struggle of listening. There
seems to come some lethargy on his sense of hearing,
which he fears will shut out from his brain the last,
lowest, sweetest strain, the very pearl of the music, for
which he has been watching with all the intensity of
prolonged desire. And then the zither is silent, and
there remains a fond memory together with a deep regret.

Herr Crippel seated himself on his stool and looked
once or twice round about upon the room almost with
dismay. Then he struck his zither, uncertainly, weakly,
and commenced the prelude of his piece. But Lotta

thought that she had never heard so sweet a sound. When he paused after a few strokes there was a noise of applause in the room, of applause intended to encourage by commemorating past triumphs. The musician looked again away from his music to his audience, and his eyes caught the eyes of the girl he loved ; and his gaze fell also upon the face of the handsome, well-dressed, young Adonis who was by her side.

He, Herr Crippel the musician, could never make himself look like that ; he could make no slightest approach to that outward triumph. But then, he could play the zither, and Fritz Planken could only play with his cane ! He would do what he could ! He would play his best ! He had once almost resolved to get up and declare that he was too tired that evening to do justice to his instrument. But there was an insolence of success about his rival's hat and trousers which spirited him on to the fight. He struck his zither again, and they who understood him and his zither knew that he was in earnest.

The old men who had listened to him for the last twenty years declared that he had never played as he played on that night. At first he was somewhat bolder, somewhat louder than was his wont; as though he were resolved to go out of his accustomed track ; but, after

awhile, he gave that up; that was simply the effect of
nervousness, and was continued only while the timidity
remained present with him. But he soon forgot everything but his zither and his desire to do it justice. The
attention of all present soon became so close that you
might have heard a pin fall. Even Fritz sat perfectly
still, with his mouth open, and forgot to play with his
cane. Lotta's eyes were quickly full of tears, and before
long they were rolling down her cheeks. Herr Crippel,
though he did not know that he looked at her, was
aware that it was so. Then came upon them all there
an ecstasy of delicious sadness. As I have said before,
every ear was struggling that no softest sound might
escape unheard. And then at last the zither was silent,
and no one could have marked the moment when it
had ceased to sing.

For a few moments there was perfect silence in the
room, and the musician still kept his seat with his face
turned upon his instrument. He knew well that he had
succeeded, that his triumph had been complete, and
every moment that the applause was suspended was an
added jewel to his crown. But it soon came, the loud
shouts of praise, the ringing bravos, the striking of
glasses, his own name repeated from all parts of the hall,
the clapping of hands, the sweet sound of women's voices,

and the waving of white handkerchiefs. Herr Crippel stood up, bowed thrice, wiped his face with a handkerchief, and then sat down on a stool in the corner of the orchestra.

" I don't know much about his being too old," said Carl Stobel.

" Nor I either," said Lotta.

" That is what I call music," said Marie Weber.

" He can play the zither, certainly," said Fritz ; " but as to the violin, it is more doubtful."

" He is excellent with both,—with both," said Lotta, angrily.

Soon after that the party got up to leave the hall, and as they went out they encountered Herr Crippel.

" You have gone beyond yourself to-night," said Marie, " and we wish you joy."

" Oh, no. It was pretty good, was it ? With the zither it depends mostly on the atmosphere; whether it is hot, or cold, or wet, or dry, or on I know not what. It is an accident if one plays well. Good-night to you. Good-night, Lotta. Good-night, Sir." And he took off his hat, and bowed,—bowed, as it were, expressly to Fritz Planken.

" Herr Crippel," said Lotta, " one word with you." And she dropped behind from Fritz, and returned to the musician. "Herr Crippel, will you meet me at Sperl's to-morrow night?"

"At Sperl's? No. I do not go to Sperl's any longer, Lotta. You told me that Marie's friend was coming to-night, but you did not tell me of your own."

"Never mind what I told you, or did not tell you. Herr Crippel, will you come to Sperl's to-morrow?"

"No; you would not dance with me, and I should not care to see you dance with anyone else."

"But I will dance with you."

"And Planken will be there?"

"Yes, Fritz will be there. He is always there; I cannot help that."

"No, Lotta; I will not go to Sperl's. I will tell you a little secret. At forty-five one is too old for Sperl's."

"There are men there every Sunday over fifty—over sixty, I am sure."

"They are men different in their ways of life from me, my dear. No, I will not go to Sperl's. When will you come and see my mother?"

Lotta promised that she would go and see the Frau Crippel before long, and then tripped off and joined her party.

Stobel and Marie had walked on, while Fritz remained a little behind for Lotta.

"Did you ask him to come to Sperl's to-morrow?" he said.

"To be sure I did.'

"Was that nice of you, Lotta?"

"Why not nice? Nice or not, I did it. Why should not I ask him, if I please?"

"Because I thought I was to have the pleasure of entertaining you; that it was a little party of my own."

"Very well, Herr Planken," said Lotta, drawing herself a little away from him; "if a friend of mine is not welcome at your little party, I certainly shall not join it myself."

"But, Lotta, does not everyone know what it is that Crippel wishes of you?"

"There is no harm in his wishing. My friends tell me that I am very foolish not to give him what he wishes. But I still have the chance."

"Oh yes, no doubt you still have the chance."

"Herr Crippel is a very good man. He is the best son in the world, and he makes two hundred florins a month."

"Oh, if that is to count!"

"Of course it is to count. Why should it not count? Would the Princess Theresa have married the other day if the young prince had had no income to support her?"

"You can do as you please, Lotta."

"Yes, I can do as I please, certainly. I suppose Adela Bruhl will be at Sperl's to-morrow?"

"I should say so, certainly. I hardly ever knew her to miss her Sunday evening."

"Nor I. I, too, am fond of dancing—very. I delight in dancing. But I am not a slave to Sperl's, and then I do not care to dance with everyone."

"Adela Bruhl dances very well," said Fritz.

"That is as one may think. She ought to; for she begins at ten, and goes on till two, always. If there is no one nice for dancing she puts up with some one that is not nice. But all that is nothing to me."

"Nothing, I should say, Lotta."

"Nothing in the world. But this is something; last Sunday you danced three times with Adela."

"Did I? I did not count."

"I counted. It is my business to watch those things, if you are to be ever anything to me, Fritz. I will not pretend that I am indifferent. I am not indifferent. I care very much about it. Fritz, if you dance to-morrow with Adela you will not dance with me again—either then or ever." And having uttered this threat she ran on and found Marie, who had just reached the door of the house in which they both lived,

Fritz, as he walked home by himself, was in doubt as to the course which it would be his duty as a man to pursue in reference to the lady whom he loved. He had distinctly heard that lady ask an old admirer of hers to go to Sperl's and dance with her; and yet, within ten minutes afterwards, she had peremptorily commanded him not to dance with another girl! Now, Fritz Planken had a very good opinion of himself, as he was well entitled to have, and was quite aware that other pretty girls besides Lotta Schmidt were within his reach. He did not receive two hundred florins a month, as did Herr Crippel, but then he was five-and-twenty instead of five-and-forty; and, in the matter of money, too, he was doing pretty well. He did love Lotta Schmidt. It would not be easy for him to part with her. But she, too, loved him, as he told himself, and she would hardly push matters to extremities. At any rate, he would not submit to a threat. He would dance with Adela Bruhl, at Sperl's. He thought, at least, that when the time should come he would find it well to dance with her.

Sperl's dancing saloon, in the Tabor Strasse, is a great institution at Vienna. It is open always of a Sunday evening, and dancing there commences at ten, and is continued till two or three o'clock in the morning. There are two large rooms, in one of which the dancers dance, and in the other the dancers and visitors who do not dance, eat, and drink, and smoke continually. But the most wonderful part of Sperl's establishment is this, that there is nothing there to offend anyone. Girls dance and men smoke, and there is eating and drinking, and everybody is as well behaved as though there was a protecting phalanx of dowagers sitting round the walls of the saloon. There are no dowagers, though there may probably be a policeman somewhere about the place. To a stranger it is very remarkable that there is so little of what we call flirting;—almost none of it. It would seem that to the girls dancing is so much a matter of business, that here at Sperl's they can think of nothing else. To mind their steps, and at the same time their dresses, lest they should be trod upon, to keep full pace with the music, to make all the proper turns at every proper time, and to have the foot fall on the floor at the exact instant; all this is enough, without further excitement. You will see a girl dancing with a man as though the man were a chair, or a stick, or some necessary piece of furniture. She condescends to use his services, but as soon as the dance is over she sends him away. She hardly speaks a word to him, if a word! She has come there to dance, and not to talk; unless, indeed, like Marie Weber and Lotta Schmidt, she has a recognised lover there of her very own.

At about half-past ten Marie and Lotta entered the saloon, and paid their kreutzers and sat themselves down on seats in the further saloon, from which through open archways they could see the dancers. Neither Carl nor Fritz had come as yet, and the girls were quite content to wait. It was to be presumed that they would be there before the men, and they both understood that the real dancing was not commenced early in the evening. It might be all very well for such as Adela Bruhl to dance with anyone who came at ten o'clock, but Lotta Schmidt would not care to amuse herself after that fashion. As to Marie, she was to be married after another week, and of course she would dance with no one but Carl Stobel.

"Look at her," said Lotta, pointing with her foot to a fair girl, very pretty, but with hair somewhat untidy, who at this moment was waltzing in the other room. "That lad is a waiter from the Minden hotel. I know him. She would dance with anyone."

"I suppose she likes dancing, and there is no harm in the boy," said Marie.

"No, there is no harm, and if she likes it I do not begrudge it her. See what red hands she has."

"She is of that complexion," said Marie.

"Yes, she is of that complexion all over; look at her

face. At any rate she might have better shoes on. Did
you ever see anybody so untidy?"

"She is very pretty," said Marie.

"Yes, she is pretty. There is no doubt she is pretty.
She is not a native here. Her people are from Munich.
Do you know, Marie, I think girls are always thought
more of in other countries than in their own."

Soon after this Carl and Fritz came in together, and
Fritz, as he passed across the end of the first saloon,
spoke a word or two to Adela. Lotta saw this, but determined that she would take no offence at so small a
matter. Fritz need not have stopped to speak, but his
doing so might be all very well. At any rate, if she did
quarrel with him she would quarrel on a plain, intelligible
ground. Within two minutes Carl and Marie were dancing, and Fritz had asked Lotta to stand up. "I will
wait a little," said she, "I never like to begin much before eleven."

"As you please," said Fritz; and he sat down in the
chair which Marie had occupied. Then he played with
his cane, and as he did so his eyes followed the steps of
Adela Bruhl.

"She dances very well," said Lotta.

"H—m—m, yes." Fritz did not choose to bestow
any strong praise on Adela's dancing.

"Yes, Fritz, she does dance well—very well, indeed. And she is never tired. If you ask me whether I like her style, I cannot quite say that I do. It is not what we do here—not exactly."

"She has lived in Vienna since she was a child."

"It is in the blood then, I suppose. Look at her fair hair, all blowing about. She is not like one of us."

"Oh no, she is not."

"That she is very pretty, I quite admit," said Lotta. "Those soft gray eyes are delicious. Is it not a pity she has no eyebrows?"

"But she has eyebrows."

"Ah! you have been closer than I, and you have seen them. I have never danced with her, and I cannot see them. Of course they are there—more or less."

After a while the dancing ceased, and Adela Bruhl came up into the supper-room, passing the seats on which Fritz and Lotta were sitting.

"Are you not going to dance, Fritz?" she said, with a smile, as she passed them.

"Go, go," said Lotta; "why do you not go? She has invited you."

"No; she has not invited me. She spoke to us both."

"She did not speak to me, for my name is not Fritz.

"He said that Herr Crippel was too old to play the zither; too old! Some people are too young to understand. I shall go home, I shall not stay to sup with you to-night."

"Lotta, you must stay for supper."

"I will not sup at his table. I have quarrelled with him. It is all over. Fritz Planken is as free as the air for me."

"Lotta, do not say anything in a hurry. At any rate do not do anything in a hurry."

"I do not mean to do anything at all. It is simply this—I do not care very much for Fritz, after all. I don't think I ever did. It is all very well to wear your clothes nicely, but if that is all, what does it come to? If he could play the zither, now!"

"There are other things except playing the zither. They say he is a good book-keeper."

"I don't like book-keeping. He has to be at his hotel from eight in the morning till eleven at night."

"You know best."

"I am not so sure of that. I wish I did know best. But I never saw such a girl as you are. How you change! It was only yesterday you scolded me because I did not wish to be the wife of your dear friend Crippel."

"Herr Crippel is a very good man."

"You go away with your good man! You have got a good man of your own. He is standing there waiting for you, like a gander on one leg. He wants you to dance; go away."

Then Marie did go away, and Lotta was left alone by herself. She certainly had behaved badly to Fritz, and she was aware of it. She excused herself to herself by remembering that she had never yet given Fritz a promise. She was her own mistress, and had, as yet, a right to do what she pleased with herself. He had asked her for her love, and she had not told him that he should not have it. That was all. Herr Crippel had asked her a dozen times, and she had at last told him definitely, positively, that there was no hope for him. Herr Crippel, of course, would not ask her again ;—so she told herself. But if there was no such person as Herr Crippel in all the world, she would have nothing more to do with Fritz Planken,—nothing more to do with him as a lover. He had given her fair ground for a quarrel, and she would take advantage of it. Then as she sat still while they were dancing, she closed her eyes and thought of the zither and of the zitherist. She remained alone for a long time. The musicians in Vienna will play a waltz for twenty minutes, and the same dancers will continue to dance almost without a pause; and then, almost immediately afterwards, there was a quadrille. Fritz, who was resolved to put down tyranny, stood up with Adela for the quadrille also. "I am so glad," said Lotta to herself. "I will wait till this is over, and then I will say good-night to Marie, and will go home." Three or four men had asked her to dance, but she had refused. She would not dance to-night at all. She was inclined, she thought, to be a little serious, and would go home. At last Fritz returned to her, and bade her come to supper. He was resolved to see how far his mode of casting off tyranny might be successful, so he approached her with a smile, and offered to take her to his table as though nothing had happened.

"My friend," she said, "your table is laid for four, and the places will all be filled."

"The table is laid for five," said Fritz.

"It is one too many. I shall sup with my friend, Herr Crippel."

"Herr Crippel is not here."

"Is he not? Ah me! then I shall be alone, and I must go to bed supperless. Thank you, no, Herr Planken."

"And what will Marie say?"

"I hope she will enjoy the nice dainties you will give her. Marie is all right. Marie's fortune is made. Woe is me! my fortune is to seek. There is one thing certain, it is not to be found here in this room."

Then Fritz turned on his heel and went away; and as he went Lotta saw the figure of a man, as he made his way slowly and hesitatingly into the saloon from the outer passage. He was dressed in a close frock-coat, and had on a hat of which she knew the shape as well as she did the make of her own gloves. " If he has not come after all!" she said to herself. Then she turned herself a little round, and drew her chair somewhat into an archway, so that Herr Crippel should not see her readily.

The other four had settled themselves at their table, Marie having said a word of reproach to Lotta as she passed. Now, on a sudden, she got up from her seat and crossed to her friend.

" Herr Crippel is here," she said.

" Of course he is here," said Lotta.

" But you did not expect him?"

" Ask Fritz if I did not say I would sup with Herr Crippel. You ask him. But I shall not, all the same. Do not say a word. I shall steal away when nobody is looking."

The musician came wandering up the room, and had looked into every corner before he had even found the supper-table at which the four were sitting. And then he did not see Lotta. He took off his hat as he addressed Marie, and asked some questions as to the absent one.

"She is waiting for you somewhere, Herr Crippel," said Fritz, as he filled Adela's glass with wine.

"For me?" said Herr Crippel as he looked round. "No, she does not expect me." And in the meantime Lotta had left her seat, and was hurrying away to the door.

"There! there!" said Marie; "you will be too late if you do not run."

Then Herr Crippel did run, and caught Lotta as she was taking her hat from the old woman, who had the girls' hats and shawls in charge near the door.

"What! Herr Crippel, you at Sperl's? When you told me expressly, in so many words, that you would not come! That is not behaving well to me, certainly."

"What, my coming? Is that behaving bad?"

"No; but why did you say you would not come when I asked you? You have come to meet some one. Who is it?"

"You, Lotta; you."

"And yet you refused me when I asked you! Well, and now you are here, what are you going to do? You will not dance."

"I will dance with you, if you will put up with me."

"No, I will not dance. I am too old. I have given it up. I shall come to Sperl's no more after this. Dancing is a folly."

"Lotta, you are laughing at me now."

"Very well; if you like, you may have it so." By this time he had brought her back into the room, and was walking up and down the length of the saloon with her. "But it is no use our walking about here," she said. "I was just going home, and now, if you please, I will go."

"Not yet, Lotta."

"Yes; now, if you please."

"But why are you not supping with them?"

"Because it did not suit me. You see there are four. Five is a foolish number for a supper party."

"Will you sup with me, Lotta?" She did not answer him at once. "Lotta," he said, "if you sup with me now you must sup with me always. How shall it be?"

"Always? No. I am very hungry now, but I do not want supper always. I cannot sup with you always, Herr Crippel."

"But you will to-night?"

"Yes, to-night."

"Then it shall be always."

And the musician marched up to a table, and threw

his hat down, and ordered such a supper that Lotta Schmidt was frightened. And when presently Carl Stobel and Marie Weber came up to their table,—for Fritz Planken did not come near them again that evening,— Herr Crippel bowed courteously to the diamond-cutter, and asked him when he was to be married. "Marie says it shall be next Sunday," said Carl.

"And I will be married the Sunday afterwards," said Herr Crippel. "Yes; and there is my wife."

And he pointed across the table with both his hands to Lotta Schmidt.

"Herr Crippel, how can you say that?" said Lotta.

"Is it not true, my dear?"

"In fourteen days! No, certainly not. It is out of the question."

But, nevertheless, what Herr Crippel said came true, and on the next Sunday but one he took Lotta Schmidt home to his house as his wife.

"It was all because of the zither," Lotta said to her old mother-in-law. "If he had not played the zither that night I should not have been here now."

THE ADVENTURES OF
FRED PICKERING.

THE ADVENTURES OF FRED PICKERING.

THERE was something almost grand in the rash courage with which Fred Pickering married his young wife, and something quite grand in her devotion in marrying him. She had not a penny in the world, and he, when he married her, had two hundred and fifty pounds, and no profession. She was the daughter of parents whom she had never seen, and had been brought up by the kindness of an aunt, who died when she was eighteen. Distant friends then told her that it was her duty to become a governess; but Fred Pickering intervened, and Mary Crofts became Mary Pickering when she was nineteen years old. Fred himself, our hero, was six years older, and should have known better and have conducted his affairs with more wisdom.

His father had given him a good education, and had articled him to an attorney at Manchester. While at Manchester he had written three or four papers in different newspapers, and had succeeded in obtaining admission for a poem in the "Free Trader," a Manchester monthly magazine, which was expected to do great things as the literary production of Lancashire. These successes, joined, no doubt, to the natural bent of his disposition, turned him against the law; and when he was a little more than twenty-five, having then been four years in the office of the Manchester attorney, he told his father that he did not like the profession chosen for him, and that he must give it up. At that time he was engaged to marry Mary Crofts; but of this fact he did not tell his father. Mr. Pickering, who was a stern man,—one not given at any time to softnesses with his children,—when so informed by his son, simply asked him what were his plans. Fred replied that he looked forward to a literary career,—that he hoped to make literature his profession. His father assured him that he was a silly fool. Fred replied that on that subject he had an opinion of his own by which he intended to be guided. Old Pickering then declared that in such circumstances he should withdraw all pecuniary assistance; and young Pickering upon this wrote an ungracious epistle, in which he expressed himself quite ready to take upon himself the burden of his own maintenance. There was one, and only one, further letter from his father, in which he told his son that the allowance made to him would be henceforth stopped. Then the correspondence between Fred and the ex-governor, as Mary used to call him, was brought to a close.

Most unfortunately there died at this time an old maiden aunt, who left four hundred pounds a-piece to twenty nephews and nieces, of whom Fred Pickering was one. The possession of this sum of money strengthened him in his rebellion against his father. Had he had nothing on which to begin, he might probably even yet have gone to the old house at home, and have had something of a fatted calf killed for him, in spite of the ungraciousness of his letter. As it was he was reliant on the resources which Fortune had sent to him, thinking that they would suffice till he had made his way to a beginning of earning money. He thought it all over for full half an hour, and then came to a decision. He would go to Mary,—his Mary,—to Mary who was about to enter the family of a very vulgar tradesman as governess to six young children with a salary of twenty-five pounds per annum, and ask her to join him in throwing all prudence to the wind. He did go to Mary; and Mary at ast consented to be as imprudent as himself, and she consented without any of that confidence which animated him. She consented simply because he asked her to do so, knowing that she was doing a thing so rash that no father or mother would have permitted it.

"Fred," she had said, half laughing as she spoke, "I am afraid we shall starve if we do."

"Starving is bad," said Fred; "I quite admit that; but there are worse things than starving. For you to be a governess at Mrs. Boullem's is worse. For me to write lawyers' letters all full of lies is worse. Of course we may come to grief. I dare say we shall come to grief. Perhaps we shall suffer awfully,—be very hungry and very cold. I am quite willing to make the worst of it. Suppose that we die in the street! Even that,—the chance of that with the chance of success on the other side, is better than Mrs. Boullem's. It always seems to me that people are too much afraid of being starved."

"Something to eat and drink is comfortable," said Mary. "I don't say that it is essential."

"If you will dare the consequences with me, I will gladly dare them with you," said Fred, with a whole rhapsody of love in his eyes. Mary had not been proof against this. She had returned the rhapsody of his eyes with a glance of her own, and then, within six weeks of that time, they were married. There were some few things to be bought, some little bills to be paid, and then there was the fortnight of honeymooning among the lakes in June. "You shall have that, though there were not another shot in the locker," Fred had said, when his bride that was to be had urged upon him the prudence of settling down into a small lodging the very day after their marriage. The fortnight of honeymooning among the lakes was thoroughly enjoyed, almost without one fearful look into the future. Indeed Fred, as he would sit in the late evening on the side of a mountain, looking down upon the lakes, and watching the fleeting brightness of the clouds, with his arm round his loving wife's waist and her head upon his shoulder, would declare that he was glad that he had nothing on which to depend except his own intellect and his own industry. "To make the score off his own bat; that should be a man's ambition, and it is that which nature must have intended for a man. She could never have meant that we should be bolstered up, one by another, from generation to generation." "You shall make the score off your own bat," Mary had said to him. Though her own heart might give way a little as she thought, when alone, of the danger of the future, she was always brave before him. So she enjoyed the fortnight of her honeymooning, and when that was over set herself to her task with infinite courage. They went up to London in a third-class carriage, and, on their arrival there went at once to lodgings which had been taken for them by a friend in Museum Street. Museum Street is not cheering by any special merits of its own ; but lodgings there were found to be cheap, and it was near to the great library by means of which, and the treasures there to be found, young Pickering meant to make himself a famous man.

He had had his literary successes at Manchester, as has been already stated, but they had not been of a re-munerative nature. He had never yet been paid for what he had written. He reaped, however, this reward, that the sub-editor of a Manchester newspaper gave him a letter to a gentleman connected with a London peri-odical, which might probably be of great service to him. It is at any rate a comfort to a man to know that he can do something towards the commencement of the work that he has in hand,—that there is a step forward which he can take. When Fred and Mary sat down to their tea and broiled ham on the first night, the letter of intro-duction was a great comfort to them, and much was said about it. The letter was addressed to Roderick Billings, Esq., office of the *Lady Bird*, 99, Catherine Street, Strand. By ten o'clock on the following morning Fred Pickering was at the office of the *Lady Bird*, and there learned that

Mr. Billings never came to the office, or almost never. He was on the staff of the paper, and the letter should be sent to him. So Fred Pickering returned to his wife; and as he was resolved that no time should be lost, he began a critical reading of Paradise Lost, with a note-book and pencil beside him, on that very day.

They were four months in London, during which they never saw Mr. Billings or any one else connected with the publishing world, and these four months were very trying to Mrs. Pickering. The study of Milton did not go on with unremitting ardour. Fred was not exactly idle, but he changed from one pursuit to another, and did nothing worthy of note except a little account of his honeymoon-ing tour in verse. In this poem the early loves of a young married couple were handled with much delicacy and some pathos of expression, so that Mary thought that her husband would assuredly drive Tennyson out of the field. But no real good had come from the poem by the end of the four months, and Fred Pickering had sometimes been very cross. Then he had insisted more than once or twice, more than four or five times, on going to the theatre; and now at last his wife had felt com-pelled to say that she would not go there with him again. They had not means, she said, for such pleasures. He did not go without her, but sometimes of an evening he was very cross. The poem had been sent to Mr. Billings, with a letter, and had not as yet been sent back. Three or four letters had been written to Mr. Billings, and one or two very short answers had been received. Mr. Billings had been out of town. " Of course all the world is out of town in September," said Fred ; " what fools we were to think of beginning just at this time of the year ! " Nevertheless he had urged plenty of reasons why the marriage should not be postponed till after June. On the first of November, however, they found that they had still a hundred and eighty pounds left. They looked their affairs in the face cheerfully, and Fred, taking upon his own shoulders all the blame of their discomfiture up to the present moment, swore that he would never be cross with his darling Molly again. After that he went out with a letter of introduction from Mr. Billings to the sub-editor of a penny newspaper. He had never seen Mr. Billings ; but Mr. Billings thus passed him on to another literary personage. Mr. Billings in his final very short note communicated to Fred his opinion that he would find "work on the penny daily press easier got."

For months Fred Pickering hung about the office of the *Morning Comet.* November went, and December, and January, and he was still hanging about the office of the *Morning Comet*. He did make his way to some acquaintance with certain persons on the staff of the *Comet*, who earned their bread, if not absolutely by literature, at least by some work cognate to literature. And when he was asked to sup with one Tom Wood on a night in January, he thought that he had really got his foot upon the threshold. When he returned home that night, or I should more properly say on the following morning, his wife hoped that many more such preliminary suppers might not be necessary for his success.

At last he did get employment at the office of the *Morning Comet*. He attended there six nights a week, from ten at night till three in the morning, and for this he received twenty shillings a week. His work was almost altogether mechanical, and after three nights disgusted him greatly. But he stuck to it, telling himself that as the day was still left to him for work he might put up with drudgery during the night. That idea, however, of working day and night soon found itself to be a false one. Twelve o'clock usually found him still in bed. After his late breakfast he walked out with his wife, and then ;— well, then he would either write a few verses or read a volume of an old novel.

"I must learn shorthand-writing," he said to his wife, one morning when he came home.

"Well, dear, I have no doubt you would learn it very quickly."

"I don't know that; I should have begun younger. It's a thousand pities that we are not taught anything useful when we are at school. Of what use is Latin and Greek to me?"

"I heard you say once that it would be of great use to you some day."

"Ah, that was when I was dreaming of what will never come to pass; when I was thinking of literature as a high vocation." It had already come to him to make such acknowledgments as this. "I must think about mere bread now. If I could report I might, at any rate, gain a living. And there have been reporters who have risen high in the profession. Dickens was a reporter. I must learn, though I suppose it will cost me twenty pounds."

He paid his twenty pounds and did learn shorthand-writing. And while he was so doing he found he might have learned just as well by teaching himself out of a book. During the period of his tuition in this art he quarrelled with his employers at the *Morning Comet*, who, as he declared, treated him with an indignity which he could not bear. "They want me to fetch and carry, and be a menial," he said to his wife. He thereupon threw

up his employment at the *Comet* office. " But now you
will get an engagement as a reporter," his wife said. He
hoped that he might get an engagement as a reporter ;
but, as he himself acknowledged, the world was all to
begin again. He was at last employed, and made his
first appearance at a meeting of discontented tidewaiters,
who were anxious to petition parliament for some improvement in their position. He worked very hard in
his efforts to take down the words of the eloquent leading
tidewaiter ; whereas he could see that two other reporters
near him did not work at all. And yet he failed. He
struggled at this work for a month, and failed at last.
" My hand is not made for it," he said to his wife, almost
in an agony of despair. " It seems to me as though
nothing would come within my reach." " My dear," she
said, " a man who can write the Braes of Birken "—the
Braes of Birken was the name of his poem on the joys of
honeymooning — " must not be ashamed of himself
because he cannot acquire a small mechanical skill." " I
am ashamed of myself all the same," said Fred.

Early in April they looked their affairs in the face
again, and found that they had still in hand something
just over a hundred pounds. They had been in London
nine months, and when they had first come up they
had expressed to each other their joint conviction that

they could live very comfortably on forty shillings a week. They had spent nearly double that over and beyond what he had earned, and after all they had not lived comfortably. They had a hundred pounds left on which they might exist for a year, putting aside all idea of comfort; and then—and then would come that starving of which Fred had once spoken so gallantly, unless some employment could in the meantime be found for him. And, by the end of the year, the starving would have to be done by three,—a development of events on which he had not seemed to calculate when he told his dearest Mary that after all there were worse things in the world than starving.

But before the end of the month there came upon them a gleam of comfort, which might be cherished and fostered till it should become a whole midday sun of nourishing heat. His friend of the *Manchester Free Trader* had become the editor of the *Salford Reformer*, a new weekly paper which had been established with the view of satisfying certain literary and political wants which the public of Salford had long experienced, and among these wants was an adequate knowledge of what was going on in London. Fred Pickering was asked whether he would write the London letter, once a week, at twenty shillings a week. Write it! Ay, that he would. There was a whole heaven of joy in the idea. This was literary work. This was the sort of thing that he could do with absolute delight. To guide the public by his own wit and discernment, as it were from behind a mask,—to be the motive power and yet unseen,—this had ever been his ambition. For three days he was in an ecstasy, and Mary was ecstatic with him. For the first time it was a joy to him that the baby was coming. A pound a week earned would of itself prolong their means of support for two years, and a pound a week so earned would surely bring other pounds. " I knew it was to be done," he said in triumph, to his wife, " if one only had the courage to make the attempt." The morning of the fourth day somewhat damped his joy, for there came a long letter of instruction from the Salford editor, in which there were hints of certain difficulties. He was told in this letter that it would be well that he should belong to a London club. Such work as was now expected from him could hardly be done under favourable circumstances unless he did belong to a club. "But as everybody now-a-days does belong to a club, you will soon get over that difficulty." So said the editor. And then the editor in his instructions greatly curtailed that liberty of the pen which Fred specially wished to enjoy. He had anticipated that in his London letter he might give free reins to his own political convictions, which were of a very Liberal nature, and therefore suitable to the *Salford Reformer.* And he had a theological bias of his own, by the putting forward of which, in strong language, among the youth of Salford, he had intended to do much towards the clearing away of prejudice and the emancipation of truth. But the editor told him that he should hardly touch politics at all in his London letter, and never lay a finger on religion. He was to tell the people of Salford what was coming out at the different theatres, how the prince and princess looked on horseback, whether the Thames Embankment made proper progress, and he was to keep his ears especially open for matters of social interest, private or general. His style was to be easy and colloquial, and above all things he was to avoid being heavy, didactic, and profound. Then there was sent to him, as a model, a column and a half cut out from a certain well-known newspaper, in which the names of people were mentioned very freely. "If you can do that sort of thing," said the editor, "we shall get on together like a house on fire."

"It is a farrago of ill-natured gossip," he said, as he chucked the fragment over to his wife.

"But you are so clever, Fred," said his wife. "You can do it without the ill-nature."

"I will do my best," he said ; "but as for telling them

about this woman and that, I cannot do it. In the first place, where am I to learn it all?" Nevertheless, the London letter to the *Salford Reformer* was not abandoned. Four or five such letters were written, and four or five sovereigns were paid into his little exchequer in return for so much work. Alas! after the four or five there came a kindly-worded message from the editor to say that the articles did not suit. Nothing could be better than Pickering's language, and his ideas were manly and for the most part good. But the *Salford Reformer* did not want that sort of thing. The *Salford Reformer* felt that Fred Pickering was too good for the work required. Fred for twenty-four hours was broken-hearted. After that he was able to resolve that he would take the thing up in the right spirit. He wrote to the editor, saying that he thought that the editor was right. The London letter required was not exactly within the compass of his ability. Then he enclosed a copy of the Braes of Birken, and expressed an opinion that perhaps that might suit a column in the *Salford Reformer*,—one of those columns which were furthest removed from the corner devoted to the London letter. The editor replied that he would publish the Braes of Birken if Pickering wished; but that they never paid for poetry. Anything being better than silence, Pickering permitted the editor to publish the Braes of Birken in the gratuitous manner suggested.

At the end of June, when tney had just been twelve months in London, Fred was altogether idle as far as any employment was concerned. There was no going to the theatre now ; and it had come to that with him, in fear of his approaching privations, that he would discuss within his own heart the expediency of taking this or that walk with reference to the effect it would have upon his shoes. In those days he strove to work hard, going on with his Milton and his notebook, and sitting for two or three hours a day over heavy volumes in the reading-room at the Museum. When he first resolved upon doing this there had come a difficulty as to the entrance. It was necessary that he should have permission to use the library, and for a while he had not known how to obtain it. Then he had written a letter to a certain gentleman well know in the literary world, an absolute stranger to him, but of whom he had heard a word or two among his newspaper acquaintances, and had asked this gentleman to give him, or to get for him, the permission needed. The gentleman having made certain enquiry, having sent for Pickering and seen him, had done as he was asked, and Fred was free of the library.

"What sort of a man is Mr. Wickham Webb ?" Mary

asked him, when he returned from the club at which, by Mr. Webb's appointment, the meeting had taken place.

"According to my ideas he is the only gentleman whom I have met since I have been in London," said Fred, who in these days was very bitter.

"Was he civil to you?"

"Very civil. He asked me what I was doing up in London, and I told him. He said that literature is the hardest profession in the world. I told him that I thought it was, but at the same time the most noble."

"What did he say to that?"

"He said that the nobler the task it was always the more difficult; and that, as a rule, it was not well that men should attempt work too difficult for their hands because of its nobility."

"What did he mean by that, Fred?"

"I knew what he meant very well. He meant to tell me that I had better go and measure ribbons behind a counter; and I don't know but what he was right."

"But yet you liked him?"

"Why should I have disliked him for giving me good advice? I liked him because his manner was kind, and because he strove hard to say an unpleasant thing in the pleasantest words that he could use. Besides, it did me good to speak to a gentleman once again."

Throughout July not a shilling was earned, nor was there any prospect of the earning of a shilling. People were then still in town, but in another fortnight London would have emptied itself of the rich and prosperous. So much Pickering had learned, little as he was qualified to write the London letter for the *Salford Reformer*. In the last autumn he had complained to his wife that circumstances had compelled him to begin at the wrong period of the year—in the dull months when there was nobody in London who could help him. Now the dull months were coming round again, and he was as far as ever from any help. What was he to do? "You said that Mr. Webb was very civil," suggested his wife: "could you not write to him and ask him to help us?"

"He is a rich man, and that would be begging," said Fred.

"I would not ask him for money," said Mary; "but perhaps he can tell you how you can get employment."

The letter to Mr. Webb was written with many throes and the destruction of much paper. Fred found it very difficult to choose words which should describe with sufficient force the extreme urgency of his position, but which should have no appearance of absolute begging.

"I hope you will understand," he said, in his last paragraph, " that what I want is simply work for which I may be paid, and that I do not care how hard I work, or how little I am paid, so that I and my wife may live. If I have taken an undue liberty in writing to you, I can only beg you to pardon my ignorance."

This letter led to another interview between our hero and Mr. Wickham Webb. Mr. Webb sent his compliments and asked Mr. Pickering to come and breakfast with him. This kindness, though it produced some immediate pleasure, created fresh troubles. Mr. Wickham Webb lived in a grand house near Hyde Park, and poor Fred was badly off for good clothes.

"Your coat does not look at all amiss," his wife said to him, comforting him; "and as for a hat, why don't you buy a new one?"

"I sha'n't breakfast in my hat," said Fred; "but look here;" and Fred exhibited his shoes.

"Get a new pair," said Mary.

"No," said he; "I've sworn to have nothing new till I've earned the money. Mr. Webb won't expect to see me very bright, I dare say. When a man writes to beg for employment, it must naturally be supposed that he will be rather seedy about his clothes." His wife did the best she could for him, and he went out to his breakfast.

Mrs. Webb was not there. Mr. Webb explained that she had already left town. There was no third person at the table, and before his first lamb-chop was eaten, Fred had told the pith of his story. He had a little money left, just enough to pay the doctor who must attend upon his wife, and carry him through the winter; and then he would be absolutely bare. Upon this Mr. Webb asked as to his relatives. "My father has chosen to quarrel with me," said Fred. "I did not wish to be an attorney, and therefore he has cast me out." Mr. Webb suggested that a reconciliation might be possible; but when Fred said at once that it was impossible, he did not recur to the subject.

When the host had finished his own breakfast he got up from his chair, and standing on the rug spoke such words of wisdom as were in him. It should be explained that Pickering, in his letter to Mr. Webb, had enclosed a copy of the Braes of Birken, another little poem in verse, and two of the London letters which he had written for the *Salford Reformer*. "Upon my word, Mr. Pickering, I do not know how to help you. I do not, indeed."

"I am sorry for that, Sir."

"I have read what you sent me, and am quite ready to acknowledge that there is enough, both in the prose and verse, to justify you in supposing it to be possible that you might hereafter live by literature as a profession; but all who make literature a profession should begin with independent means."

"That seems to be hard on the profession as well as on the beginner."

"It is not the less true; and is, indeed, true of most other professions as well. If you had stuck to the law your father would have provided you with the means of living till your profession had become profitable."

"Is it not true that many hundreds in London live on literature?" said our hero.

"Many hundreds do so, no doubt. They are of two sorts, and you can tell yourself whether you belong to either. There are they who have learned to work in accordance with the directions of others. The great bulk of what comes out to us almost hourly in the shape of newspapers is done by them. Some are very highly paid, many are paid liberally, and a great many are paid scantily. There is that side of the profession, and you say that you have tried it and do not like it. Then there are those who do their work independently; who write either books or articles which find acceptance in magazines."

"It is that which I would try if the opportunity were given me."

"But you have to make your own opportunity," said

Mr. Wickham Webb. "It is the necessity of the position that it should be so. What can I do for you?"

"You know the editors of magazines?"

"Granted that I do, can I ask a man to buy what he does not want because he is my friend?"

"You could get your friend to read what I write."

It ended in Mr. Webb strongly advising Fred Pickering to go back to his father, and in his writing two letters of introduction for him, one to the editor of the *Inter national*, a weekly gazette of mixed literature, and the other to Messrs. Brook and Boothby, publishers in St. James's Street. Mr. Webb, though he gave the letters open to Fred, read them to him with the view of explaining to him how little and how much they meant. "I do not know that they can do you the slightest service," said he; "but I give them to you because you ask me. I strongly advise you to go back to your father; but if you are still in town next spring, come and see me again." Then the interview was over, and Fred returned to his wife, glad to have the letters; but still with a sense of bitterness against Mr. Webb. When one word of encouragement would have made him so happy, might not Mr. Webb have spoken it? Mr. Webb had thought that he had better not speak any such word. And Fred, when he read the letters of introduction over to his wife. found them to be very cold.

"I don't think I'll take them," he said.

But he did take them, of course, on the very next day, and saw Mr. Boothby, the publisher, after waiting for half-an-hour in the shop. He swore to himself that the time was an hour and a half, and became sternly angry at being so treated. It did not occur to him that Mr. Boothby was obliged to attend to his own business, and that he could not put his other visitors under the counter, or into the cupboards, in order to make way for Mr. Pickering. The consequence was that poor Fred was seen at his worst, and that the Boothbyan heart was not much softened towards him. "There are so many men of this kind who want work," said Mr. Boothby, "and so very little work to give them!"

"It seems to me," said Pickering, "that the demand for the work is almost unlimited." As he spoke, he looked at a hole in his boot, and tried to speak in a tone that should show that he was above his boots.

"It may be so," said Boothby; "but if so, the demands do not run in my way. I will, however, keep Mr. Webb's note by me, and if I find I can do anything for you, I will. Good-morning."

Then Mr. Boothby got up from his chair, and Fred

Pickering understood that he was told to go away. He was furious in his abuse of Boothby as he described the interview to his wife that evening.

The editor of the *International* he could not get to see; but he got a note from him. The editor sent his compliments, and would be glad to read the article to which Mr. W. W—— had alluded. As Mr. W. W—— had alluded to no article, Fred saw that the editor was not inclined to take much trouble on his behalf. Nevertheless, an article should be sent. An article was written to which Fred gave six weeks of hard work, and which contained an elaborate criticism on the Samson Agonistes. Fred's object was to prove that Milton had felt himself to be a superior Samson—blind, indeed, in the flesh, as Samson was blind, but not blind in the spirit, as was Samson when he crushed the Philistines. The poet had crushed his Philistines with all his intellectual eyes about him. Then there was a good deal said about the Philistines of those days as compared with the other Philistines, in all of which Fred thought that he took much higher ground than certain other writers in magazines on the same subject. The editor sent back his compliments, and said that the *International* never admitted reviews of old books.

"Insensate idiot!" said Fred, tearing the note asunder,

and then tearing his own hair, on both sides of his head. "And these are the men who make the world of letters! Idiot!—thick-headed idiot!"

"I suppose he has not read it," said Mary.

"Then why hasn't he read it? Why doesn't he do the work for which he is paid? If he has not read it, he is a thief as well as an idiot."

Poor Fred had not thought much of his chance from the *International* when he first got the editor's note; but as he had worked at his Samson he had become very fond of it, and golden dreams had fallen on him, and he had dared to whisper to himself words of wondrous praise which might be forthcoming, and to tell himself of enquiries after the unknown author of the great article about the Philistines. As he had thought of this, and as the dreams and the whispers had come to him, he had re-written his essay from the beginning, making it grander, bigger, more eloquent than before. He became very eloquent about the Philistines, and mixed with his eloquence some sarcasm which could not, he thought, be without effect even in dull-brained, heavy-livered London. Yes; he had dared to hope. And then his essay—such an essay as this—was sent back to him with a notice that the *International* did not insert reviews of old books. Hideous, brainless, meaningless idiot! Fred in his fury tore his article into a hundred fragments; and poor Mary was employed, during the whole of the next week, in making another copy of it from the original blotted sheets, which had luckily been preserved.

"Pearls before swine!" Fred said to himself, as he slowly made his way up to the library of the Museum on the last day of that week.

That was in the end of October. He had not then earned a single shilling for many months, and the nearer prospect of that starvation of which he had once spoken so cheerily was becoming awfully frightful to him. He had said that there were worse fates than to starve. Now, as he looked at his wife, and thought of the baby that was to be added to them, and counted the waning heap of sovereigns, he began to doubt whether there was in truth anything worse than to starve. And now, too, idleness made his life more wretched to him than it had ever been. He could not bring himself to work when it seemed to him that his work was to have no result; literally none.

"Had you not better write to your father?" said Mary.

He made no reply, but went out and walked up and down Museum Street.

He had been much disgusted by the treatment he had received from Mr. Boothby, the publisher; but in November he brought himself to write to Mr. Boothby, and ask him whether some employment could not be found.

"You will perhaps remember Mr. Wickham Webb's letter," wrote Fred, "and the interview which I had with you last July."

His wife had wished him to speak more civilly, and to refer to the pleasure of the interview. But Fred had declined to condescend so far. There were still left to them some thirty pounds.

A fortnight afterwards, when December had come, he got a reply from Mr. Boothby, in which he was asked to call at a certain hour at the shop in St. James's Street. This he did, and saw the great man again. The great man asked him whether he could make an index to an historical work. Fred of course replied that he could do that—that or anything else. He could make the index; or, if need was, write the historical work itself. That, no doubt, was his feeling. Ten pounds would be paid for the index if it was approved. Fred was made to understand that payment was to depend altogether on approval of the work. Fred took away the sheets confided to him without any doubt as to the ultimate approval. It would be odd indeed if he could not make an index.

"That young man will never do any good," said Mr Boothby to his foreman, as Fred took his departure. "He thinks he can do everything, and I doubt very much whether he can do anything as it should be done."

Fred worked very hard at the index, and the baby was born to him as he was doing it. A fortnight, however, finished the index, and if he could earn money at the rate of ten pounds a fortnight he might still live. So he took his index to St. James's Street, and left it for approval. He was told by the foreman that if he would call again in a week's time he should hear the result. Of course he called on that day week. The work had not yet been examined, and he must call again after three days. He did call again; and Mr. Boothby told him that his index was utterly useless,—that, in fact, it was not an index at all.

"You couldn't have looked at any other index, I think," said Mr. Boothby.

"Of course you need not take it," said Fred; "but I believe it to be as good an index as was ever made."

Mr. Boothby, getting up from his chair, declared that there was nothing more to be said. The gentleman for whom the work had been done begged that Mr. Pickershould receive five pounds for his labour,—which unfortunately had been thus thrown away. And in saying this Mr. Boothby tendered a five-pound note to Fred. Fred pushed the note away from him, and left the room with a tear in his eye. Mr. Boothby saw the tear, and ten pounds was sent to Fred on the next day, with the gentleman's compliments. Fred sent the ten pounds back. There was still a shot in the locker, and he could not as yet take money for work that he had not done.

By the end of January Fred had retreated with his wife and child to the shelter of a single small bed-room. Hitherto there had been a sitting-room and a bed-room; but now there were but five pounds between him and that starvation which he had once almost coveted, and every shilling must be strained to the utmost. His wife's confinement had cost him much of his money, and she was still ill. Things were going very badly with him, and among all the things that were bad with him, his own idleness was probably the worst. When starvation was so near to him, he could not seat himself in the Museum library and read to any good purpose. And, indeed, he had no purpose. Milton was nothing to him now, as his lingering shillings became few, and still fewer. He could only sit brooding over his misfortunes, and cursing his fate. And every day, as he sat eating his scraps of food over the morsel of fire in his wife's bed-room, she would implore him to pocket his pride and write to his father.

"He would do something for us, so that baby should not die," Mary said to him. Then he went into Museum Street, and bethought himself whether it would not be a manly thing for him to cut his throat. At any rate there would be much relief in such a proceeding.

One day as he was sitting over the fire while his wife still lay in bed, the servant of the house brought up word that a gentleman wanted to see him. "A gentleman! what gentleman?" The girl could not say who was the gentleman, so Fred went down to receive his visitor at the door of the house. He met an old man of perhaps seventy years of age, dressed in black, who with much politeness asked him whether he was Mr. Frederick Pickering. Fred declared himself to be that unfortunate man, and explained that he had no apartment in which to be seen. "My wife is in bed up stairs, ill; and there is not a room in the house to which I can ask you." So the old gentleman and Fred walked up Museum Street and had their conversation on the pavement. "I am Mr. Burnaby, for whose book you made an index," said the old man.

Mr. Burnaby was an author well-known in those days, and Fred, in the midst of his misfortunes, felt that he was honoured by the visit.

"I was sorry that my index did not suit you," said Fred.

"It did not suit at all," said Mr. Burnaby. "Indeed it was no index. An index should comprise no more than words and figures. Your index conveyed opinions, and almost criticism."

"If you suffered inconvenience, I regret it much," said Fred. "I was punished at any rate by my lost labour."

"I do not wish you to be punished at all," said Mr. Burnaby, "and therefore I have come to you with the price in my hand. I am quite sure that you worked hard to do your best." Then Mr. Burnaby's fingers went into his waistcoat pocket, and returned with a crumpled note.

"Certainly not, Mr. Burnaby," said Fred. "I can take nothing that I have not earned."

"Now my dear young friend, listen to me. I know that you are poor."

"I am very poor."

"And I am rich."

"That has nothing to do with it. Can you put me in the way of earning anything by literature? I will accept any such kindness as that at your hand; but nothing else."

"I cannot. I have no means of doing so."

"You know so many authors and so many publishers."

"Though I knew all the authors and all the publishers, what can I do? Excuse me if I say that you have not served the apprenticeship that is necessary."

"And do all authors serve apprenticeships?"

"Certainly not. And it may be that you will rise to wealth and fame without apprenticeship;—but if so you must do it without help."

After that they walked silently together half the length of the street before Fred spoke again. "You mean," said he, "that a man must be either a genius or a journeyman."

"Yes, Mr. Pickering; that, or something like it, is what I mean."

Fred told Mr. Burnaby his whole story, walking up and down Museum Street,—even to that early assurance given to his young bride that there were worse things in the world than starvation. And then Mr. Burnaby asked him what were his present intentions. "I suppose we shall try it," said Pickering with a forced laugh.

"Try what?" said Mr. Burnaby.

"Starvation," said Fred.

"What! with your baby,—with your wife and baby? Come; you must take my ten-pound note at any rate. And while you are spending it write home to your father. Heaven and earth! is a man to be ashamed to tell his father that he has been wrong?" When Fred said that his father was a stern man, and one whose heart would not be melted into softness at the tale of a baby's sufferings, Mr. Burnaby went on to say that the attempt should at any rate be made. "There can be no doubt what duty requires of you, Mr. Pickering. And, upon my word, I do not see what other step you can take. You are not, I suppose, prepared to send your wife and child to the poor-house." Then Fred Pickering burst into tears, and Mr. Burnaby left him at the corner of Great Russell Street, after cramming the ten-pound note into his hand.

To send his wife and child to the poor-house! In all his misery that idea had never before presented itself to Fred Pickering. He had thought of starvation, or rather of some high-toned extremity of destitution, which might be borne with an admirable and perhaps sublime magnanimity. But how was a man to bear with magnanimity a poor-house jacket, and the union mode of hair-cutting? It is not easy for a man with a wife and baby to starve in this country, unless he be one to whom starvation has come very gradually. Fred saw it all now. The police would come to him, and take his wife and baby away into the workhouse, and he would follow them. It might be that this was worse than starvation, but it lacked all that melodramatic grandeur to which he had looked forward almost with satisfaction.

"Well," said Mary to him, when he returned to her bedside, "who was it? Has he told you of anything? Has he brought you anything to do?"

"He has given me that," said Fred, throwing the bank-note on to the bed, "—out of charity! I may as well go out into the streets and beg now. All the pride has gone out of me." Then he sat over the fire crying, and there he sat for hours.

"Fred," said his wife to him, "if you do not write to your father to-morrow I will write."

He went again to every person connected in the slightest degree with literature of whom he had the smallest knowledge; to Mr. Roderick Billings, to the teacher who had instructed him in shorthand-writing, to all those whom he had ever seen among the newspapers, to the editor of the *International*, and to Mr. Boothby. Four different visits he made to Mr. Boothby, in spite of his previous anger, but it was all to no purpose. No one could find him employment for which he was suited. He wrote to Mr. Wickham Webb, and Mr. Wickham Webb sent him a five-pound note. His heart was, I think, more broken by his inability to refuse charity than by anything else that had occurred to him.

His wife had threatened to write to his father, but she had not carried her threat into execution. It is not by such means that a young wife overcomes her husband. He had looked sternly at her when she had so spoken, and she had known that she could not bring herself to do such a thing without his permission. But when she fell ill, wanting the means of nourishment for her child, and in her illness begged of him to implore succour from his father for her baby when she should be gone, then his pride gave way, and he sat down and wrote his letter. When he went to his ink-bottle it was dry. It was nearly two months since he had made any attempt at working in that profession to which he had intended to devote himself.

He wrote to his father, drinking to the dregs the bitter cup of broken pride. It always seems to me that the prodigal son who returned to his father after feeding with the swine suffered but little mortification in his repentant submission. He does, indeed, own his unworthiness, but the calf is killed so speedily that the pathos of the young man's position is lost in the hilarity of the festival. Had he been compelled to announce his coming by post; had he been driven to beg permission to return, and been forced to wait for a reply, his punishment, I think, would have been more severe. To Fred Pickering the punishment was very severe, and indeed for him no fatted calf was killed at last. He received without delay a very cold letter from his father, in which he was told that his father would consider the matter. In the meanwhile thirty shillings a week should be allowed him. At the end of a fortnight he received a further letter, in which he was informed that if he would return to Manchester he would be taken in at the attorney's office which he had left. He must not, however, hope to become himself an attorney ; he must look forward to be a paid attorney's clerk, and in the meantime his father would continue to allow him thirty shillings a week. "In the present position of affairs," said his father, " I do not feel that anything would be gained by our seeing each other." The calf which was thus killed for poor Fred Pickering was certainly by no means a fatted calf.

Of course he had to do as he was directed. He took his wife and baby back to Manchester, and returned with sad eyes and weary feet to the old office which he had in former days not only hated but despised. Then he had been gallant and gay among the other young men, thinking himself to be too good for the society of those around him; now he was the lowest of the low, if not the humblest of the humble.

He told his whole story by letters to Mr. Burnaby, and

received some comfort from the kindness of that gentleman's replies. "I still mean," he said, in one of those letters, "to return some day to my old aspirations; but I will endeavour first to learn my trade as a journeyman of literature."

THE TWO GENERALS.

THE TWO GENERALS.

CHRISTMAS of 1860 is now three years past, and the civil war which was then being commenced in America is still raging without any apparent sign of an end.* The prophets of that time who prophesied the worst never foretold anything so black as this. On that Christmas-day, Major Anderson, who then held the command of the forts in Charleston harbour on the part of the United States Government, removed his men and stores from Fort Moultrie to Fort Sumter, thinking that he might hold the one, though not both, against any attack from the people of Charleston, whose state, that of South Carolina, had seceded five days previously. That was in truth the beginning of the war, though at

* This story was first published in December, 1863.

that time Mr. Lincoln was not yet president. He became so on the 4th of March, 1861, and on the 15th April following Fort Sumter was evacuated by Major Anderson, on the part of the United States Government, under fire from the people of Charleston. So little bloody however, was that affair, that no one was killed in the assault; though one poor fellow perished in the saluting fire with which the retreating officer was complimented as he retired with the so called honours of war. During the three years that have since passed, the combatants have better learned the use of their weapons of war. No one can now laugh at them for their bloodless battles. Never have the shores of any stream been so bathed in blood, as have the shores of those Virginian rivers whose names have lately become familiar to us. None of those old death-doomed generals of Europe, whom we have learned to hate for the cold-blooded energy of their trade,—Tilly, Gustavus Adolphus, Frederic, or Napoleon,—none of these ever left so many carcasses to the kites as have the Johnsons, Jacksons, and Hookers of the American armies, who come and go so fast that they are almost forgotten before the armies they have led have melted into clay.

Of all the states of the old Union, Virginia has probably suffered the most, but Kentucky has least deserved the suffering which has fallen to her lot. In Kentucky the war has raged hither and thither, every town having been subject to inroads from either army. But she would have been loyal to the Union if she could ;—nay, on the whole she has been loyal. She would have thrown off the plague chain of slavery if the prurient virtue of New England would have allowed her to do so by her own means; but virtuous New England was too proud of her own virtue to be content that the work of abolition should thus pass from her hands. Kentucky, when the war was beginning, desired nothing but to go on in her own course. She wished for no sudden change. She grew no cotton. She produced corn and meat, and was a land flowing with milk and honey. Her slaves were not as the slaves of the Southern States. They were few in number; tolerated for a time because their manumission was understood to be of all questions the most difficult,—rarely or never sold from the estates to which they belonged. When the war broke out Kentucky said that she would be neutral. Neutral, and she lying on the front lines of the contest ! Such neutrality was impossible to her,—impossible to any of her children !

Near to the little state capital of Frankfort, there lived at that Christmas time of 1860 an old man, Major Reckenthorpe by name, whose life had been marked by many circumstances which had made him well-known throughout Kentucky.   He had sat for nearly thirty years in the congress of the United States at Washington, representing his own state sometimes as senator and sometimes in the Lower House.   Though called a major he was by profession a lawyer, and as such had lived successfully.   Time had been when friends had thought it possible that he might fill the president's chair; but his name had been too much and too long in men's mouths for that.   Who had heard of Lincoln, Pierce, or Polk, two years before they were named as candidates for the presidency ?   But Major Reckenthorpe had been known and talked of in Washington longer perhaps than any other living politician.

Upon the whole he had been a good man, serving his country as best he knew how, and adhering honestly to his own political convictions.   He had been, and now was, a slave-owner, but had voted in the congress of his own state for the abolition of slavery in Kentucky.   He had been a passionate man, and had lived not without the stain of blood on his hands; for duels had been familiar to him.   But he had lived in a time and in a country in which it had been hardly possible for a leading public man not to be familiar with a pistol.   He had been known as one whom no man could attack with impunity; but he had also been known as one who would not willingly attack any one. Now, at the time of which I am writing, he was old,—almost on the shelf,—past his duellings and his strong short invectives on the floors of congress; but he was a man whom no age could tame, and still he was ever talking, thinking, and planning for the political well-being of his state.

In person he was tall, still upright, stiff, and almost ungainly in his gait, with eager gray eyes that the waters of age could not dim, with short, thick,. grizzled hair which age had hardly thinned, but which ever looked rough and uncombed, with large hands, which he stretched out with extended fingers when he spoke vehemently;—and of the major it may be said that he always spoke with vehemence. But now he was slow in his steps, and infirm on his legs. He suffered from rheumatism, sciatica, and other maladies of the old, which no energy of his own could repress. In these days he was a stern, unhappy, all but broken-hearted old man; for he saw that the work of his life had been wasted.

And he had another grief, which at this Christmas of 1860 had already become terrible to him, and which afterwards bowed him with sorrow to the ground. He had two sons, both of whom were then at home with him, having come together under the family roof-tree that they might discuss with their father the political position of their country, and especially the position of Kentucky. South Carolina had already seceded, and other Slave States were talking of Secession. What should Kentucky do? So the major's sons, young men of eight and twenty and five and twenty, met together at their father's house; — they met and quarrelled deeply, as their father had well known would be the case.

The eldest of these sons was at that time the owner of the slaves and land which his father had formerly possessed and farmed. He was a Southern gentleman, living on the produce of slave labour, and as such had learned to vindicate, if not love, that social system which has produced as its result the war which is still raging at this Christmas of 1863. To him this matter of Secession or Non-Secession was of vital import. He was prepared to declare that the wealth of the South was derived from its agriculture, and that its agriculture could only be supported by its slaves. He went further than this, and declared also, that no further league was possible between a Southern gentleman and a Puritan from New England. His father, he said, was an old man, and might be excused by reason of his age from any active part in the contest that was coming. But for himself there could be but one duty,—that of supporting the new Confederacy, to which he would belong, with all his strength and with whatever wealth was his own.

The second son had been educated at Westpoint, the great military school of the old United States, and was now an officer in the national army. Not on that account need it be supposed that he would, as a matter of course, join himself to the Northern side in the war,— to the side which, as being in possession of the capital and the old government establishments, might claim to possess a right to his military services. A large proportion of the officers in the pay of the United States leagued themselves with Secession,—and it is difficult to see why such an act would be more disgraceful in them than in others. But with Frank Reckenthorpe such was not the case. He declared that he would be loyal to the government which he served, and in saying so, seemed to imply that the want of such loyalty in any other person, soldier, or non-soldier, would be disgraceful, as in his opinion it would have been disgraceful in himself.

" I can understand your feeling," said his brother, who was known as Tom Reckenthorpe " on the assumption that you think more of being a soldier than of being a a man ; but not otherwise."

"Even if I were no soldier, I would not be a rebel," said Frank.

"How a man can be a rebel for sticking to his own country, I cannot understand," said Tom.

"Your own country !" said Frank. "Is it to be Kentucky or South Carolina ? And is it to be a republic or a monarchy ? Or shall we hear of Emperor Davis ? You already belong to the greatest nation on the earth, and you are preparing yourself to belong to the least ;—that is, if you should be successful. Luckily for yourself, you have no chance of success."

"At any rate, I will do my best to fight for it."

"Nonsense, Tom," said the old man, who was sitting by.

"It is no nonsense, Sir. A man can fight without having been at Westpoint. Whether he can do so after having his spirit drilled and drummed out of him there, I don't know."

"Tom !" said the old man.

"Don't mind him, father," said the younger. "His appetite for fighting will soon be over. Even yet I doubt whether we shall ever see a regiment in arms sent from the Southern States against the Union."

"Do you?" said Tom. "If you stick to your colours, as you say you will, your doubts will be soon set at rest. And I'll tell you what, if your regiment is brought into the field, I trust that I may find myself opposite to it. You have chosen to forget that we are brothers, and you shall find that I can forget it also."

"Tom!" said the father, "you should not say such words as that ; at any rate, in my presence."

"It is true, Sir," said he. "A man who speaks as he speaks does not belong to Kentucky, and can be no brother of mine. If I were to meet him face to face, I would as soon shoot him as another ;—sooner, because he is a renegade."

"You are very wicked,—very wicked," said the old man, rising from his chair,—"very wicked." And then, leaning on his stick, he left the room.

"Indeed, what he says is true," said a sweet, soft voice from a sofa in the far corner of the room. "Tom, you are very wicked to speak to your brother thus. Would you take on yourself the part of Cain?"

"He is more silly than wicked, Ada," said the soldier. "He will have no chance of shooting me, or of seeing me shot. He may succeed in getting himself locked up as a rebel ; but I doubt whether he'll ever go beyond that."

"If I ever find myself opposite to you with a pistol in my grasp," said the elder brother, "may my right hand——"

But his voice was stopped, and the imprecation remained unuttered. The girl who had spoken rushed from her seat, and put her hand before his mouth.

"Tom," she said, "I will never speak to you again if you utter such an oath,—never !"

And her eyes flashed fire at his and made him dumb.

Ada Forster called Mrs. Reckenthorpe her aunt, but the connexion between them was not so near as that of aunt and niece. Ada nevertheless lived with the Reckenthorpes, and had done so for the last two years. She was an orphan, and on the death of her father had followed her father's sister-in-law from Maine down to Kentucky ;—for Mrs. Reckenthorpe had come from that farthest and most strait-laced state of the Union, in which people bind themselves by law to drink neither beer, wine, nor spirits, and all go to bed at nine o'clock. But Ada Forster was an heiress, and therefore it was thought well by the elder Reckenthorpes that she should marry one of their sons. Ada Forster was also a beauty, with slim, tall form, very pleasant to the eye ; with bright, speaking eyes and glossy hair ; with ivory teeth of the whitest,—only to be seen now and then when a smile could be won from her; and therefore such a match was thought desirable also by the younger Reckenthorpes. But unfortunately it had been thought desirable by each of them, whereas the father and mother had intended Ada for the soldier.

I have not space in this short story to tell how progress had been made in the troubles of this love affair. So it was now, that Ada had consented to become the wife of the elder brother,—of Tom Reckenthorpe, with his home among the slaves,—although she, with all her New England feelings strong about her, hated slavery and all its adjuncts. But when has love stayed to be guided by any such consideration as that? Tom Reckenthorpe was a handsome, high-spirited, intelligent man. So was his brother Frank. But Tom Reckenthorpe could be soft to a woman, and in that, I think, had he found the means of his success. Frank Reckenthorpe was never soft.

Frank had gone angrily from home when, some three months since, Ada had told him her determination. His brother had been then absent, and they had not met till this their Christmas meeting. Now it had been understood between them, by the intervention of their mother, that they would say nothing to each other as to Ada Forster. The elder had, of course, no cause for saying aught, and Frank was too proud to wish to speak on such a matter before his successful rival. But Frank had not given up the battle. When Ada had made her speech to him, he had told her that he would not take it as conclusive.

"The whole tenor of Tom's life," he had said to her, "must be distasteful to you. It is impossible that you should live as the wife of a slave-owner."

"In a few years there will be no slaves in Kentucky," she had answered.

"Wait till then," he had answered; "and I also will wait."

And so he had left her, resolving that he would bide his time. He thought that the right still remained to him of seeking Ada's hand, although she had told him that she loved his brother.

"I know that such a marriage would make each of them miserable," he said to himself over and over again. And now that these terrible times had come upon them, and that he was going one way with the Union, while his brother was going the other way with Secession, he felt more strongly than ever that he might still be successful The political predilections of American women are as strong as those of American men. And Frank Reckenthorpe knew that all Ada's feelings were as strongly in favour of the Union as his own. Had not she been born and bred in Maine? Was she not ever keen for total abolition, till even the old major, with all his gallantry for womanhood and all his love for the young girl who had come to his house in his old age, would be driven occasionally by stress of feeling to rebuke her? Frank Reckenthorpe was patient, hopeful, and firm. The time must come when Ada would learn that she could not be a fit wife for his brother. The time had, he thought, perhaps come already; and so he spoke to her a word or two on the evening of that day on which she had laid her hand upon his brother's mouth.

"Ada," he had said, "there are bad times coming to us."

"Good times, I hope," she had answered. "No one could expect that the thing could be done without some struggle. When the struggle has passed we shall say that good times have come." The thing of which she spoke was that little thing of which she was ever thinking — the enfranchisement of four millions of slaves.

"I fear that there will be bad times first. Of course I am thinking of you now."

"Bad or good, they will not be worse to me than to others."

"They would be very bad to you if this state were to secede, and if you were to join your lot to my brother's. In the first place, all your fortune would be lost to him and to you."

"I do not see that; but of course I will caution him that it may be so. If it alters his views, I shall hold him free to act as he chooses."

"But, Ada, should it not alter yours?"

"What,—because of my money?—or because Tom could not afford to marry a girl without a fortune?"

"I did not mean that. He might decide that for himself. But your marriage with him under such circumstances as those which he now contemplates, would be as though you married a Spaniard or a Greek adventurer. You would be without country, without home, without fortune, and without standing-ground in the world. Look you, Ada, before you answer. I frankly own that I tell you this because I want you to be my wife, and not his."

"Never, Frank; I shall never be your wife, whether I marry him or no."

"All I ask of you now is to pause. This is no time for marrying or for giving in marriage."

"There I agree with you; but as my word is pledged to him, I shall let him be my adviser in that."

Late on that same night Ada saw her betrothed and bade him adieu. She bade him adieu with many tears, for he came to tell her that he intended to leave Frankfort very early on the following morning.

"My staying here now is out of the question," said he. "I am resolved to secede, whatever the state may do. My father is resolved against Secession. It is necessary, therefore, that we should part. I have already left my father and mother, and now I have come to say good-bye to you."

"And your brother, Tom?"

"I shall not see my brother again."

"And is that well after such words as you have spoken to each other? Perhaps it may be that you will never see him again. Do you remember what you threatened?"

"I do remember what I threatened."

"And did you mean it?"

"No; of course I did not mean it. You, Ada, have heard me speak many angry words, but I do not think that you have known me do many angry things."

"Never one, Tom:—never. See him then before you go, and tell him so."

"No,—he is hard as iron, and would take any such telling from me amiss. He must go his way, and I mine."

"But though you differ as men, Tom, you need not hate each other as brothers."

"It will be better that we should not meet again. The truth is, Ada, that he always despises any one who does not think as he does. If I offered him my hand he would take it, but while doing so he would let me know that he thought me a fool. Then I should be angry, and threaten him again, and things would be worse. You must not quarrel with me, Ada, if I say that he has all the faults of a Yankee."

"And the virtues too, Sir, while you have all the faults of a Southern —— But, Tom, as you are going from us, I will not scold you. I have, too, a word of business to say to you."

"And what's the word of business, dear?" said Tom, getting nearer to her, as a lover should do, and taking her hand in his.

"It is this. You and those who think like you are dividing yourselves from your country. As to whether that be right or wrong, I will say nothing now,—nor will I say anything as to your chance of success. But I am told that those who go with the South will not be able to hold property in the North."

"Did Frank tell you that?"

"Never mind who told me, Tom."

"And is that to make a difference between you and me?"

"That is just the question that I am asking you. Only you ask me with a reproach in your tone, and I ask you with none in mine. Till we have mutually agreed to break our engagement you shall be my adviser. If you think it better that it should be broken,—better for your own interest, be man enough to say so."

But Tom Reckenthorpe either did not think so, or else he was not man enough to speak his thoughts. Instead of doing so, he took the girl in his arms and kissed her, and swore that, whether with fortune or no fortune, she should be his, and his only. But still he had to go,—to go now, within an hour or two of the very moment at which they were speaking. They must part, and before parting must make some mutual promise as to their future meeting. Marriage now, as things stood at this Christmas time, could not be thought of even by Tom Reckenthorpe. At last he promised that if he were then alive he would be with her again, at the old family-house at Frankfort, on the next coming Christmas-day. So he went, and as he let himself out of the old house, Ada, with her eyes full of tears, took herself up to her bed-room.

During the year that followed,—the year 1861,—the American war progressed only as a school for fighting,

The most memorable action was that of Bull's Run, in
which both sides ran away, not from individual cowardice
in either set of men, but from that feeling of panic which
is engendered by ignorance and inexperience. Men saw
wagons rushing hither and thither, and thought that all
was lost.   After that the year was passed in drilling and
in camp-making,—in the making of soldiers, of gun-
powder, and of cannons. But of all the articles of war
made in that year, the article that seemed easiest of fabri-
cation was a general officer. Generals were made with
the greatest rapidity, owing their promotion much more
frequently to local interest than to military success. Such
a state sent such and such regiments, and therefore must
be rewarded by having such and such generals nominated
from among its citizens. The wonder, perhaps, is that
with armies so formed battles should have been fought so
well.

Before the end of 1861, both Major Reckenthorpe's
sons had become general officers. That Frank, the
soldier, should have been so promoted was, at such a
period as this, nothing strange. Though a young man
he had been a soldier, or learning the trade of a soldier,
for more than ten years, and such service as that might
well be counted for much in the sudden construction of
an army intended to number seven hundred thousand

troops, and which at one time did contain all those soldiers. Frank, too, was a clever fellow, who knew his business, and there were many generals made in those days who understood less of their work than he did. As much could not be said for Tom's quick military advancement. But this could be said for them in the South,— that unless they did make their generals in this way, they would hardly have any generals at all, and General Reckenthorpe, as he so quickly became,—General Tom as they used to call him in Kentucky,—recommended himself specially to the Confederate leaders by the warmth and eagerness with which he had come among them. The name of the old man so well known throughout the Union, who had ever loved the South without hating the North, would have been a tower of strength to them. Having him they would have thought that they might have carried the state of Kentucky into open Secession. He was now worn-out and old, and could not be expected to take upon his shoulders the crushing burden of a new contest. But his eldest son had come among them eagerly, with his whole heart; and so they made him a general.

The poor old man was in part proud of this and in part grieved.

"I have a son a general in each army," he said to a

stranger who came to his house in those days; "but what strength is there in a fagot when it is separated? Of what use is a house that is divided against itself? The boys would kill each other if they met."

"It is very sad," said the stranger.

"Sad!" said the old man. "It is as though the devil were let loose upon the earth;—and so he is; so he is."

The family came to understand that General Tom was with the Confederate army which was confronting the Federal army of the Potomac and defending Richmond; whereas it was well known that Frank was in Kentucky with the army on the Green River, which was hoping to make its way into Tennessee, and which did so early in the following year. It must be understood that Kentucky, though a slave state, had never seceded, and that therefore it was divided off from the Southern States, such as Tennessee and that part of Virginia which had seceded, by a cordon of pickets; so that there was no coming up from the Confederate army to Frankfort, in Kentucky. There could, at any rate, be no easy or safe coming up for such a one as General Tom, seeing that being a soldier he would be regarded as a spy, and certainly treated as a prisoner if found within the Northern lines. Nevertheless, general as he was, he kept his engagement with Ada, and made his way into the gardens of his father's house on the night of Christmas-eve. And Ada was the first who knew that he was there. Her ear first caught the sound of his footsteps, and her hand raised for him the latch of the garden door.

"Oh, Tom, it is not you?"

"But it is though, Ada, my darling!" Then there was a little pause in his speech. "Did I not tell you that I should see you to-day?"

"Hush. Do you know who is here? Your brother came across to us from the Green River yesterday."

"The mischief he did! Then I shall never find my way back again. If you knew what I have gone through for this!"

Ada immediately stepped out through the door and on to the snow, standing close up against him as she whispered to him, "I don't think Frank would betray you," she said. "I don't think he would."

"I doubt him,—doubt him hugely. But I suppose I must trust him. I got through the pickets close to Cumberland Gap, and I left my horse at Stoneley's half way between this and Lexington. I cannot go back to-night now that I have come so far!"

"Wait, Tom; wait a minute, and I will go in and tell your mother. But you must be hungry. Shall I bring you food?"

"Hungry enough, but I will not eat my father's victuals out here in the snow."

"Wait a moment, dearest, till I speak to my aunt."

Then Ada slipped back into the house and soon managed to get Mrs. Reckenthorpe away from the room in which the major and his second son were sitting.

"Tom is here," she said, "in the garden. He had encountered all this danger to pay us a visit because it is Christmas. Oh, aunt, what are we to do? He says that Frank would certainly give him up!"

Mrs. Reckenthorpe was nearly twenty years younger than her husband, but even with this advantage on her side Ada's tidings were almost too much for her. She, however, at last managed to consult the major, and he resolved upon appealing to the generosity of his younger son. By this time the Confederate general was warming himself in the kitchen, having declared that his brother might do as he pleased;—he would not skulk away from his father's house in the night.

"Frank," said the father, as his younger son sat silently thinking of what had been told him, "it cannot be your duty to be false to your father in his own house."

"It is not always easy, Sir, for a man to see what is his duty. I wish that either he or I had not come here."

"But he is here; and you, his brother, would not take

advantage of his coming to his father's house?" said the old man.

"Do you remember, Sir, how he told me last year that if ever he met me on the field he would shoot me like a dog?"

"But, Frank, you know that he is the last man in the world to carry out such a threat. Now he has come here with great danger."

"And I have come with none; but I do not see that that makes any difference."

"He has put up with it all that he may see the girl he loves."

"Psha!" said Frank, rising up from his chair. "When a man has work to do, he is a fool to give way to play. The girl he loves! Does he not know that it is impossible that she should ever marry him? Father, I ought to insist that he should leave this house as a prisoner. I know that that would be my duty."

"You would have, Sir, to bear my curse."

"I should not the less have done my duty. But, father, independently of your threat, I will neglect that duty. I cannot bring myself to break your heart and my mother's. But I will not see him. Good-bye, Sir. I will go up to the hotel, and will leave the place before daybreak to-morrow."

After some few further words Frank Reckenthorpe left the house without encountering his brother. He also had not seen Ada Forster since that former Christmas when they had all been together, and he had now left his camp and come across from the army much more with the view of inducing her to acknowledge the hopelessness of her engagement with his brother, than from any domestic idea of passing his Christmas at home. He was a man who would not have interfered with his brother's prospects, as regarded either love or money, if he had thought that in doing so he would in truth have injured his brother. He was a hard man, but one not wilfully unjust. He had satisfied himself that a marriage between Ada and his brother must, if it were practicable, be ruinous to both of them. If this were so, would not it be better for all parties that there should be another arrangement made? North and South were as far divided now as the two poles. All Ada's hopes and feelings were with the North. Could he allow her to be taken as a bride among perishing slaves and ruined whites?

But when the moment for his sudden departure came he knew that it would be better that he should go without seeing her. His brother Tom had made his way to her through cold, and wet, and hunger, and through infinite perils of a kind sterner even than these. Her heart now

would be full of softness towards him. So Frank Reckenthorpe left the house without seeing anyone but his
mother. Ada, as the front door closed behind him, was
still standing close by her lover over the kitchen fire,
while the slaves of the family, with whom Master Tom
had always been the favourite, were administering to his
little comforts.

Of course General Tom was a hero in the house for
the few days that he remained there, and of course the
step he had taken was the very one to strengthen for him
the affection of the girl whom he had come to see.

North and South were even more bitterly divided now
than they had been when the former parting had taken
place. There were fewer hopes of reconciliation; more
positive certainty of war to the knife; and they who
adhered strongly to either side—and those who did not
adhere strongly to either side were very few,—held their
opinions now with more acrimony than they had then
done. The peculiar bitterness of civil war, which adds
personal hatred to national enmity, had come upon the
minds of the people. And here, in Kentucky, on the
borders of the contest, members of the same household
were, in many cases, at war with each other.

Ada Forster and her aunt were passionately Northern,
while the feelings of the old man had gradually turned

themselves to that division in the nation to which he naturally belonged. For months past the matter on which
they were all thinking—the subject which filled their
minds morning, noon, and night,—was banished from
their lips because it could not be discussed without the
bitterness of hostility. But, nevertheless, there was no
word of bitterness between Tom Reckenthorpe and Ada
Forster. While these few short days lasted it was all
love. Where is the woman whom one touch of romance
will not soften, though she be ever so impervious to
argument? Tom could sit up stairs with his mother and
his betrothed, and tell them stories of the gallantry of the
South,—of the sacrifices women were making, and of the
deeds men were doing,—and they would listen and smile
and caress his hand, and all for awhile would be pleasant;
while the old major did not dare to speak before them of
his Southern hopes. But down in the parlour, during the
two or three long nights which General Tom passed in
Frankfort, open Secession was discussed between the two
men. The old man now had given away altogether. The
Yankees, he said, were too bitter for him.

"I wish I had died first; that is all," he said. "I
wish I had died first. Life is wretched now to a man
who can do nothing."

His son tried to comfort him, saying that Secession

would certainly be accomplished in twelve months, and that every Slave State would certainly be included in the Southern Confederacy. But the major shook his head. Though he hated the political bitterness of the men whom he called Puritans and Yankees, he knew their strength and acknowledged their power.

"Nothing good can come in my time," he said; "not in my time,—not in my time."

In the middle of the fourth night General Tom took his departure. An old slave arrived with his horse a little before midnight, and he started on his journey.

"Whatever turns up, Ada," he said, "you will be true to me."

"I will; though you are a rebel all the same for that."

"So was Washington."

"Washington made a nation;—you are destroying one."

"We are making another, dear; that's all. But I won't talk Secesh to you out here in the cold. Go in, and be good to my father; and remember this, Ada, I'll be here again next Christmas-eve, if I'm alive."

So he went, and made his journey back to his own camp in safety. He slept at a friend's house during the following day, and on the next night again made his way through the Northern lines back into Virginia. Even at that time there was considerable danger in doing this, although the frontier to be guarded was so extensive. This arose chiefly from the paucity of roads, and the impossibility of getting across the country where no roads existed. But General Tom got safely back to Richmond, and no doubt found that the tedium of his military life had been greatly relieved by his excursion.

Then, after that, came a year of fighting,—and there has since come another year of fighting; of such fighting that we, hearing the accounts from day to day, have hitherto failed to recognise its extent and import. Every now and then we have even spoke of the inaction of this side or of that, as though the drawn battles which have lasted for days, in which men have perished by tens of thousands, could be renewed as might the old German battles, in which an Austrian general would be ever retreating with infinite skill and military efficacy. For constancy, for blood, for hard determination to win at any cost of life or material, history has known no such battles as these. That the South have fought the best as regards skill no man can doubt. As regards pluck and resolution there has not been a pin's choice between them. They have both fought as Englishmen fight when they are equally in earnest. As regards result, it has been almost altogether in favour of the North, because they have so vast a superiority in numbers and material.

General Tom Reckenthorpe remained during the year in Virginia, and was attached to that corps of General Lee's army which was commanded by Stonewall Jackson. It was not probable, therefore, that he would be left without active employment. During the whole year he was fighting, assisting in the wonderful raids that were made by that man whose loss was worse to the Confederates than the loss of Vicksburg or of New Orleans. And General Tom gained for himself mark, name, and glory,— but it was the glory of a soldier rather than of a general. No one looked upon him as the future commander of an army; but men said that if there was a rapid stroke to be stricken, under orders from some more thoughtful head, General Tom was the hand to strike it. Thus he went on making wonderful rides by night, appearing like a warrior ghost leading warrior ghosts in some quiet valley of the Federals, seizing supplies and cutting off cattle, till his name came to be great in the State of Kentucky, and Ada Forster, Yankee though she was, was proud of her rebel lover.

And Frank Reckenthorpe, the other general, made progress also, though it was progress of a different kind. Men did not talk of him so much as they did of Tom;

but the War Office at Washington knew that he was useful,—and used him. He remained for a long time attached to the Western army, having been removed from Kentucky to St. Louis, in Missouri, and was there when his brother last heard of him.

"I am fighting day and night," he once said to one who was with him from his own state, "and, as far as I can learn, Frank is writing day and night. Upon my word, I think that I have the best of it."

It was but a couple of days after this, the time then being about the latter end of September, that Tom Reckenthorpe found himself on horseback at the head of three regiments of cavalry, near the foot of one of those valleys which lead up into the Blue Mountain ridge of Virginia. He was about six miles in advance of Jackson's army, and had pushed forward with the view of intercepting certain Federal supplies which he and others had hoped might be within his reach. He had expected that there would be fighting, but he had hardly expected so much fighting as came that day in his way. He got no supplies. Indeed, he got nothing but blows, and though on that day the Confederates would not admit that they had been worsted, neither could they claim to have done more than hold their own. But General Tom's fighting was on that day brought to an end.

It must be understood that there was no great battle fought on this occasion. General Reckenthorpe, with about 1500 troopers, had found himself suddenly compelled to attack about double that number of Federal infantry.

He did so once, and then a second time, but on each occasion without breaking the lines to which he was opposed; and towards the close of the day he found himself unhorsed, but still unwounded, with no weapon in his hand but his pistol, immediately surrounded by about a dozen of his own men, but so far in advance of the body of his troops as to make it almost impossible that he should find his way back to them.

As the smoke cleared away and he could look about him, he saw that he was close to an uneven, irregular line of Federal soldiers. But there was still a chance, and he had turned for a rush, with his pistol ready for use in his hand, when he found himself confronted by a Federal officer. The pistol was already raised, and his finger was on the trigger, when he saw that the man before him was his brother.

" Your time is come," said Frank, standing his ground very calmly. He was quite unarmed, and had been separated from his men and ridden over; but hitherto had not been hurt.

"Frank!" said Tom, dropping his pistol arm, "is that you?"

"And you are not going to do it, then?" said Frank.

"Do what?" said Tom, whose calmness was altogether gone. But he had forgotten that threat as soon as it had been uttered, and did not even know to what his brother was alluding.

But Tom Reckenthorpe, in his confusion at meeting his brother, had lost whatever chance there remained to him of escaping. He stood for a moment or two, looking at Frank, and wondering at the coincidence which had brought them together, before he turned to run. Then it was too late. In the hurry and scurry of the affair all but two of his own men had left him, and he saw that a rush of Federal soldiers was coming up around him.

Nevertheless he resolved to start for a run.

"Give me a chance, Frank," he said, and prepared to run. But as he went,—or rather before he had left the ground on which he was standing before his brother, a shot struck him, and he was disabled. In a minute he was as though he were stunned; then he smiled faintly, and slowly sunk upon the ground.

"It's all up, Frank," he said, "and you are in at the death."

Frank Reckenthorpe was soon kneeling beside his brother, amidst a crowd of his own men.

"Spurrell," he said to a young officer who was close to him, "it is my own brother."

"What, General Tom?" said Spurrell. "Not danger-ously, I hope?"

By this time the wounded man had been able, as it were, to feel himself and to ascertain the amount of the damage done him.

"It's my right leg," he said: "just on the knee. If you'll believe me, Frank, I thought it was my heart at first. I don't think much of the wound, but I suppose you won't let me go."

Of course they wouldn't let him go, and indeed if they had been minded so to do, he could not have gone. The wound was not fatal, as he had at first thought; but neither was it a matter of little consequence, as he after-wards asserted. His fighting was over, unless he could fight with a leg amputated between the knee and the hip.

Before nightfall General Tom found himself in his brother's quarters, a prisoner on parole, with his leg all but condemned by the surgeon. The third day after that saw the leg amputated. For three weeks the two brothers remained together, and after that the elder was taken to Washington,—or rather to Alexandria, on the

other side of the Potomac, as a prisoner, there to
await his chance of exchange. At first the intercourse
between the two brothers was cold, guarded, and uncomfortable; but after a while it became more kindly
than it had been for many a day. Whether it were
cold or kindly, its nature, we may be sure, was such
as the younger brother made it. Tom was ready enough
to forget all personal animosity as soon as his brother
would himself be willing to do so; though he was willing
enough also to quarrel,—to quarrel bitterly as ever, if
Frank should give him occasion. As to that threat of
the pistol, it had passed away from Tom Reckenthorpe,
as all his angry words passed from him. It was clean
forgotten. It was not simply that he had not wished
to kill his brother, but that such a deed was impossible
to him. The threat had been like a curse that means
nothing,—which is used by passion as its readiest
weapon when passion is impotent. But with Frank
Reckenthorpe words meant what they were intended
to mean. The threat had rankled in his bosom from
the time of its utterance, to that moment when a strange
coincidence had given the threatener the power of ex-
ecuting it. The remembrance of it was then strong
upon him, and he had expected that his brother would
have been as bad as his word. But his brother had

spared him; and now, slowly, by degrees, he began to remember that also.

"What are your plans, Tom?" he said, as he sat one day by his brother's bed before the removal of the prisoner to Alexandria. "Plans?" said Tom. "How should a poor fellow like me have plans? To eat bread and water in prison at Alexandria, I suppose?"

"They'll let you up to Washington on your parole, I should think. Of course, I can say a word for you."

"Well, then, do say it. I'd have done as much for you, though I don't like your Yankee politics."

"Never mind my politics now, Tom."

"I never did mind them. But at any rate, you see I can't run away."

It should have been mentioned a little way back in this story that the poor old major had been gathered to his fathers during the past year. As he had said himself, it would be better for him that he should die. He had lived to see the glory of his country, and had gloried in it. If further glory, or even further gain, were to come out of this terrible war,—as great gains to men and nations do come from contests which are very terrible while they last,—he at least would not live to see it. So when he was left by his sons, he turned his face to the wall and died. There had of course been much said on this subject between the two brothers when they were together, and Frank had declared how special orders had been given to protect the house of the widow, if the waves of the war in Kentucky should surge up around Frankfort. Land very near to Frankfort had become debateable between the two armies, and the question of flying from their house had more than once been mooted between the aunt and her niece ; but, so far, that evil day had been staved off, and as yet Frankfort, the little capital of the state, was Northern territory.

"I suppose you will get home," said Frank, after musing awhile, "and look after my mother and Ada?"

"If I can I shall, of course. What else can I do with one leg?"

"Nothing in this war, Tom, of course."

Then there was another pause between them.

"What will Ada do?" said Frank.

"What will Ada do? Stay at home with my mother."

"Ay,—yes. But she will not remain always as Ada Forster."

"Do you mean to ask whether I shall marry her ;— because of my one leg? If she will have me, I certainly shall."

"And will she? Ought you to ask her?"

"If I found her seamed all over with small-pox, with

her limbs broken, blind, disfigured by any misfortune which could have visited her, I would take her as my wife all the same. If she were penniless it would make no difference. She shall judge for herself; but I shall expect her to act by me as I would have acted by her." Then there was another pause. "Look here, Frank," continued General Tom, "if you mean that I am to give her up as a reward to you for being sent home, I will have nothing to do with the bargain."

"I had intended no such bargain," said Frank, gloomily.

"Very well; then you can do as you please. If Ada will take me, I shall marry her as soon as she will let me. If my being sent home depends upon that, you will know how to act now."

Nevertheless he was sent home. There was not another word spoken between the two brothers about Ada Forster. Whether Frank thought that he might still have a chance through want of firmness on the part of the girl; or whether he considered that in keeping his brother away from home he could at least do himself no good; or whether, again, he resolved that he would act by his brother as a brother should act, without reference to Ada Forster, I will not attempt to say. For a day or two after the above conversation he was somewhat

sullen, and did not talk freely with his brother. After
that he brightened up once more, and before long the
two parted on friendly terms. General Frank remained
with his command, and General Tom was sent to the
hospital at Alexandria,—or to such hospitalities as he
might be able to enjoy at Washington in his mutilated
state,—till that affair of his exchange had been arranged.

In spite of his brother's influence at head-quarters this
could not be done in a day; nor could permission be
obtained for him to go home to Kentucky till such
exchange had been effected. In this way he was kept
in terrible suspense for something over two months, and
mid-winter was upon him before the joyful news arrived
that he was free to go where he liked. The officials in
Washington would have sent him back to Richmond
had he so pleased, seeing that a Federal general officer,
supposed to be of equal weight with himself, had been
sent back from some Southern prison in his place; but
he declined any such favour, declaring his intention of
going home to Kentucky. He was simply warned that
no pass South could after this be granted to him, and
then he went his way.

Disturbed as was the state of the country, nevertheless
railways ran from Washington to Baltimore, from Baltimore to Pittsburgh, from Pittsburgh to Cincinnati, and

from Cincinnati to Frankfort. So that General Tom's journey home, though with but one leg, was made much faster, and with less difficulty, than that last journey by which he reached the old family house. And again he presented himself on Christmas-eve. Ada declared that he remained purposely at Washington, so that he might make good his last promise to the letter; but I am inclined to think that he allowed no such romantic idea as that to detain him among the amenities of Washington.

He arrived again after dark, but on this occasion did not come knocking at the back door. He had fought his fight, had done his share of the battle, and now had reason to be afraid of no one. But again it was Ada who opened the door for him, "Oh, Tom; oh, my own one!" There never was a word of question between them as to whether that unseemly crutch and still unhealed wound was to make any difference between them. General Tom found before three hours were over that he lacked the courage to suggest that he might not be acceptable to her as a lover with one leg. There are times in which girls throw off all their coyness, and are as bold in their loves as men. Such a time was this with Ada Forster. In the course of another month the elder general simply sent word to the younger that they intended to be married in May, if the war did not prevent them; and the younger general simply sent back word that his duties at head-quarters would prevent his being present at the ceremony.

And they were married in May, though the din of war was going on around them on every side. And from that time to this the din of war is still going on, and they are in the thick of it. The carnage of their battles, and the hatreds of their civil contests, are terrible to us when we think of them: but may it not be that the beneficent power of Heaven, which they acknowledge as we do, is thus cleansing their land from that stain of slavery, to abolish which no human power seemed to be sufficient?

FATHER GILES OF BALLYMOY.

FATHER GILES OF BALLYMOY.

T is nearly thirty years since I, Archibald Green, first entered the little town of Ballymoy, in the west of Ireland, and became acquainted with one of the honestest fellows and best Christians whom it has ever been my good fortune to know. For twenty years he and I were fast friends, though he was much my elder. As he has now been ten years beneath the sod, I may tell the story of our first meeting.

Ballymoy is a so-called town,—or was in the days of which I am speaking,—lying close to the shores of Lough Corrib, in the county of Galway. It is on the road to no place, and, as the end of a road, has in itself nothing to attract a traveller. The scenery of Lough Corrib is grand ; but the lake is very large, and the fine

scenery is on the side opposite to Ballymoy, and hardly
to be reached, or even seen, from that place. There is
fishing,—but it is lake fishing. The salmon fishing of
Lough Corrib is far away from Ballymoy, where the little
river runs away from the lake down to the town of
Galway. There was then in Ballymoy one single street,
of which the characteristic at first sight most striking to
a stranger was its general appearance of being thoroughly
wet through. It was not simply that the rain water was
generally running down its unguttered streets in muddy,
random rivulets, hurrying towards the lake with true
Irish impetuosity, but that each separate house looked as
though the walls were reeking with wet; and the alter-
nated roofs of thatch and slate,—the slated houses being
just double the height of those that were thatched,—
assisted the eye and mind of the spectator in forming
this opinion. The lines were broken everywhere, and at
every break it seemed as though there was a free
entrance for the waters of heaven. The population of
Ballymoy was its second wonder. There had been no
famine then; no rot among the potatoes; and land
around Ballymoy had been let for nine, ten, and even
eleven pounds an acre. At all hours of the day, and at
nearly all hours of the night, able-bodied men were to be
seen standing in the streets, with knee-breeches un-

buttoned, with stockings rolled down over their brogues, and with swallow-tailed frieze coats. Nor, though thus idle, did they seem to suffer any of the distress of poverty. There were plenty of beggars, no doubt, in Ballymoy, but it never struck me that there was much distress in those days. The earth gave forth its potatoes freely, and neither man nor pig wanted more.

It was to be my destiny to stay a week at Ballymoy, on business, as to the nature of which I need not trouble the present reader. I was not, at that time, so well acquainted with the manners of the people of Connaught as I became afterwards, and I had certain misgivings as I was driven into the village on a jaunting-car from Tuam. I had just come down from Dublin, and had been informed there that there were two "hotels" in Ballymoy, but that one of the "hotels" might, perhaps, be found deficient in some of those comforts which I, as an Englishman, might require. I was therefore to ask for the "hotel" kept by Pat Kirwan. The other hotel was kept by Larry Kirwan; so that it behoved me to be particular. I had made the journey down from Dublin in a night and a day, travelling, as we then did travel in Ireland, by canal boats and by Bianconi's long cars; and I had dined at Tuam, and been driven over, after dinner

on an April evening; and when I reached Ballymoy I
was tired to death and very cold.

"Pat Kirwan's hotel," I said to the driver, almost
angrily. "Mind you don't go to the other."

"Shure, yer honour, and why not to Larry's? You'd
be getting better enthertainment at Larry's, because of
Father Giles."

I understood nothing about Father Giles, and wished
to understand nothing. But I did understand that I was
to go to Pat Kirwan's "hotel," and thither I insisted on
being taken.

It was dusk at this time, and the wind was blowing
down the street of Ballymoy, carrying before it wild
gusts of rain. In the west of Ireland March weather
comes in April, and it comes with a violence of its own,
though not with the cruelty of the English east wind.
At this moment my neck was ricked by my futile
endeavours to keep my head straight on the side car,
and the water had got under me upon the seat, and the
horse had come to a stand-still half-a-dozen times in the
last two minutes, and my apron had been trailed in the
mud, and I was very unhappy. For the last ten minutes
I had been thinking evil of everything Irish, and
especially of Connaught.

I was driven up to a queerly-shaped, three-cornered

house, that stood at the bottom of the street, and which seemed to possess none of the outside appurtenances of an inn.

"Is this Pat Kirwan's hotel?" said I.

"Faix, and it is then, yer honour," said the driver. "And barring only that Father Giles——"

But I had rung the bell, and as the door was now opened by a barefooted girl, I entered the little passage without hearing anything further about Father Giles.

"Could I have a bed-room immediately, with a fire in it?"

Not answering me directly, the girl led me into a sitting-room, in which my nose was at once greeted by that peculiar perfume which is given out by the relics of hot whisky-punch mixed with a great deal of sugar, and there she left me,

"Where is Pat Kirwan himself?" said I, coming to the door, and blustering somewhat. For, let it be re-membered, I was very tired; and it may be a fair question whether in the far west of Ireland a little bluster may not sometimes be of service. "If you have not a room ready, I will go to Larry Kirwan's," said I, showing that I understood the bearings of the place.

"It's right away at the furder end then, yer honour,"

said the driver, putting in his word, "and we comed by it ever so long since. But shure yer honour wouldn't think of leaving this house for that?"

This he said because Pat Kirwan's wife was close behind him.

Then Mrs. Kirwan assured me that I could and should be accommodated. The house, to be sure, was crowded, but she had already made arrangements, and had a bed ready. As for a fire in my bed-room, she could not recommend that, "becase the wind blew so mortial sthrong down the chimney since the pot had blown off,—bad cess to it; and that loon, Mick Hackett, wouldn't lend a hand to put it up again, becase there were jobs going on at the big house,—bad luck to every joint of his body, thin," said Mrs. Kirwan, with great energy. Nevertheless, she and Mick Hackett the mason were excellent friends.

I professed myself ready to go at once to the bed-room without the fire, and was led away up stairs. I asked where I was to eat my breakfast and dine on the next day, and was assured that I should have the room so strongly perfumed with whisky all to myself. I had been rather cross before, but on hearing this, I became decidedly sulky. It was not that I could not eat my breakfast in the chamber in question, but that I saw before me seven days of absolute misery, if I could have no other place of refuge for myself than a room in which, as was too plain, all Ballymoy came to drink and smoke. But there was no alternative, at any rate for that night and the following morning, and I therefore gulped down my anger without further spoken complaint, and followed the barefooted maiden up stairs, seeing my portmanteau carried up before me.

Ireland is not very well known now to all Englishmen, but it is much better known than it was in those days. On this my first visit into Connaught, I own that I was somewhat scared lest I should be made a victim to the wild lawlessness and general savagery of the people; and I fancied, as in the wet, windy gloom of the night, I could see the crowd of natives standing round the doors of the inn, and just discern their naked legs and old battered hats, that Ballymoy was probably one of those places so far removed from civilisation and law, as to be an unsafe residence for an English Protestant. I had undertaken the service on which I was employed, with my eyes more or less open, and was determined to go through with it;—but I confess that I was by this time alive to its dangers. It was an early resolution with me that I would not allow my portmanteau to be out of my sight. To that I would cling; with that ever close to me

would I live; on that, if needful, would I die. I therefore required that it should be carried up the narrow
stairs before me, and I saw it deposited safely in the bed-
room.

The stairs were very narrow and very steep. Ascend-
ing them was like climbing into a loft. The whole house
was built in a barbarous, uncivilised manner, and as fit
to be an hotel as it was to be a church. It was triangular
and all corners,—the most uncomfortably arranged building I had ever seen. From the top of the stairs I was
called upon to turn abruptly into the room destined for
me; but there was a side step which I had not noticed
under the glimmer of the small tallow candle, and I
stumbled headlong into the chamber, uttering impreca-
tions against Pat Kirwan, Ballymoy, and all Connaught.

I hope the reader will remember that I had travelled
for thirty consecutive hours, had passed sixteen in a
small comfortless canal boat without the power of stretch-
ing my legs, and that the wind had been at work upon
me sideways for the last three hours. I was terribly tired,
and I spoke very uncivilly to the young woman.

"Shure, yer honour, it's as clane as clane, and as dhry
as dhry, and has been slept in every night since the big
storm," said the girl, good-humouredly. Then she went
on to tell me something more about Father Giles, **of**

which, however, I could catch nothing, as she was bending over the bed, folding down the bedclothes. "Feel of 'em," said she, "they's dhry as dhry."

I did feel them, and the sheets were dry and clean, and the bed, though very small, looked as if it would be comfortable. So I somewhat softened my tone to her, and bade her call me the next morning at eight.

"Shure, yer honour, and Father Giles will call yer hisself," said the girl.

I begged that Father Giles might be instructed to do no such thing. The girl, however, insisted that he would, and then left me. Could it be that in this savage place, it was considered to be the duty of the parish priest to go round, with matins perhaps, or some other abominable papist ceremony, to the beds of all the strangers? My mother, who was a strict woman, had warned me vehemently against the machinations of the Irish priests, and I, in truth, had been disposed to ridicule her. Could it be that there were such machinations? Was it possible that my trousers might be refused me till I had taken mass? Or that force would be put upon me in some other shape, perhaps equally disagreeable?

Regardless of that and other horrors, or rather, I should perhaps say, determined to face manfully whatever horrors the night or morning might bring upon me, I

began to prepare for bed. There was something pleasant in the romance of sleeping at Pat Kirwan's house in
Ballymoy, instead of in my own room in Keppel Street,
Russell Square. So I chuckled inwardly at Pat Kirwan's
idea of an hotel, and unpacked my things.

There was a little table covered with a clean cloth, on
which I espied a small comb. I moved the comb carefully without touching it, and brought the table up to my
bedside. I put out my brushes and clean linen for the
morning, said my prayers, defying Father Giles and his
machinations, and jumped into bed. The bed certainly
was good, and the sheets were very pleasant. In five
minutes I was fast asleep.

How long I had slept when I was awakened, I never
knew. But it was at some hour in the dead of night,
when I was disturbed by footsteps in my room, and on
jumping up, I saw a tall, stout, elderly man standing with
his back towards me, in the middle of the room, brushing
his clothes with the utmost care. His coat was still on
his back, and his pantaloons on his legs; but he was
most assiduous in his attention to every part of his body
which he could reach.

I sat upright, gazing at him, as I thought then, for ten
minutes,—we will say that I did so perhaps for forty
seconds,—and of one thing I became perfectly certain,—

namely, that the clothes-brush was my own! Whether, according to Irish hotel law, a gentleman would be justified in entering a stranger's room at midnight for the sake of brushing his clothes, I could not say; but I felt quite sure that in such a case, he would be bound at least to use the hotel brush or his own. There was a manifest trespass in regard to my property.

"Sir," said I, speaking very sharply, with the idea of startling him, "what are you doing here in this chamber?"

"Deed, then, and I'm sorry I've waked ye, my boy," said the stout gentleman.

"Will you have the goodness, Sir, to tell me what you are doing here?"

"Bedad, then, just at this moment it's brushing my clothes, I am. It was badly they wanted it."

"I dare say they did. And you were doing it with my clothes-brush."

"And that's thrue too. And if a man hasn't a clothes-brush of his own, what else can he do but use somebody else's?"

"I think it's a great liberty, Sir," said I.

"And I think it's a little one. It's only in the size of it we differ. But I beg your pardon. There is your brush. I hope it will be none the worse."

Then he put down the brush, seated himself on one of the two chairs which the room contained, and slowly proceeded to pull off his shoes, looking me full in the face all the while.

" What are you going to do, Sir ? " said I, getting a little further out from under the clothes, and leaning over the table.

" I am going to bed," said the gentleman.

" Going to bed ! where ? "

" Here," said the gentleman ; and he still went on untying the knot of his shoe-string.

It had always been a theory with me, in regard not only to my own country, but to all others, that civilisation displays itself never more clearly than when it ordains that every man shall have a bed for himself. In older days Englishmen of good position,—men supposed to be gentlemen,—would sleep together and think nothing of it, as ladies, I am told, will still do. And in outlandish regions, up to this time, the same practice prevails. In parts of Spain you will be told that one bed offers sufficient accommodation for two men, and in Spanish America the traveller is considered to be fastidious who thinks that one on each side of him is oppressive. Among the poorer classes with ourselves this grand touchstone of civilisation has not yet made itself felt. For aught I know there might be no such touchstone in Connaught at all. There clearly seemed to be none such at Ballymoy.

"You can't go to bed here," said I, sitting bolt upright on the couch.

"You'll find you are wrong there, my friend," said the elderly gentleman. "But make yourself aisy, I won't do you the least harm in life, and I sleep as quiet as a mouse."

It was quite clear to me that time had come for action. I certainly would not let this gentleman get into my bed. I had been the first comer, and was for the night, at least, the proprietor of this room. Whatever might be the custom of this country in these wild regions, there could be no special law in the land justifying the landlord in such treatment of me as this.

"You won't sleep here, Sir," said I, jumping out of the bed, over the table, on to the floor, and confronting the stranger just as he had succeeded in divesting himself of his second shoe. "You won't sleep here to-night, and so you may as well go away."

With that I picked up his two shoes, took them to the door, and chucked them out. I heard them go rattling down the stairs, and I was glad that they made so much noise. He would see that I was quite in earnest.

"You must follow your shoes," said I, "and the sooner the better."

I had not even yet seen the man very plainly, and even now, at this time, I hardly did so, though I went close up to him and put my hand upon his shoulder. The light was very imperfect, coming from one small farthing candle, which was nearly burnt out in the socket. And I, myself, was confused, ill at ease, and for the moment unobservant. I knew that the man was older than myself, but I had not recognised him as being old enough to demand or enjoy personal protection by reason of his age. He was tall, and big, and burly,—as he appeared to me then. Hitherto, till his shoes had been chucked away, he had maintained imperturbable good-humour. When he heard the shoes clattering down stairs, it seemed that he did not like it, and he began to talk fast and in an angry voice. I would not argue with him, and I did not understand him, but still keeping my hand on the collar of his coat, I insisted that he should not sleep there. Go away out of that chamber he should.

"But it's my own," he said, shouting the words a dozen times. "It's my own room. It's my own room."

So this was Pat Kirwan himself,—drunk probably, or mad.

"It may be your own," said I; "but you've let it to

me for to-night, and you sha'n't sleep here;" so saying I backed him towards the door, and in so doing I trod upon his unguarded toe.

"Bother you, thin, for a pig-headed Englishman!" said he. "You've kilt me entirely now. So take your hands off my neck, will ye, before you have me throttled outright?"

I was sorry to have trod on his toe, but I stuck to him all the same. I had him near the door now, and I was determined to put him out into the passage. His face was very round and very red, and I thought that he must be drunk; and since I had found out that it was Pat Kirwan the landlord, I was more angry with the man than ever.

"You sha'n't sleep here, so you might as well go," I said, as I backed him away towards the door. This had not been closed since the shoes had been thrown out, and with something of a struggle between the doorposts, I got him out. I remembered nothing whatever as to the suddenness of the stairs. I had been fast asleep since I came up them, and hardly even as yet knew exactly where I was. So, when I got him through the aperture of the door, I gave him a push, as was most natural, I think, for me to do. Down he went backwards, —down the stairs, all in a heap, and I could hear that in his fall he had stumbled against Mrs. Kirwan, who was coming up, doubtless to ascertain the cause of all the trouble above her head.

A hope crossed my mind that the wife might be of assistance to her husband in this time of his trouble. The man had fallen very heavily, I knew, and had fallen backwards. And I remembered then how steep the stairs were. Heaven and earth! Suppose that he were killed, — or even seriously injured in his own house. What, in such case as that, would my life be worth in that wild country? Then I began to regret that I had been so hot. It might be that I had murdered a man on my first entrance into Connaught!

For a moment or two I could not make up my mind what I would first do. I was aware that both the land-lady and the servant were occupied with the body of the ejected occupier of my chamber, and I was aware also that I had nothing on but my night-shirt. I returned, therefore, within the door, but could not bring myself to shut myself in and return to bed without making some enquiry as to the man's fate. I put my head out, there-fore, and did make enquiry.

"I hope he is not much hurt by his fall," I said.

"Ochone, ochone! murdher, murdher! Spake, Father Giles, dear, for the love of God!" Such and many such exclamations I heard from the women at the bottom of the stairs.

"I hope he is not much hurt," I said again, putting my head out from the doorway; "but he shouldn't have forced himself into my room."

"His room, the omadhaun!—the born idiot!" said the landlady.

"Faix, Ma'am, and Father Giles is a dead man," said the girl, who was kneeling over the prostrate body in the passage below.

I heard her say Father Giles as plain as possible, and then I became aware that the man whom I had thrust out was not the landlord, but the priest of the parish! My heart became sick within me as I thought of the troubles around me. And I was sick also with fear lest the man who had fallen should be seriously hurt. But why—why—why had he forced his way into my room? How was it to be expected that I should have remembered that the stairs of the accursed house came flush up to the door of the chamber?

"He shall be hanged if there's law in Ireland," said a voice down below; and as far as I could see it might be that I should be hung. When I heard that last voice I began to think that I had in truth killed a man, and a cold sweat broke out all over me, and I stood for awhile shivering where I was. Then I remembered that it behoved me as a man to go down among my enemies below, and to see what had really happened, to learn whom I had hurt—let the consequences to myself be what they might. So I quickly put on some of my clothes—a pair of trousers, a loose coat, and a pair of slippers, and I descended the stairs. By this time they had taken the priest into the whisky-perfumed chamber below, and although the hour was late, there were already six or seven persons with him. Among them was the real Pat Kirwan himself, who had not been so particular about his costume as I had.

Father Giles—for indeed it was Father Giles, the priest of the parish—had been placed in an old arm-chair, and his head was resting against Mrs. Kirwan's body. I could tell from the moans which he emitted that there was still, at any rate, hope of life.

Pat Kirwan, who did not quite understand what had happened, and who was still half asleep, and as I afterwards learned, half tipsy, was standing over him wagging his head. The girl was also standing by, with an old woman and two men who had made their way in through the kitchen.

"Have you sent for a doctor?" said I.

"Oh, you born blagghuard!" said the woman. "You

thief of the world! That the like of you should ever have darkened my door!"

"You can't repent it more than I do, Mrs. Kirwan; but hadn't you better send for the doctor?"

"Faix, and for the police too, you may be shure of that, young man. To go and chuck him out of the room like that—his own room too, and he a priest and an ould man—he that had given up the half of it, though I axed him not to do so, for a sthranger as nobody knowed nothing about."

The truth was coming out by degrees. Not only was the man I had put out Father Giles, but he was also the proper occupier of the room. At any rate somebody ought to have told me all this before they put me to sleep in the same bed with the priest.

I made my way round to the injured man, and put my hand upon his shoulder, thinking that perhaps I might be able to ascertain the extent of the injury. But the angry woman, together with the girl, drove me away, heaping on me terms of reproach, and threatening me with the gallows at Galway.

I was very anxious that a doctor should be brought as soon as possible; and as it seemed that nothing was being done, I offered to go and search for one. But I was given to understand that I should not be allowed to leave the house until the police had come. I had therefore to remain there for half-an-hour, or nearly so, till a sergeant, with two other policemen, really did come. During this time I was in a most wretched frame of mind. I knew no one at Ballymoy or in the neighbourhood. From the manner in which I was addressed, and also threatened by Mrs. Kirwan and by those who came in and out of the room, I was aware that I should encounter the most intense hostility. I had heard of Irish murders, and heard also of the love of the people for their priests, and I really began to doubt whether my life might not be in danger.

During this time, while I was thus waiting, Father Giles himself recovered his consciousness. He had been stunned by the fall, but his mind came back to him, though by no means all at once; and while I was left in the room with him he hardly seemed to remember all the events of the past hour.

I was able to discover from what was said that he had been for some days past, or, as it afterwards turned out, for the last month, the tenant of the room, and that when I arrived he had been drinking tea with Mrs. Kirwan. The only other public bed-room in the hotel was occupied, and he had with great kindness given the landlady permission to put the Saxon stranger into his chamber. All this came out by degrees, and I could see how the idea of my base and cruel ingratitude rankled in the heart of Mrs. Kirwan. It was in vain that I expostulated and explained, and submitted myself humbly to everything that was said around me.

"But, Ma'am," I said, "if I had only been told that it was the reverend gentleman's bed!"

"Bed, indeed! To hear the blagghuard talk you'd think it was axing Father Giles to sleep along with the likes of him we were. And there's two beds in the room as dacent as any Christian iver stretched in."

It was a new light to me. And yet I had known over night, before I undressed, that there were two bedsteads in the room! I had seen them, and had quite forgotten the fact in my confusion when I was woken. I had been very stupid, certainly. I felt that now. But I had truly believed that that big man was going to get into my little bed. It was terrible as I thought of it now. The good-natured priest, for the sake of accommodating a stranger, had consented to give up half of his room, and had been repaid for his kindness by being—perhaps murdered! And yet, though just then I hated myself cordially, I could not quite bring myself to look at the matter as they looked at it. There were excuses to be made, if only I could get anyone to listen to them.

" He was using my brush—my clothes-brush—indeed he was," I said.   " Not but what he'd be welcome ; but it made me think he was an intruder."

"And wasn't it too much honour for the likes of ye ? " said one of the women, with infinite scorn in the tone of her voice.

" I did use the gentleman's clothes-brush, certainly," said the priest.   They were the first collected words he had spoken, and I felt very grateful to him for them.   It seemed to me that a man who could condescend to re-member that he had used a clothes-brush could not really be hurt to death, even though he had been pushed down such very steep stairs as those belonging to Pat Kirwan's hotel.

" And I'm sure you were very welcome, Sir," said I. " It wasn't that I minded the clothes-brush.   It wasn't, indeed ; only I thought—indeed, I did think that there was only one bed.   And they had put me into the room, and had not said anything about anybody else.   And what was I to think when I woke up in the middle of the night ? "

" Faix, and you'll have enough to think of in Galway gaol, for that's where you're going to," said one of the bystanders.

I can hardly explain the bitterness that was displayed

against me. No violence was absolutely shown to me, but I could not move without eliciting a manifest determination that I was not to be allowed to stir out of the room. Red angry eyes were glowering at me, and every word I spoke called down some expression of scorn and ill-will. I was beginning to feel glad that the police were coming, thinking that I needed protection. I was thoroughly ashamed of what I had done, and yet I could not discover that I had been very wrong at any particular moment. Let any man ask himself the question, what he would do, if he supposed that a stout old gentleman had entered his room at an inn and insisted on getting into his bed? It was not my fault that there had been no proper landing-place at the top of the stairs.

Two sub-constables had been in the room for some time before the sergeant came, and with the sergeant arrived also the doctor, and another priest — Father Columb he was called—who, as I afterwards learned, was curate or coadjutor to Father Giles. By this time there was quite a crowd in the house, although it was past one o'clock, and it seemed that all Ballymoy knew that its priest had been foully misused. It was manifest to me that there was something in the Roman Catholic religion which made the priests very dear to the people; for I doubt whether in any village in England, had such an accident happened to the rector, all the people would have roused themselves at midnight to wreak their vengeance on the assailant. For vengeance they were now beginning to clamour, and even before the sergeant of police had come, the two sub-constables were standing over me; and I felt that they were protecting me from the people in order that they might give me up—to the gallows!

I did not like the Ballymoy doctor at all—then, or even at a later period of my visit to that town. On his arrival he made his way up to the priest through the crowd, and would not satisfy their affection or my anxiety by declaring at once that there was no danger. Instead of doing so he insisted on the terrible nature of the outrage and the brutality shown by the assailant. And at every hard word he said, Mrs. Kirwan would urge him on.

"That's thrue for you, doctor!" "'Deed, and you may say that, doctor; two as good beds as ever Christian stretched in!" "'Deed, and it was just Father Giles's own room, as you may say, since the big storm fetched the roof off his riverence's house below there."

Thus gradually I was learning the whole history. The roof had been blown off Father Giles's own house, and therefore he had gone to lodge at the inn! He had been willing to share his lodging with a stranger, and this had been his reward!

"I hope, doctor, that the gentleman is not much hurt," said I, very meekly.

"Do you suppose a gentleman like that, Sir, can be thrown down a long flight of stairs without being hurt?" said the doctor, in an angry voice. "It is no thanks to you, Sir, that his neck has not been sacrificed."

Then there arose a hum of indignation, and the two policemen standing over me bustled about a little, coming very close to me, as though they thought they should have something to do to protect me from being torn to pieces.

I bethought me that it was my special duty in such a crisis to show a spirit, if it were only for the honour of my Saxon blood among the Celts. So I spoke up again, as loud as I could well speak.

"No one in this room is more distressed at what has occurred than I am. I am most anxious to know, for the gentleman's sake, whether he has been seriously hurt?"

"Very seriously hurt indeed," said the doctor; "very seriously hurt. The vertebræ may have been injured for aught I know at present."

"Arrah, blazes, man," said a voice, which I learned

afterwards had belonged to an officer of the revenue corps of men which was then stationed at Ballymoy, a gentleman with whom I became afterwards familiarly acquainted; Tom Macdermot was his name, Captain Tom Macdermot, and he came from the county of Leitrim,— "Arrah, blazes, man; do ye think a gentleman's to fall sthrait headlong backwards down such a ladder as that, and not find it inconvanient? Only that he's the priest, and has had his own luck, sorrow a neck belonging to him there would be this minute."

"Be aisy, Tom," said Father Giles himself; and I was delighted to hear him speak. Then there was a pause for a moment. "Tell the gentleman I aint so bad at all," said the priest; and from that moment I felt an affection to him which never afterwards waned.

They got him up stairs back into the room from which he had been evicted, and I was carried off to the police-station, where I positively spent the night. What a night it was! I had come direct from London, sleeping on my road but once in Dublin, and now I found myself accommodated with a stretcher in the police barracks at Ballymoy! And the worst of it was that I had business to do at Ballymoy which required that I should hold up my head and make much of myself. The few words which had been spoken by the priest had comforted me and had enabled me to think again of my own position. Why was I locked up? No magistrate had committed me. It was really a question whether I had done anything illegal. As that man whom Father Giles called Tom had very properly explained, if people will have ladders instead of staircases in their houses, how is anybody to put an intruder out of the room without risk of breaking the intruder's neck? And as to the fact—now an undoubted fact—that Father Giles was no intruder, the fault in that lay with the Kirwans, who had told me nothing of the truth. The boards of the stretcher in the police-station were very hard, in spite of the blankets with which I had been furnished; and as I lay there I began to remind myself that there certainly must be law in county Galway. So I called to the attendant policeman and asked him by whose authority I was locked up.

"Ah, thin, don't bother," said the policeman; "shure, and you've given throuble enough this night!" The dawn was at that moment breaking, so I turned myself on the stretcher, and resolved that I would put a bold face on it all when the day should come.

The first person I saw in the morning was Captain Tom, who came into the room where I was lying, followed by a little boy with my portmanteau. The sub-inspector of police who ruled over the men at Ballymoy lived, as I afterwards learned, at Oranmore, so that I had not, at this conjuncture, the honour of seeing him. Captain Tom assured me that he was an excellent fellow, and rode to hounds like a bird. As in those days I rode to hounds myself—as nearly like a bird as I was able—I was glad to have such an account of my head-gaoler. The sub-constables seemed to do just what Captain Tom told them, and there was, no doubt, a very good understanding between the police force and the revenue officer.

"Well, now, I'll tell you what you must do, Mr. Green," said the captain.

"In the first place," said I, "I must protest that I'm now locked up here illegally."

"Oh, bother; now don't make yourself unaisy."

"That's all very well, Captain——. I beg your pardon, Sir, but I didn't catch any name plainly except the Christian name."

"My name is Macdermot—Tom Macdermot. They call me captain—but that's neither here nor there."

"I suppose, Captain Macdermot, the police here cannot lock up anybody they please, without a warrant?"

"And where would you have been if they hadn't locked you up? I'm blessed if they wouldn't have had you into the Lough before this time."

There might be something in that, and I therefore resolved to forgive the personal indignity which I had suffered, if I could secure something like just treatment for the future. Captain Tom had already told me that Father Giles was doing pretty well.

"He's as sthrong as a horse, you see, or, sorrow a doubt, he'd be a dead man this minute. The back of his neck is as black as your hat with the bruises, and it's the same way with him all down his loins. A man like that, you know, not just as young as he was once, falls mortial heavy. But he's as jolly as a four-year old," said Captain Tom, "and you're to go and ate your breakfast with him, in his bed-room, so that you may see with your own eyes that there are two beds there."

"I remembered it afterwards quite well," said I.

"'Deed, and Father Giles got such a kick of laughter this morning, when he came to understand that you thought he was going to get into bed alongside of you, that he strained himself all over again, and I thought he'd have frightened the house, yelling with the pain. But anyway you've to go over and see him. So now you'd better get yourself dressed."

This announcement was certainly very pleasant. Against Father Giles, of course, I had no feeling of bitterness. He had behaved well throughout, and I was quite alive to the fact that the light of his countenance would afford me a better ægis against the ill-will of the people of Ballymoy, than anything the law would do for me. So I dressed myself in the barrack-room, while Captain Tom waited without, and then I sallied out under his guidance to make a second visit to Pat Kirwan's hotel. I was amused to see that the police, though by no means subject to Captain Tom's orders, let me go without the least difficulty, and that the boy was allowed to carry my portmanteau away with him.

"Oh, it's all right," said Captain Tom when I alluded to this. "You're not down in the sheet. You were only there for protection, you know."

Nevertheless, I had been taken there by force, and had been locked up by force. If, however, they were disposed to forget all that, so was I. I did not return to the barracks again ; and when, after that, the policemen whom I had known met me in the street, they always accosted me as though I were an old friend ; hoping my honour had found a better bed than when they last saw me. They had not looked at me with any friendship in their eyes when they had stood over me in Pat Kirwan's parlour.

This was my first view of Ballymoy, and of the "hotel" by daylight. I now saw that Mrs. Pat Kirwan kept a grocery establishment, and that the three-cornered house which had so astonished me was very small. Had I seen it before I entered it, I should hardly have dared to look there for a night's lodging. As it was, I stayed there for a fortnight, and was by no means uncomfortable. Knots of men and women were now standing in groups round the door, and, indeed, the lower end of the street was almost crowded.

"They're all here," whispered Captain Tom, "because they've heard how Father Giles has been murdered during the night by a terrible Saxon; and there isn't a man or woman among them who doesn't know that you are the man who did it."

"But they know also, I suppose," said I, "that Father Giles is alive."

"Bedad, yes, they know that, or I wouldn't be in your skin, my boy. But come along. We mustn't keep the priest waiting for his breakfast."

I could see that they all looked at me, and there were some of them, especially among the women, whose looks I did not even yet like. They spoke among each other in Gaelic, and I could perceive that they were talking of me.

"Can't you understand, then," said Captain Tom, speaking to them aloud, just as he entered the house, "that father Giles, the Lord be praised, is as well as ever he was in his life? Shure it was only an accident."

"An accident done on purpose, Captain Tom," said one person.

"What is it to you how it was done, Mick Healy? If Father Giles is satisfied, isn't that enough for the likes of you? Get out of that, and let the gentleman pass." Then Captain Tom pushed Mick away roughly, and the others let us enter the house. "Only they wouldn't do it unless somebody gave them the wink, they'd pull you in pieces this moment for a dandy of punch—they would, indeed."

Perhaps Captain Tom exaggerated the prevailing feeling, thinking thereby to raise the value of his own service in protecting me; but I was quite alive to the fact that I had done a most dangerous deed, and had a most narrow escape.

I found Father Giles sitting up in his bed, while Mrs. Kirwan was rubbing his shoulder diligently with an embrocation of arnica. The girl was standing by with a basin half full of the same, and I could see that the priest's neck and shoulders were as red as a raw beefsteak. He winced grievously under the rubbing, but he bore it like a man.

"And here comes the hero," said Father Giles. "Now

stop a minute or two, Mrs. Kirwan, while we have a
mouthful of breakfast, for I'll go bail that Mr. Green is
hungry after his night's rest. I hope you got a better
bed, Mr. Green, than the one I found you in when I was
unfortunate enough to waken you last night. There it
is, all ready for you still," said he; "and if you accept of
it to-night, take my advice and don't let a trifle stand in
the way of your dhraims."

"I hope, thin, the gintleman will contrive to suit
hisself elsewhere," said Mrs. Kirwan.

"He'll be very welcome to take up his quarters here
if he likes," said the priest. "And why not? But,
bedad, Sir, you'd better be a little more careful the next
time you see a stranger using your clothes-brush. They
are not so strict here in their ideas of *meum* and *tuum* as
they are perhaps in England; and if you had broken my
neck for so small an offence, I don't know but what they'd
have stretched your own."

We then had breakfast together, Father Giles, Captain
Tom, and I; and a very good breakfast we had. By
degrees even Mrs. Kirwan was induced to look favour-
ably at me, and before the day was over I found myself
to be regarded as a friend in the establishment. And as
a friend I certainly was regarded by Father Giles—then,
and for many a long day afterwards. And many times

when he has, in years since that, but years nevertheless which are now long back, come over and visited me in my English home, he has told the story of the manner in which we first became acquainted. "When you find a gentleman asleep," he would say, "always ask his leave before you take a liberty with his clothes-brush."

MALACHI'S COVE.

MALACHI'S COVE.

ON the northern coast of Cornwall, between Tintagel and Bossiney, down to the very margin of the sea, there lived not long since an old man who got his living by saving seaweed from the waves, and selling it for manure. The cliffs there are bold and fine, and the sea beats in upon them from the north with a grand violence. I doubt whether it be not the finest morsel of cliff scenery in England, though it is beaten by many portions of the west coast of Ireland, and perhaps also by spots in Wales and Scotland. Cliffs should be nearly precipitous, they should be broken in their outlines, and should barely admit here and there of an insecure passage from the summit of the sand at their feet. The sea should come, if not up to them, at least very near to them, and then, above all things, the water

below them should be blue, and not of that dead leaden
colour which is so familiar to us in England. At Tintagel
all these requisites are there, except that bright blue colour
which is so lovely. But the cliffs themselves are bold and
well broken, and the margin of sand at high water is very
narrow,—so narrow that at spring-tides there is barely a
footing there.

Close upon this margin was the cottage or hovel
of Malachi Trenglos, the old man of whom I have
spoken.

But Malachi, or old Glos, as he was commonly called by
the people around him, had not built his house absolutely
upon the sand. There was a fissure in the rock so great
that at the top it formed a narrow ravine, and so complete
from the summit to the base that it afforded an opening
for a steep and rugged track from the top of the rock to
the bottom. This fissure was so wide at the bottom that
it had afforded space for Trenglos to fix his habitation
on a foundation of rock, and here he had lived for many
years. It was told of him that in the early days of his
trade he had always carried the weed in a basket on his
back to the top, but latterly he had been possessed of a
donkey, which had been trained to go up and down the
steep track with a single pannier over his loins, for the
rocks would not admit of panniers hanging by his side;

and for this assistant he had built a shed adjoining his own, and almost as large as that in which he himself resided.

But as years went on, old Glos procured other assistance than that of the donkey, or, as I should rather say, Providence supplied him with other help; and, indeed, had it not been so, the old man must have given up his cabin and his independence and gone into the workhouse at Camelford. For rheumatism had afflicted him, old age had bowed him till he was nearly double, and by degrees he became unable to attend the donkey on its upward passage to the world above, or even to assist in rescuing the coveted weed from the waves.

At the time to which our story refers Trenglos had not been up the cliff for twelve months, and for the last six months he had done nothing towards the further-ance of his trade, except to take the money and keep it, if any of it was kept, and occasionally to shake down a bundle of fodder for the donkey. The real work of the business was done altogether by Mahala Trenglos, his granddaughter.

Mally Trenglos was known to all the farmers round the coast, and to all the small tradespeople in Camelford. She was a wild-looking, almost unearthly creature, with wild flowing, black, uncombed hair, small in stature, with small hands and bright black eyes; but people said that she was very strong, and the children around declared that she worked day and night and knew nothing of fatigue. As to her age there were many doubts. Some said she was ten, and others five-and-twenty, but the reader may be allowed to know that at this time she had in truth passed her twentieth birthday. The old people spoke well of Mally, because she was so good to her grandfather; and it was said of her that though she carried to him a little gin and tobacco almost daily, she bought nothing for herself;—and as to the gin, no one who looked at her would accuse her of meddling with that. But she had no friends and but few acquaintances among people of her own age. They said that she was fierce and ill-natured, that she had not a good word for anyone, and that she was, complete at all points, a thorough little vixen. The young men did not care for her; for, as regarded dress, all days were alike with her. She never made herself smart on Sundays. She was generally without stockings, and seemed to care not at all to exercise any of those feminine attractions which might have been hers had she studied to attain them. All days were the same to her in regard to dress; and, indeed, till lately, all days had, I fear, been the same to her in other respects. Old Malachi had never been seen inside a place of worship since he had taken to live under the cliff.

But within the last two years Mally had submitted herself to the teaching of the clergyman at Tintagel, and had appeared at church on Sundays, if not absolutely with punctuality, at any rate so often that no one who knew the peculiarity of her residence was disposed to quarrel with her on that subject. But she made no difference in her dress on these occasions. She took her place on a low stone seat just inside the church door, clothed as usual in her thick red serge petticoat and loose brown serge jacket, such being the apparel which she had found to be best adapted for her hard and perilous work among the waters. She had pleaded to the clergyman when he attacked her on the subject of church attendance with vigour that she had got no church-going clothes. He had explained to her that she would be received there without distinction to her clothing. Mally had taken him at his word, and had gone, with a courage which certainly deserved admiration, though I doubt whether there was not mingled with it an obstinacy which was less admirable.

For people said that old Glos was rich, and that Mally might have proper clothes if she chose to buy them. Mr. Polwarth, the clergyman, who, as the old man could not come to him, went down the rocks to the old man, did make some hint on the matter in Mally's absence. But old Glos, who had been patient with him on other matters, turned upon him so angrily when he made an allusion to money, that Mr. Polwarth found himself obliged to give that matter up, and Mally continued to sit upon the stone bench in her short serge petticoat, with her long hair streaming down her face. She did so far sacrifice to decency as on such occasions to tie up her back hair with an old shoestring. So tied it would remain through the Monday and Tuesday, but by Wednesday afternoon Mally's hair had generally managed to escape.

As to Mally's indefatigable industry there could be no manner of doubt, for the quantity of seaweed which she and the donkey amassed between them was very surprising. Old Glos, it was declared, had never collected half what Mally gathered together; but then the article was becoming cheaper, and it was necessary that the exertion should be greater. So Mally and the donkey toiled and toiled, and the seaweed came up in heaps which surprised those who looked at her little hands and light form. Was there not some one who helped her at nights, some fairy, or demon, or the like? Mally was so snappish in her answers to people that she had no right to be surprised if illnatured things were said of her.

No one ever heard Mally Trenglos complain of her work, but about this time she was heard to make great and loud complaints of the treatment she received from some of her neighbours. It was known that she went with her plaints to Mr. Polwarth; and when he could not help her, or did not give her such instant help as she needed, she went—ah, so foolishly! to the office of a certain attorney at Camelford, who was not likely to prove himself a better friend than Mr. Polwarth.

Now the nature of her injury was as follows. The place in which she collected her seaweed was a little cove ;—the people had come to call it Malachi's Cove from the name of the old man who lived there ;—which was so formed, that the margin of the sea therein could only be reached by the passage from the top down to Trenglos's hut. The breadth of the cove when the sea was out might perhaps be two hundred yards, and on each side the rocks ran out in such a way that both from north and south the domain of Trenglos was guarded from intruders. And this locality had been well chosen for its intended purpose.

There was a rush of the sea into the cove, which carried there large, drifting masses of seaweed, leaving

them among the rocks when the tide was out. During
the equinoctial winds of the spring and autumn the
supply would never fail; and even when the sea was
calm, the long, soft, salt-bedewed, trailing masses of the
weed, could be gathered there when they could not be
found elsewhere for miles along the coast. The task of
getting the weed from the breakers was often difficult and
dangerous,—so difficult that much of it was left to be
carried away by the next incoming tide.

Mally doubtless did not gather half the crop that was
there at her feet. What was taken by the returning
waves she did not regret; but when interlopers came
upon her cove, and gathered her wealth,—her grandfather's wealth, beneath her eyes, then her heart was
broken. It was this interloping, this intrusion, that drove
poor Mally to the Camelford attorney. But, alas, though
the Camelford attorney took Mally's money, he could do
nothing for her, and her heart was broken !

She had an idea, in which no doubt her grandfather
shared, that the path to the cove was, at any rate, their
property. When she was told that the cove, and sea
running into the cove, were not the freeholds of her
grandfather, she understood that the statement might be
true. But what then as to the use of the path ? Who
had made the path what it was ? Had she not painfully,

wearily, with exceeding toil, carried up bits of rock with her own little hands, that her grandfather's donkey might have footing for his feet? Had she not scraped together crumbs of earth along the face of the cliff that she might make easier to the animal the track of that rugged way? And now, when she saw big farmers' lads coming down with other donkeys,—and, indeed, there was one who came with a pony; no boy, but a young man, old enough to know better than rob a poor old man and a young girl,—she reviled the whole human race, and swore that the Camelford attorney was a fool.

Any attempt to explain to her that there was still weed enough for her was worse than useless. Was it not all hers and his, or, at any rate, was not the sole way to it his and hers? And was not her trade stopped and impeded? Had she not been forced to back her laden donkey down, twenty yards she said, but it had, in truth, been five, because Farmer Gunliffe's son had been in the way with his thieving pony? Farmer Gunliffe had wanted to buy her weed at his own price, and because she had refused he had set on his thieving son to destroy her in this wicked way.

"I'll hamstring the beast the next time as he's down here!" said Mally to old Glos, while the angry fire literally streamed from her eyes.

Farmer Gunliffe's small homestead,—he held about fifty acres of land,—was close by the village of Tintagel, and not a mile from the cliff. The sea-wrack, as they call it, was pretty well the only manure within his reach, and no doubt he thought it hard that he should be kept from using it by Mally Trenglos and her obstinacy.

"There's heaps of other coves, Barty," said Mally to Barty Gunliffe, the farmer's son.

"But none so nigh, Mally, nor yet none that fills 'emselves as this place."

Then he explained to her that he would not take the weed that came up close to hand. He was bigger than she was, and stronger, and would get it from the outer rocks, with which she never meddled. Then, with scorn in her eye, she swore that she could get it where he durst not venture, and repeated her threat of hamstringing the pony. Barty laughed at her wrath, jeered her because of her wild hair, and called her a mermaid.

"I'll mermaid you!" she cried. "Mermaid, indeed! I wouldn't be a man to come and rob a poor girl and an old cripple. But you're no man, Barty Gunliffe! You're not half a man."

Nevertheless, Bartholomew Gunliffe was a very fine young fellow as far as the eye went. He was about five feet eight inches high, with strong arms and legs, with light curly brown hair and blue eyes. His father was but in a small way as a farmer, but, nevertheless, Barty Gunliffe was well thought of among the girls around. Everybody like Barty,—excepting only Mally Trenglos, and she hated him like poison.

Barty, when he was asked why so good natured a lad as he persecuted a poor girl and an old man, threw himself upon the justice of the thing. It wouldn't do at all, according to his view, that any single person should take upon himself to own that which God Almighty sent as the common property of all. He would do Mally no harm, and so he had told her. But Mally was a vixen, —a wicked little vixen ; and she must be taught to have a civil tongue in her head. When once Mally would speak him civil as he went for weed, he would get his father to pay the old man some sort of toll for the use of the path.

"Speak him civil?" said Mally. "Never; not while I have a tongue in my mouth !" And I fear old Glos encouraged her rather than otherwise in her view of the matter.

But her grandfather did not encourage her to hamstring the pony. Hamstringing a pony would be a serious thing, and old Glos thought it might be very awkward for both of them if Mally were put into prison. He suggested, therefore, that all manner of impediments should be put in the way of the pony's feet, surmising that the well-trained donkey might be able to work in spite of them. And Barty Gunliffe, on his next descent, did find the passage very awkward when he came near to Malachi's hut, but he made his way down, and poor Mally saw the lumps of rock at which she had laboured so hard pushed on one side or rolled out of the way with a steady persistency of injury towards herself that almost drove her frantic.

"Well, Barty, you're a nice boy," said old Glos, sitting in the doorway of the hut, as he watched the intruder.

"I aint a doing no harm to none as doesn't harm me," said Barty. "The sea's free to all, Malachi."

"And the sky's free to all, but I mustn't get up on the top of your big barn to look at it," said Mally, who was standing among the rocks with a long hook in her hand. The long hook was the tool with which she worked in dragging the weed from the waves. "But you aint got no justice, nor yet no sperrit, or you wouldn't come here to vex an old man like he."

"I didn't want to vex him, nor yet to vex you, Mally. You let me be for a while, and we'll be friends yet."

"Friends!" exclaimed Mally. "Who'd have the likes of you for a friend? What are you moving them stones for? Them stones belongs to grandfather." And in her wrath she made a movement as though she were going to fly at him.

"Let him be, Mally," said the old man; "let him be. He'll get his punishment. He'll come to be drowned some day if he comes down here when the wind is in shore."

"That he may be drowned then!" said Mally, in her anger. "If he was in that big hole there among the rocks, and the sea running in at half tide, I wouldn't lift a hand to help him out."

"Yes you would, Mally; you'd fish me up with your hook like a big stick of seaweed."

She turned from him with scorn as he said this, and went into the hut. It was time for her to get ready for her work, and one of the great injuries done her lay in this,—that such a one as Barty Gunliffe should come and look at her during her toil among the breakers.

It was an afternoon in April, and the hour was something after four o'clock. There had been a heavy wind from the north-west all the morning, with gusts of rain, and the sea-gulls had been in and out of the cove all the day, which was a sure sign to Mally that the incoming tide would cover the rocks with weed.

The quick waves were now returning with wonderful

celerity over the low reefs, and the time had come at
which the treasure must be seized, if it was to be garnered
on that day. By seven o'clock it would be growing dark,
at nine it would be high water, and before daylight the
crop would be carried out again if not collected. All
this Mally understood very well, and some of this Barty
was beginning to understand also.

As Mally came down with her bare feet, bearing her
long hook in her hand, she saw Barty's pony standing
patiently on the sand, and in her heart she longed to
attack the brute. Barty at this moment, with a common
three-pronged fork in his hand, was standing down on a
large rock, gazing forth towards the waters. He had
declared that he would gather the weed only at places
which were inaccessible to Mally, and he was looking out
that he might settle where he would begin.

"Let un be, let un be," shouted the old man to Mally,
as he saw her take a step towards the beast, which she
hated almost as much as she hated the man.

Hearing her grandfather's voice through the wind, sne
desisted from her purpose, if any purpose she had had,
and went forth to her work. As she passed down the
cove, and scrambled in among the rocks, she saw Barty
still standing on his perch; out beyond, the white-curling
waves were cresting and breaking themselves with

violence, and the wind was howling among the caverns and abutments of the cliff.

Every now and then there came a squall of rain, and though there was sufficient light, the heavens were black with clouds. A scene more beautiful might hardly be found by those who love the glories of the coast. The light for such objects was perfect. Nothing could exceed the grandeur of the colours,—the blue of the open sea, the white of the breaking waves, the yellow sands, or the streaks of red and brown which gave such richness to the cliff.

But neither Mally nor Barty were thinking of such things as these. Indeed they were hardly thinking of their trade after its ordinary forms. Barty was meditating how he could best accomplish his purpose of working beyond the reach of Mally's feminine powers, and Mally was resolving that wherever Barty went she would go farther.

And, in many respects, Mally had the advantage. She knew every rock in the spot, and was sure of those which gave a good foothold, and sure also of those which did not. And then her activity had been made perfect by practice for the purpose to which it was to be devoted. Barty, no doubt, was stronger than she, and quite as active. But Barty could not jump among the waves from one stone to another as she could do, nor was he as yet able to get aid in his work from the very force of the water as she could get it. She had been hunting seaweed in that cove since she had been an urchin of six years old, and she knew every hole and corner and every spot of vantage. The waves were her friends, and she could use them. She could measure their strength, and knew when and where it would cease.

Mally was great down in the salt pools of her own cove,—great, and very fearless. As she watched Barty make his way forward from rock to rock, she told herself, gleefully, that he was going astray. The curl of the wind as it blew into the cove would not carry the weed up to the northern buttresses of the cove ; and then there was the great hole just there,—the great hole of which she had spoken when she wished him evil.

And now she went to work, hooking up the dishevelled hairs of the ocean, and landing many a cargo on the extreme margin of the sand, from whence she would be able in the evening to drag it back before the invading waters would return to reclaim the spoil.

And on his side also Barty made his heap up against the northern buttresses of which I have spoken. Barty's heap became big and still bigger, so that he knew, let the pony work as he might, he could not take it all up that evening. But still it was not as large as Mally's heap. Mally's hook was better than his fork, and Mally's skill was better than his strength. And when he failed in some haul Mally would jeer him with a wild, weird laughter, and shriek to him through the wind that he was not half a man. At first he answered her with laughing words, but before long, as she boasted of her success and pointed to his failure, he became angry, and then he answered her no more. He became angry with himself, in that he missed so much of the plunder before him.

The broken sea was full of the long straggling growth which the waves had torn up from the bottom of the ocean, but the masses were carried past him, away from him,—nay, once or twice over him; and then Mally's weird voice would sound in his ear, jeering him. The gloom among the rocks was now becoming thicker and thicker, the tide was beating in with increased strength, and the gusts of wind came with quicker and greater violence. But still he worked on. While Mally worked he would work, and he would work for some time after she was driven in. He would not be beaten by a girl.

The great hole was now full of water, but of water which seemed to be boiling as though in a pot. And the pot was full of floating masses,—large treasures of seaweed which were thrown to and fro upon its surface, but lying there so thick that one would seem almost able to rest upon it without sinking.

Mally knew well how useless it was to attempt to rescue aught from the fury of that boiling caldron. The hole went in under the rocks, and the side of it towards the shore lay high, slippery, and steep. The hole, even at low water, was never empty; and Mally believed that there was no bottom to it. Fish thrown in there could escape out to the ocean, miles away,—so Mally in her softer moods would tell the visitors to the cove. She knew the hole well. Poulnadioul she was accustomed to call it; which was supposed, when translated, to mean that this was the hole of the Evil One. Never did Mally attempt to make her own of weed which had found its way into that pot.

But Barty Gunliffe knew no better, and she watched him as he endeavoured to steady himself on the treacherously slippery edge of the pool. He fixed himself there and made a haul, with some small success. How he managed it she hardly knew, but she stood still for a while watching him anxiously, and then she saw him slip. He slipped, and recovered himself;—slipped again, and again recovered himself.

"Barty, you fool!" she screamed, "if you get yourself pitched in there, you'll never come out no more."

Whether she simply wished to frighten him, or whether her heart relented and she had thought of his danger with dismay, who shall say? She could not have told herself. She hated him as much as ever,—but she could hardly have wished to see him drowned before her eyes.

"You go on, and don't mind me," said he, speaking in a hoarse angry tone.

"Mind you!—who minds you?" retorted the girl. And then she again prepared herself for her work.

But as she went down over the rocks with her long hook balanced in her hands, she suddenly heard a splash, and, turning quickly round, saw the body of her enemy tumbling amidst the eddying waves in the pool. The tide had now come up so far that every succeeding wave washed into it and over it from the side nearest to the sea, and then ran down again back from the rocks, as the rolling wave receded, with a noise like the fall of a cataract. And then, when the surplus water had retreated for a moment, the surface of the pool would be partly calm, though the fretting bubbles would still boil up and down, and there was ever a simmer on the surface, as though, in truth, the caldron were heated. But

this time of comparative rest was but a moment, for
the succeeding breaker would come up almost as soon
as the foam of the preceding one had gone, and then
again the waters would be dashed upon the rocks,
and the sides would echo with the roar of the angry
wave.

Instantly Mally hurried across to the edge of the pool,
crouching down upon her hands and knees for security
as she did so. As a wave receded, Barty's head and
face was carried round near to her, and she could see
that his forehead was covered with blood. Whether he
were alive or dead she did not know. She had seen nothing but his blood, and the light-coloured hair of his
head lying amidst the foam. Then his body was drawn
along by the suction of the retreating wave; but the mass
of water that escaped was not on this occasion large
enough to carry the man out with it.

Instantly Mally was at work with her hook, and
getting it fixed into his coat, dragged him towards the
spot on which she was kneeling. During the half
minute of repose she got him so close that she could
touch his shoulder. Straining herself down, laying herself over the long bending handle of the hook, she strove
to grasp him with her right hand. But she could not do
it; she could only touch him.

Then came the next breaker, forcing itself on with a roar, looking to Mally as though it must certainly knock her from her resting-place, and destroy them both. But she had nothing for it but to kneel, and hold by her hook.

What prayer passed through her mind at that moment for herself or for him, or for that old man who was sitting unconsciously up at the cabin, who can say? The great wave came and rushed over her as she lay almost prostrate, and when the water was gone from her eyes, and the tumult of the foam, and the violence of the roaring breaker had passed by her, she found herself at her length upon the rock, while his body had been lifted up, free from her hook, and was lying upon the slippery ledge, half in the water and half out of it. As she looked at him, in that instant, she could see that his eyes were open and that he was struggling with his hands.

"Hold by the hook, Barty," she cried, pushing the stick of it before him, while she seized the collar of his coat in her hands.

Had he been her brother, her lover, her father, she could not have clung to him with more of the energy of despair. He did contrive to hold by the stick which she had given him, and when the succeeding wave had passed by, he was still on the ledge. In the next moment she was seated a yard or two above the hole, in comparative safety, while Barty lay upon the rocks with his still bleeding head resting upon her lap.

What could she do now? She could not carry him; and in fifteen minutes the sea would be up where she was sitting. He was quite insensible, and very pale, and the blood was coming slowly,—very slowly,—from the wound on his forehead. Ever so gently she put her hand upon his hair to move it back from his face; and then she bent over his mouth to see if he breathed, and as she looked at him she knew that he was beautiful.

What would she not give that he might live? Nothing now was so precious to her as his life,—as this life which she had so far rescued from the waters. But what could she do? Her grandfather could scarcely get himself down over the rocks, if indeed he could succeed in doing so much as that. Could she drag the wounded man backwards, if it were only a few feet, so that he might lie above the reach of the waves till further assistance could be procured?

She set herself to work and she moved him, almost lifting him. As she did so she wondered at her own strength, but she was very strong at that moment. Slowly, tenderly, falling on the rocks herself so that he might fall on her, she got him back to the margin of the sand, to a spot which the waters would not reach for the next two hours.

Here her grandfather-met them, having seen at last what had happened from the door.

"Dada," she said, "he fell into the pool yonder, and was battered against the rocks. See there at his forehead."

"Mally, I'm thinking that he's dead already," said old Glos, peering down over the body.

"No, dada; he is not dead; but mayhap he's dying. But I'll go at once up to the farm."

"Mally," said the old man, "look at his head. They'll say we murdered him."

"Who'll say so? Who'll lie like that? Didn't I pull him out of the hole?"

"What matters that? His father'll say we killed him."

It was manifest to Mally that whatever any one might say hereafter, her present course was plain before her. She must run up the path to Gunliffe's farm and get necessary assistance. If the world were as bad as her grandfather said, it would be so bad that she would not care to live longer in it. But be that as it might, there was no doubt as to what she must do now.

So away she went as fast as her naked feet could carry her up the cliff. When at the top she looked round to see if any person might be within ken, but she saw no one. So she ran with all her speed along the headland of the corn-field which led in the direction of old Gunliffe's house, and as she drew near to the homestead she saw that Barty's mother was leaning on the gate. As she approached she attempted to call, but her breath failed her for any purpose of loud speech, so she ran on till she was able to grasp Mrs. Gunliffe by the arm.

"Where's himself?" she said, holding her hand upon her beating heart that she might husband her breath.

"Who is it you mean?" said Mrs. Gunliffe, who participated in the family feud against Trenglos and his granddaughter. "What does the girl clutch me for in that way?"

"He's dying then, that's all."

"Who is dying? Is it old Malachi? If the old man's bad, we'll send some one down."

"It aint dada; it's Barty! Where's himself? where's the master?" But by this time Mrs. Gunliffe was in an agony of despair, and was calling out for assistance lustily. Happily Gunliffe, the father, was at hand, and with him a man from the neighbouring village.

" Will you not send for the doctor ? " said Mally.
" Oh, man, you should send for the doctor ! "

Whether any orders were given for the doctor she did
not know, but in a very few minutes she was hurrying
across the field again towards the path to the cove, and
Gunliffe with the other man and his wife were following
her.

As Mally went along she recovered her voice, for their
step was not so quick as hers, and that which to them
was a hurried movement, allowed her to get her breath
again. And as she went she tried to explain to the
father what had happened, saying but little, however, of
her own doings in the matter. The wife hung behind
listening, exclaiming every now and again that her boy
was killed, and then asking wild questions as to his
being yet alive. The father, as he went, said little. He
was known as a silent, sober man, well spoken of for
diligence and general conduct, but supposed to be stern
and very hard when angered.

As they drew near to the top of the path the other
man whispered something to him, and then he turned
round upon Mally and stopped her.

" If he has come by his death between you, **your**
blood shall be taken for his," said he.

Then the wife shrieked out that her child had been

murdered, and Mally, looking round into the faces of the three, saw that her grandfather's words had come true. They suspected her of having taken the life, in saving which she had nearly lost her own.

She looked round at them with awe in her face, and then, without saying a word, preceded them down the path. What had she to answer when such a charge as that was made against her? If they chose to say that she pushed him into the pool and hit him with her hook as he lay amidst the waters, how could she show that it was not so?

Poor Mally knew little of the law of evidence, and it seemed to her that she was in their hands. But as she went down the steep track with a hurried step,—a step so quick that they could not keep up with her,—her heart was very full,—very full and very high. She had striven for the man's life as though he had been her brother. The blood was yet not dry on her own legs and arms, where she had torn them in his service. At one moment she had felt sure that she would die with him in that pool. And now they said that she had murdered him! It may be that he was not dead, and what would he say if ever he should speak again? Then she thought of that moment when his eyes had opened, and he had seemed to see her. She had no fear for her

self, for her heart was very high. But it was full also,—
full of scorn, disdain, and wrath.

When she had reached the bottom, she stood close
to the door of the hut waiting for them, so that
they might precede her to the other group, which
was there in front of them, at a little distance on
the sand.

"He is there, and dada is with him. Go and look at
him," said Mally.

The father and mother ran on stumbling over the
stones, but Mally remained behind by the door of the
hut.

Barty Gunliffe was lying on the sand where Mally had
left him, and old Malachi Trenglos was standing over
him, resting himself with difficulty upon a stick.

"Not a move he's moved since she left him," said he;
"not a move. I put his head on the old rug as you see,
and I tried 'un with a drop of gin, but he wouldn't take
it,—he wouldn't take it."

"Oh, my boy! my boy!" said the mother, throwing
herself beside her son upon the sand.

"Haud your tongue, woman," said the father, kneeling
down slowly by the lad's head, "whimpering that way
will do 'un no good."

Then having gazed for a minute or two upon the pale

face beneath him, he looked up sternly into that of
Malachi Trenglos.

The old man hardly knew how to bear this terrible in-
quisition.

"He would come," said Malachi; "he brought it all
upon hisself."

"Who was it struck him?" said the father.

"Sure he struck hisself, as he fell among the breakers."

"Liar!" said the father, looking up at the old man.

"They have murdered him! — they have murdered
him!" shrieked the mother.

"Haud your peace, woman!" said the husband again.
"They shall give us blood for blood."

Mally, leaning against the corner of the hovel, heard it
all, but did not stir. They might say what they liked.
They might make it out to be murder. They might drag
her and her grandfather to Camelford Gaol, and then to
Bodmin, and the gallows; but they could not take from
her the conscious feeling that was her own. She had
done her best to save him,—her very best. And she had
saved him!

She remembered her threat to him before they had
gone down on the rocks together, and her evil wish.
Those words had been very wicked; but since that she
had risked her life to save his. They might say what

they pleased of her, and do what they pleased. She knew what she knew.

Then the father raised his son's head and shoulders in his arms, and called on the others to assist him in carrying Barty towards the path. They raised him between them carefully and tenderly, and lifted their burden on towards the spot at which Mally was standing. She never moved, but watched them at their work; and the old man followed them, hobþling after them with his crutch.

When they had reached the end of the hut she looked upon Barty's face, and saw that it was very pale. There was no longer blood upon the forehead, but the great gash was to be seen there plainly, with its jagged cut, and the skin livid and blue round the orifice. His light brown hair was hanging back, as she had made it to hang when she had gathered it with her hand after the big wave had passed over them. Ah, how beautiful he was in Mally's eyes with that pale face, and the sad scar upon his brow! She turned her face away, that they might not see her tears; but she did not move, nor did she speak.

But now, when they had passed the end of the hut, shuffling along with their burden, she heard a sound which stirred her. She roused herself quickly from her leaning

posture, and stretched forth her head as though to listen;
then she moved to follow them.   Yes, they had stopped
at the bottom of the path, and had again laid the body
on the rocks.   She heard that sound again, as of a long,
long sigh, and then, regardless of any of them, she ran to
the wounded man's head.

"He is not dead," she said.   "There; he is not dead."

As she spoke Barty's eyes opened, and he looked about
him.

"Barty, my boy, speak to me," said the mother.

Barty turned his face upon his mother, smiled, and
then stared about him wildly.

"How is it with thee, lad?" said his father.   Then
Barty turned his face again to the latter voice, and as he
did so his eyes fell upon Mally.

"Mally!" he said, "Mally!"

It could have wanted nothing further to any of those
present to teach them that, according to Barty's own
view of the case, Mally had not been his enemy; and, in
truth, Mally herself wanted no further triumph.   That
word had vindicated her, and she withdrew back to the
hut.

"Dada," she said, "Barty is not dead, and I'm thinking they won't say anything more about our hurting him."

Old Glos shook his head.   He was glad the lad hadn't

met his death there; he didn't want the young man's blood, but he knew what folk would say. The poorer he was the more sure the world would be to trample on him. Mally said what she could to comfort him, being full of comfort herself.

She would have crept up to the farm if she dared, to ask how Barty was. But her courage failed her when she thought of that, so she went to work again, dragging back the weed she had saved to the spot at which on the morrow she would load the donkey. As she did this she saw Barty's pony still standing patiently under the rock; so she got a lock of fodder and threw it down before the beast.

It had become dark down in the cove, but she was still dragging back the seaweed, when she saw the glimmer of a lantern coming down the pathway. It was a most unusual sight, for lanterns were not common down in Malachi's Cove. Down came the lantern rather slowly,—much more slowly than she was in the habit of descending, and then through the gloom she saw the figure of a man standing at the bottom of the path. She went up to him, and saw that it was Mr. Gunliffe, the father.

"Is that Mally?" said Gunliffe.

"Yes, it is Mally; and how is Barty, Mr. Gunliffe?"

"You must come to 'un yourself, now at once," said the farmer. "He won't sleep a wink till he's seed you. You must not say but you'll come."

"Sure I'll come if I'm wanted," said Mally.

Gunliffe waited a moment, thinking that Mally might have to prepare herself, but Mally needed no preparation. She was dripping with salt water from the weed which she had been dragging, and her elfin locks were streaming wildly from her head; but, such as she was, she was ready.

"Dada's in bed," she said, "and I can go now if you please."

Then Gunliffe turned round and followed her up the path, wondering at the life which this girl led so far away from all her sex. It was now dark night, and he had found her working at the very edge of the rolling waves by herself, in the darkness, while the only human being who might seem to be her protector had already gone to his bed.

When they were at the top of the cliff Gunliffe took her by her hand, and led her along. She did not comprehend this, but she made no attempt to take her hand from his. Something he said about falling on the cliffs, but it was muttered so lowly that Mally hardly understood him. But in truth the man knew that she had saved his boy's life, and that he had injured her instead of thanking her. He was now taking her to his heart, and as words were wanting to him, he was showing his love after this silent fashion. He held her by the hand as though she were a child, and Mally tripped along at his side asking him no questions.

When they were at the farm-yard gate he stopped there for a moment.

"Mally, my girl," he said, "he'll not be content till he sees thee, but thou must not stay long wi' him, lass. Doctor says he's weak like, and wants sleep badly."

Mally merely nodded her head, and then they entered the house. Mally had never been within it before, and looked about with wondering eyes at the furniture of the big kitchen. Did any idea of her future destiny flash upon her then, I wonder? But she did not pause here a moment, but was led up to the bed-room above stairs, where Barty was lying on his mother's bed.

"Is it Mally herself?" said the voice of the weak youth.

"It's Mally herself," said the mother, "so now you can say what you please."

"Mally," said he, "Mally, it's along of you that I'm alive this moment."

"I'll not forget it on her," said the father, with his eyes turned away from her. "I'll never forget it on her."

"We hadn't a one but only him," said the mother, with her apron up to her face.

"Mally, you'll be friends with me now?" said Barty.

To have been made lady of the manor of the cove for ever, Mally couldn't have spoken a word now. It was not only that the words and presence of the people there cowed her and made her speechless, but the big bed, and the looking-glass, and the unheard-of wonders of the chamber, made her feel her own insignificance. But she crept up to Barty's side, and put her hand upon his.

"I'll come and get the weed, Mally; but it shall all be for you," said Barty.

"Indeed, you won't then, Barty dear," said the mother; "you'll never go near the awsome place again. What would we do if you were took from us?"

"He mustn't go near the hole if he does," said Mally, speaking at last in a solemn voice, and imparting the knowledge which she had kept to herself while Barty was her enemy; "'specially not if the wind's any way from the nor'rard."

"She'd better go down now," said the father.

Barty kissed the hand which he held, and Mally, looking at him as he did so, thought that he was like an angel.

"You'll come and see us to-morrow, Mally?" said he.

To this she made no answer, but followed Mrs. Gunliffe out of the room. When they were down in the kitchen the mother had tea for her, and thick milk, and a hot cake,—all the delicacies which the farm could afford. I don't know that Mally cared much for the eating and drinking that night, but she began to think that the Gunliffes were good people,—very good people. It was better thus, at any rate, than being accused of murder and carried off to Camelford prison.

"I'll never forget it on her—never," the father had said.

Those words stuck to her from that moment, and seemed to sound in her ears all the night. How glad she was that Barty had come down to the cove,—oh, yes, how glad! There was no question of his dying now, and as for the blow on his forehead, what harm was that to a lad like him?

"But father shall go with you," said Mrs. Gunliffe, when Mally prepared to start for the cove by herself. Mally, however, would not hear of this. She could find her way to the cove whether it was light or dark.

"Mally, thou art my child now, and I shall think of thee so," said the mother, as the girl went off by herself.

Mally thought of this, too, as she walked home. How could she become Mrs. Gunliffe's child; ah, how?

I need not, I think, tell the tale any further. That Mally did become Mrs. Gunliffe's child, and how she became so the reader will understand; and in process of time the big kitchen and all the wonders of the farm-house were her own. The people said that Barty Gunliffe had married a mermaid out of the sea; but when it was said in Mally's hearing I doubt whether she liked it; and when Barty himself would call her a mermaid she would frown at him, and throw about her black hair, and pretend to cuff him with her little hand.

Old Glos was brought up to the top of the cliff, and lived his few remaining days under the roof of Mr. Gunliffe's house; and as for the cove and the right of sea-weed, from that time forth all that has been supposed to attach itself to Gunliffe's farm, and I do not know that any of the neighbours are prepared to dispute the right.

THE WIDOW'S MITE.

THE WIDOW'S MITE.

"BUT I'm not a widow, and I haven't got two mites."

"My dear, you are a widow, and you have got two mites."

"I'll tell both of you something that will astonish you. I've made a calculation, and I find that if everybody in England would give up their Christmas dinner—that is, in Scotland, and Ireland too——"

"They never have any in Ireland, Bob."

"Hold your tongue till I've done, Charley. They do have Christmas dinners in Ireland. It's pretty nearly the only day that they do, and I don't count much upon them either. But if everybody gave up his special Christmas dinner, and dined as he does on other days the saving would amount to two millions and a half."

Charley whistled.

"Two millions and a half is a large sum of money," said Mrs. Granger, the elder lady of the party.

"Those calculations never do any good," said the younger lady, who had declared herself not to be a widow.

"Those calculations do a great deal of good," continued Bob, carrying on his argument with continued warmth. "They show us what a great national effort would do."

"A little national effort, I should call that," said Mrs. Granger, "but I should doubt the two millions and a half."

"Half-a-crown a-head on thirty million people would do it. You are to include all the beer, wine, and whisky. But suppose you take off one-fifth for the babies and young girls, who don't drink."

"Thank you, Bob," said the younger lady—Nora Field by name.

"And two more fifths for the poor, who haven't got the half-crown a-head," said the elder lady.

"And you'd ruin the grocer and butcher," said Charley.

"And never get your half-crown, after all," said Nora.

It need hardly be said that the subject under discussion was the best mode of abstracting from the pockets of the non-suffering British public a sufficiency of money to sustain the suffering portion during the period of the cotton famine.

Mr. Granger was the rector of Plumstock, a parish in Cheshire, sufficiently near to the manufacturing districts to give to every incident of life at that time a colouring taken from the distress of the neighbourhood; which had not, however, itself ever depended on cotton, — for Plumstock boasted that it was purely agricultural. Mr. Granger was the chairman of a branch relief committee, which had its centre in Liverpool; and the subject of the destitution, with the different modes by which it might be, should be, or should not be relieved, were constantly under discussion in the rectory. Mr. Granger himself was a practical man, somewhat hard in his manners, but by no means hard in his heart, who had in these times taken upon himself the business of alms-begging on a large scale. He declined to look at the matter in a political, statistical, or economical point of view, and answered all questions as to rates, rates in aid, loans, and the Consolidated Fund, with a touch of sarcasm, which showed the bent of his own mind.

"I've no doubt you'll have settled all that in the wisest possible way by the time that the war is over, and the river full of cotton again."

"Father," Bob replied, pointing across the Cheshire

flats to the Mersey, "that river will never again be full of American cotton."

"It will be all the same for the present purpose, if it comes from India," said the rector, declining all present argument on the great American question.

To collect alms was his immediate work, and he would do nothing else. Five-pound notes, sovereigns, half-crowns, shillings, and pence ! In search of these he was urgent, we may almost say day and night, begging with a pertinacity which was disagreeable, but irresistible. The man who gave him five sovereigns instantly became the mark for another petition.

"When you have got your dinner, you have not done with the butcher for ever," he would say in answer to reproaches. "Of course, we must go on as long as this thing lasts."

Then his friends and neighbours buttoned up their pockets ; but Mr. Granger would extract coin from them even when buttoned.

The two young men who had taken part in the above argument were his sons. The elder, Charles, was at Oxford, but now in these Christmas days—for Christmas was close at hand—had come home. Bob, the second son, was in a merchant's house in Liverpool, intending to become, in the fulness of time, a British merchant prince.

It had been hinted to him, however, more than once, that if he would talk a little less and work a little harder, the path to his princedom would be quicker found than if his present habits were maintained. Nora Field was Mrs. Granger's niece. She was Miss Field, and certainly not a widow in the literal sense of the word; but she was about to become a bride a few weeks after Christmas.

"It is spoil from the Amalekites," Mr. Granger had said, when she had paid in some contribution from her slender private stores to his treasury:—"spoil from the Amalekites, and therefore the more precious." He had called Nora Field's two sovereigns spoil from the Amalekites, because she was about to marry an American.

Frederic Frew, or Frederic F. Frew, as he delighted to hear himself called, for he had been christened Franklin as well as Frederic,—and to an American it is always a point of honour that, at any rate, the initial of his second Christian name should be remembered by all men,—was a Pennsylvanian from Philadelphia; a strong Democrat, according to the politics of his own country, hating the Republicans, as the Tories used to hate the Whigs among us before political feeling had become extinct; speaking against Lincoln the president, and Seward his minister, and the Fremonts, and Sumners, and Philipses, and Beechers of the Republican party, fine hard racy words of powerful condemnation, such as used to be spoken against Earl Grey and his followers, but nevertheless as steady for the war as Lincoln, or Seward, or any Republican of them all;—as steady for the war, and as keen in his bitterness against England.

His father had been a partner in a house of business, of which the chief station had been in Liverpool. That house had now closed its transactions, and young Frew was living and intended to live an easy idle life on the moderate fortune which had been left to him; but the circumstances of his family affairs had made it necessary for him to pass many months in Liverpool, and during that sojourn he had become engaged to Nora Field. He had travelled much, going everywhere with his eyes open, as Americans do. He knew many things, had read many books, and was decided in his opinion on most subjects. He was good-looking too, and well-mannered; was kindly-hearted, and capable of much generosity. But he was hard, keen in his intelligence, but not broad in genius, thin and meagre in his aspirations,—not looking to or even desirous of anything great, but indulging a profound contempt for all that is very small. He was a well-instructed, but by no means learned man, who greatly despised those who were ignorant. I fear that he hated England in his heart; but he did not hate Nora Field, and was about to make her his wife in three or four weeks from the present time.

When Nora declared to her aunt that she was not a widow, and that she possessed no two mites, and when her aunt flatly contradicted her, stating that she was a widow, and did possess two mites, they had not intended to be understood by each other literally. It was an old dispute between them.

"What the widow gave," said Nora, "she gave off her own poor back, and therefore was very cold. She gave it out of her own poor mouth, and was very hungry afterwards in consequence. I have given my two pounds, but I shall not be cold or hungry. I wish I was a widow with two mites! only, the question is whether I should not keep them for my own back after all, and thus gain nothing by the move."

"As to that," replied her aunt, "I cannot speak. But the widowhood and the two mites are there for us all, if we choose to make use of them."

"In these days," said Bob, "the widows with two mites should not be troubled at all. We can do it all without them, if we go to work properly."

"If you had read your Bible properly, Sir," said Mrs. Granger, "you would understand that the widows would not thank you for the exemption."

"I don't want the widows to thank me. I only want to live, and allow others to live according to the existing circumstances of the world." It was manifest from Bob's tone that he regarded his mother as little better than an old fogey.

In January, Nora was to become Mrs. Frederic F. Frew, and be at once taken away to new worlds, new politics, and new loves and hatreds. Like a true, honest-hearted girl as she was, she had already become half an American in spirit. She was an old Union American, and as such was strong against the South; and in return for her fervour in that matter, her future husband consented to abstain from any present loud abuse of things English, and generously allowed her to defend her own country when it was abused. This was much as coming from an American. Let us hope that the same privilege may be accorded to her in her future home in Philadelphia. But in the meantime, during these last weeks of her girlhood, these cold, cruel weeks of desperate want, she strove vigorously to do what little might be in her power for the poor of the country she was leaving. All this want had been occasioned by the wretched rebels of the South.

This was her theory. And she was right in much of this. Whether the Americans of the South are wretched or are rebels we will not say here; but of this there can be no doubt, that they created all the misery which we then endured.

"But I have no way of making myself a widow," she said again. "Uncle Robert would not let me give away the cloak he gave me the other day."

"He would have to give you another," said Mrs. Granger.

"Exactly. It is not so easy, after all, to be a widow with two mites!"

Nora Field had no fortune of her own, nor was her uncle in a position to give her any. He was not a poor man; but like many men who are not poor, he had hardly a pound of his own in the shape of ready money.

To Nora and to her cousins, and to certain other first cousins of the same family, had been left, some eighteen months since, by a grand-aunt, a hundred pounds a-piece, and with this hundred pounds Nora was providing for herself her wedding trousseau.

A hundred pounds do not go far in such provision, as some young married women who may read this will perhaps acknowledge; but Mr. Frederic F. Frew had been told all about it, and he was contented. Miss Field was fond of nice clothes, and had been tempted more than once to wish that her great-aunt had left them all two hundred pounds a-piece instead of one.

"If I were to cast in my wedding veil?" said Nora.

"That will be your husband's property," said her aunt.

"Ah, but before I'm married."

"Then why have it at all?"

"It is ordered, you know."

"Couldn't you bedizen yourself with one made of false lace?" said her uncle. "Frew would never find it out, and that would be a most satisfactory spoiling of the Amalekite."

"He isn't an Amalekite, uncle Robert. Or if he is, I'm another."

"Just so; and therefore false lace will be quite good enough for you. Molly,"—Mrs. Granger's name was Molly,—"I've promised to let them have the use of the great boiler in the back kitchen once a-week, and you are to furnish them with fuel."

"Oh, dear!" said Mrs. Granger, upon whose active charity this loan of her own kitchen boiler made a strain that was almost too severe. But she recovered herself in half a minute. "Very well, my dear; but you won't expect any dinner on that day."

"No; I shall expect no dinner; only some food in the rough. You may boil that in the copper too if you like it."

"You know, my dear, you don't like anything boiled."

" As for that, Molly, I don't suppose any of them like
it. They'd all prefer roast mutton."

" The copper will be your two mites," whispered the
niece.

" Only I have not thrown them in of my own accord,"
said Mrs. Granger.

Mr. Frew, who was living in Liverpool, always came
over to Plumstock on Friday evening, and spent Saturday
and Sunday with the rector and his family. For him
those Saturdays were happy days, for Frederick F. Frew
was a good lover. He liked to be with Nora, to walk
with her, and to talk with her; he liked to show her
that he loved her, and to make himself gracious and
pleasant. I am not so sure that his coming was
equally agreeable to Mr. Granger. Mr. Frew would
talk about American politics, praising the feeling and
spirit of his countrymen in the North; whereas Mr.
Granger, when driven into the subject, was constrained
to make a battle for the South. All his prejudices, and
what he would have called his judgment, went with the
South, and he was not ashamed of his opinion; but he
disliked arguing with Frederic F. Frew. I fear it must
be confessed that Frederic F. Frew was too strong for
him in such arguments. Why it should be so I cannot
say; but an American argues more closely on politics

than does an Englishman. His convictions are not the truer on that account; very often the less true, as are the conclusions of a logician, because he trusts to syllogisms which are often false, instead of to the experience of his life and daily workings of his mind. But though not more true in his political convictions than an English-man, he is more unanswerable, and therefore Mr. Granger did not care to discuss the subject of the American war with Frederic F. Frew.

" It riles me," Frew said, as he sat after dinner in the Plumstock drawing-room on the Friday evening before Christmas Day, " to hear your folks talking of our elec-tions. They think the war will come to an end, and the rebels of the South have their own way, because the Democrats have carried their ticket."

" It will have that tendency," said the parson.

" Not an inch; any more than your carrying the Re-form Bill or repealing the Corn Laws had a tendency to put down the throne. It's the same sort of argument. Your two parties were at daggers drawn about the Reform Bill; but that did not cause you to split on all other matters."

" But the throne wasn't in question," said the par-son.

" Nor is the war in question; not in that way. The

most popular Democrat in the States at this moment is
M'Clellan."

"And they say no one is so anxious to see the war
ended."

"Whoever says so slanders him. If you don't trust his
deeds, look at his words."

"I believe in neither," said the parson.

"Then put him aside as a nobody. But you can't do
that, for he is the man whom the largest party in the
Northern States trusts most implicitly. The fact is, Sir,"
and Frederic F. Frew gave the proper twang to the last
letter of the last word, "you, none of you here, understand our politics. You can't realise the blessing of
a——"

"Molly, give me some tea," said the rector in a loud
voice. When matters went as far as this he did not care
by what means he stopped the voice of his future relative.

"All I say is this," continued Frew, "you will find
out your mistake if you trust to the Democratic elections
to put an end to the war, and bring cotton back to
Liverpool."

"And what is to put an end to the war?" asked Nora.

"Victory and union," said Frederic F. Frew

"Exhaustion," said Charley, from Oxford.

"Compromise," said Bobby, from Liverpool.

"The Lord Almighty, when He shall have done His work," said the parson. "And, in the meantime, Molly, do you keep plenty of fire under the kitchen boiler."

That was clearly the business of the present hour, for all in Mr. Granger's part of the country;—we may say, indeed, for all on Mr. Granger's side of the water. It mattered little, then, in Lancashire, whether New York might have a Democratic or a Republican governor. The old cotton had been burned; the present crop could not be garnered; the future crop—the crop which never would be future, could not get itself sown.

Mr. Granger might be a slow politician, but he was a practical man, understanding the things immediately around him; and they all were aware, Frederic F. Frew with the rest of them, that he was right when he bade his wife keep the fire well hot beneath the kitchen boiler.

"Isn't it almost wicked to be married in such a time as this?" It was much later in the evening when Nora, still troubled in her mind about her widow's mite, whispered these words into her lover's ears. If she were to give up her lover for twelve months, would not that be a throwing in of something to the treasury from off her own back and out of her own mouth? But then this matter of her marriage had been so fully settled that she feared to think of disturbing it. He would never consent to such a postponement. And then the offering, to be of avail for her, must be taken from her own back, not from his; and Nora had an idea that in the making of such an offering as that suggested, Mr. Frederic F. Frew would conceive that he had contributed by far the greater part. Her uncle called him an Amalekite, and she doubted whether it would be just to spoil an Amalekite after such a fashion as that. Nevertheless, into his ears she whispered her little proposition.

"Wicked to get married!" said Frederic; "not according to my idea of the Christian religion."

"Oh! but you know what I mean," and she gave his arm a slight caressing pinch.

At this time her uncle had gone to his own room; her cousins had gone to their studies, by which I believe they intended to signify the proper smoking of a pipe of tobacco in the rectory kitchen; and Mrs. Granger, seated in her easy chair, had gone to her slumbers, dreaming of the amount of fuel with which that kitchen boiler must be supplied.

"I shall bring a breach of promise against you," said Frederic, "if you don't appear in church with bridal array on Monday, the 12th of January, and pay the penalty into the war-treasury. That would be a spoiling of the Amalekite."

Then he got hold of the fingers which had pinched him.

"Of course I sha'n't put it off, unless you agree."

"Of course you won't."

"But, dear Fred, don't you think we ought?"

"No; certainly not. If I thought you were in earnest I would scold you."

"I am in earnest, quite. You need not look in that way, for you know very well how truly I love you. You know I want to be your wife above all things."

"Do you?"

And then he began to insinuate his arm round her waist; but she got up and moved away, not as in anger at his caress, but as showing that the present moment was unfit for it.

"I do," she said, "above all things. I love you so well that I could hardly bear to see you go away again without taking me with you. I could hardly bear it—but I could bear it."

"Could you? Then I couldn't. I'm a weaker vessel than you, and your strength must give way to my weakness."

"I know I've no right to tax you, if you really care about it."

Frederic F. Frew made no answer to this in words, but

pursued her in her retreat from the sofa on which they had sat.

"Don't, Fred. I am so much in earnest! I wish I knew what I ought to do to throw in my two mites."

"Not throw me over, certainly, and break all the promises you have made for the last twelve months. You can't be in earnest. It's out of the question, you know."

"Oh! I am in earnest."

"I never heard of such a thing in my life. What good would it do? It wouldn't bring the cotton in. It wouldn't feed the poor. It wouldn't keep your aunt's boiler hot."

"No; that it wouldn't," said Mrs. Granger, starting up; "and coals are such a terrible price."

Then she went to sleep again, and ordered in large supplies in her dreams.

"But I should have done as much as the widow did. Indeed I should, Fred. Oh, dear! to have to give you up! But I only meant for a year."

"As you are so very fond of me——"

"Of course I'm fond of you. Should I let you do like that if I was not?"

At the moment of her speaking he had again got his arm round her waist.

"Then I'm too charitable to allow you to postpone your happiness for a day.   We'll look at it in that way."

"You won't understand me, or rather you do understand me, and pretend that you don't, which is very wrong."

"I always was very wicked."

"Then why don't you make yourself better?   Do not you too wish to be a widow?   You ought to wish it."

"I should like to have an opportunity of trying married life first."

"I won't stay any longer with you, Sir, because you are scoffing.   Aunt, I'm going to bed."   Then she returned again across the room, and whispered to her lover, "I'll tell you what, Sir, I'll marry you on Monday, the 12th of January, if you'll take me just as I am now; with a bonnet on, and a shawl over my dress, exactly as I walked out with you before dinner.   When I made the promise, I never said anything about fine clothes."

"You may come in an old red cloak, if you like it."

"Very well; now mind I've got your consent.   Good-night, Sir.   After all it will only be half a mite."

She had turned towards the door, and had her hand upon the lock, but she came back into the room, close up to him.

"It will not be a quarter of a mite," she said.   "How

can it be anything if I get you!" Then she kissed him, and hurried away out of the room, before he could again speak to her.

"What, what, what!" said Mrs. Granger, waking up. "So Nora has gone, has she?"

"Gone; yes, just this minute," said Frew, who had turned his face to the fire, so that the tear in his eyes might not be seen. As he took himself off to his bed, he swore to himself that Nora Field was a trump, and that he had done well in securing for himself such a wife; but it never occurred to him that she was in any way in earnest about her wedding dress. She was a trump because she was so expressive in her love to himself, and because her eyes shone so brightly when she spoke eagerly on any matter; but as to her appearing at the altar in a red cloak, or, as was more probable, in her own customary thick woollen shawl, he never thought about it. Of course she would be married as other girls are married.

Nor had Nora thought of it till that moment in which she made the proposition to her lover. As she had said before, her veil was ordered, and so was her white silk dress. Her bonnet also had been ordered, with its bridal wreath, and the other things assorting therewith. A vast hole was to be made in her grand-aunt's legacy for the

payment of all this finery; but, as Mrs. Granger had said
to her, in so spending it, she would best please her future
husband. He had enough of his own, and would not
care that she should provide herself with articles which
he could afterwards give her, at the expense of that little
smartness at his wedding which an American likes, at any
rate, as well as an Englishman. Nora, with an honesty
which some ladies may not admire, had asked her lover
the question in the plainest language.

"You will have to buy my things so much the sooner,"
she had said.

"I'd buy them all to-morrow, only you'll not let me."

"I should rather think not, Master Fred."

Then she had gone off with her aunt, and ordered her
wedding-clothes. But now as she prepared for bed, after
the conversation which has just been recorded, she began
to think in earnest whether it would not be well to dispense with white silk and orange-wreaths while so many
were dispensing with—were forced to dispense with—
bread and fuel. Could she bedizen herself with finery
from Liverpool, while her uncle was, as she well knew,
refusing himself a set of new shirts which he wanted
sorely, in order that he might send to the fund at Liverpool the money which they would cost him. He was
throwing in his two mites daily, as was her aunt, who

toiled unceasingly at woollen shawls and woollen stock-ings, so that she went on knitting even in her sleep. But she, Nora, since the earnestness of these bad days began, had done little or nothing. Her needle, indeed, had been very busy, but it had been busy in preparation for Mr. Frederic F. Frew's nuptials. Even Bob and Charley worked for the Relief Committee; but she had done no-thing—nothing but given her two pounds. She had offered four, but her uncle, with a self-restraint never be-fore or afterwards practised by him, had chucked her back two, saying that he would not be too hard even upon an Amalekite. As she thought of the word, she asked herself whether it was not more incumbent on her, than on any one else, to do something in the way of self-sacrifice. She was now a Briton, but would shortly be an American. Should it be said of her that the distress of her own countrywomen—the countrywomen whom she was leaving—did not wring her heart? It was not without a pang that she prepared to give up that nationality, which all its owners rank as the first in the world, and most of those who do not own it, rank, if not as the first, then as the second. Now it seemed to her as though she were deserting her own family in its distress, deserting her own ship in the time of its storm, and she was going over to those from whom this dis-

tress and this storm had come! Was it not needful
that she should do something—that she should satisfy
herself that she had been willing to suffer in the cause?

She would throw in her two mites if she did but
know where to find them.

"I could only do it, in truth," she said to herself, as
she rose from her prayers, "by throwing in him. I
have got one very great treasure, but I have not got
anything else that I care about. After all, it isn't so
easy to be a widow with two mites."

Then she sat down and thought about it. As to post-
poning her marriage, that she knew to be in truth quite
out of the question. Even if she could bring herself to
do it, everybody about her would say that she was mad,
and Mr. Frederic F. Frew might not impossibly destroy
himself with one of those pretty revolvers which he sometimes brought out from Liverpool for her to play with.
But was it not practicable for her to give up her wedding-
clothes? There would be considerable difficulty even in
this. As to their having been ordered, that might be
overcome by the sacrifice of some portion of the price.
But then her aunt, and even her uncle, would oppose
her; her cousins would cover her with ridicule; in the
latter she might, however, achieve something of her
widowhood;—and, after all, the loss would fall more

upon F. F. Frew than upon herself. She really did not care for herself, in what clothes she was married, so that she was made his wife. But as regarded him, might it not be disagreeable to him to stand before the altar with a dowdy creature in an old gown? And then there was one other consideration. Would it not seem that she was throwing in her two mites publicly, before the eyes of all men, as a Pharisee might do it? Would there not be an ostentation in her widowhood? But as she continued to reflect, she cast this last thought behind her. It might be so said of her, but if such saying were untrue, if the offering were made in a widow's spirit, and not in the spirit of a Pharisee, would it not be cowardly to regard what men might say? Such false accusation would make some part of the two mites.

"I'll go into Liverpool about it on Monday," she said to herself as she finally tucked the clothes around her.

Early in the following morning she was up and out of her room, with a view of seeing her aunt before she came down to breakfast; but the first person she met was her uncle. He accosted her in one of the passages.

"What, Nora, this is early for you! Are you going to have a morning lovers' walk with Frederic Franklin?"

"Frederic Franklin, as you choose to call him, uncle,"

said Nora, "never comes out of his room much before breakfast time. And it's raining hard."

"Such a lover as he is ought not to mind rain."

"But I should mind it, very much. But, uncle, I want to speak to you, very seriously. I have been making up my mind about something."

"There's nothing wrong; is there, my dear?"

"No; there's nothing very wrong. It is not exactly about anything being wrong. I hardly know how to tell you what it is."

And then she paused, and he could see by the light of the candle in his hand that she blushed.

"Hadn't you better speak to your aunt?" said Mr. Granger.

"That's what I meant to do when I got up," said Nora; "but as I have met you, if you don't mind ——"

He assured her that he did not mind, and putting his hand upon her shoulder caressingly, promised her any assistance in his power.

"I'm not afraid that you will ask anything I ought not to do for you."

Then she revealed to him her scheme, turning her face away from him as she spoke. "It will be so horrid," she said, "to have a great box of finery coming home when

you are all giving up everything for the poor people. And if you don't think it would be wrong——"

"It can't be wrong," said her uncle. "It may be a question whether it would be wise."

"I mean wrong to him. If it was to be any other clergyman, I should be ashamed of it. But as you are to marry us——"

"I don't think you need mind about the clergyman."

"And of course I should tell the Foster girls."

"The Foster girls ?"

"Yes; they are to be my bridesmaids, and I am nearly sure they have not bought anything new yet. Of course they would think it all very dowdy, but I don't care a bit about that. I should just tell them that we had all made up our minds that we couldn't afford wedding-clothes. That would be true ; wouldn't it ? "

"But the question is about that wild American ? "

"He isn't a wild American."

"Well, then, about that tamed American. What will he say ? "

"He said I might come in an old cloak."

"You have told him, then ? "

"But I am afraid he thought I was only joking. But uncle, if you'll help me, I think I can bring him round."

"I dare say you can—to anything, just at present."

"I didn't at all mean that. Indeed, I'm sure I couldn't bring him round to putting off the marriage."

"No, no, no; not to that; to anything else."

"I know you are laughing at me, but I don't much mind being laughed at. I should save very nearly fifteen pounds, if not quite. Think of that!"

"And you'd give it all to the soup kitchen?"

"I'd give it all to you for the distress."

Then her uncle spoke to her somewhat gravely.

"You're a good girl, Nora,—a dear good girl. I think I understand your thoughts on this matter, and I love you for them. But I doubt whether there be any necessity for you to make this sacrifice. A marriage should be a gala festival according to the means of the people married, and the bridegroom has a right to expect that his bride shall come to him fairly arrayed, and bright with wedding trappings. I think we can do, my pet, without robbing you of your little braveries."

"Oh, as for that, of course you can do without me."

There was a little soreness in her tone; not because she was feeling herself to be misunderstood, but because she knew that she could not explain herself further. She could not tell her uncle that the poor among the Jews might have been relieved without the contribution of those two mites, but that the widow would have lost all had she not so contributed. She had hardly arranged her thoughts as to the double blessing of charity, and certainly could not express them with reference to her own case; but she felt the need of giving in this time of trouble something that she herself valued. She was right when she had said that it was hard to be a widow. How many among us, when we give, give from off our own backs, and from out of our own mouths? Who can say that he has sacrificed a want of his own; that he has abandoned a comfort; that he has worn a threadbare coat, when coats with their gloss on have been his customary wear; that he has fared roughly on cold scraps, whereas a well-spread board has been his usual daily practice? He who has done so has thrown in his two mites, and for him will charity produce her double blessing.

Nora thought that it was not well in her uncle to tell her that he could do without her wedding clothes. Of course he could do without them. But she soon threw those words behind her, and went back upon the words which had preceded them. "The bridegroom has a right to expect that the bride shall come to him fairly arrayed." After all, that must depend upon circumstances. Suppose the bride had no means of arraying herself fairly without getting into debt; what would the bridegroom expect in that case?

"If he'll consent, you will?" she said, as she prepared to leave her uncle.

"You'll drive him to offer to pay for the thing himself."

"I dare say he will, and then he'll drive me to refuse. You may be quite sure of this, uncle, that whatever clothes I do wear, he will never see the bill of them;" and then that conference was ended.

"I've made that calculation again," said Bob at breakfast, and I feel convinced that if an act of parliament could be passed restricting the consumption of food in Christmas week,—the entire week, mind,—to that of ordinary weeks, we should get two millions of money, and that those two millions would tide us over till the Indian cotton comes in. Of course I mean by food, butchers' meat, groceries, spirits, and wines. Only think, that by one measure, which would not entail any real disappointment on any one, the whole thing would be done."

"But the act of parliament wouldn't give us the money," said his father.

"Of course I don't really mean an act of parliament; that would be absurd. But the people might give up their Christmas dinners."

"A great many will, no doubt. Many of those most in earnest are pretty nearly giving up their daily dinners. Those who are indifferent will go on feasting the same as ever. You can't make a sacrifice obligatory."

"It would be no sacrifice if you did," said Nora, still thinking of her wedding clothes.

"I doubt whether sacrifices ever do any real good," said Frederick F. Frew.

"Oh, Fred!" said Nora.

"We have rather high authority as to the benefit of self-denial," said the parson.

"A man who can't sacrifice himself must be selfish," said Bobby; "and we are all agreed to hate selfish people."

"And what about the widow's mite?" said Mrs. Granger.

"That's all very well, and you may knock me down with the Bible if you like, as you might do also if I talked about pre-Adamite formations. I believe every word of the Bible, but I do not believe that I understand it all thoroughly."

"You might understand it better if you studied it more," said the parson.

"Very likely. I won't be so uncourteous as to say the same thing of my elders. But now about these sacrifices

You wouldn't wish to keep people in distress that you might benefit yourself by releasing them?"

"But the people in distress are there," said Nora.

"They oughtn't to be there; and as your self-sacrifices, after all, are very insufficient to prevent distress, there certainly seems to be a question open whether some other mode should not be tried. Give me the country in which the humanitarian principle is so exercised that no one shall be degraded by the receipt of charity. It seems to me that you like poor people here in England that you may gratify yourselves by giving them, not as much to eat as they want, but just enough to keep their skins from falling off their bones. Charity may have its double blessing, but it may also have its double curse."

"Not charity, Mr. Frew," said Mrs. Granger.

"Look at your Lady Bountifuls."

"Of course it depends on the heart," continued the lady; "but charity, if it be charity——"

"I'll tell you what," said Frederic F. Frew interrupting her. "In Philadelphia, which in some matters is the best organised city I know——"

"I'm going down to the village," said the parson jumping up. "Who is to come with me?" and he escaped out of the room before Frew had had an opportunity of saying a word further about Philadelphia.

"That's the way with your uncle always," said he, turning to Nora, almost in anger. "It certainly is the most conclusive argument I know — that of running away."

"Mr. Granger meant it to be conclusive," said the elder lady.

"But the pity is that it never convinces."

"Mr. Granger probably had no desire of convincing."

"Ah! Well, it does not signify," said Frew. "When a man has a pulpit of his own, why should he trouble himself to argue in any place where counter arguments must be met and sustained?"

Nora was almost angry with her lover, whom she regarded as stronger and more clever than any of her uncle's family, but tyrannical and sometimes overbearing in the use of his strength. One by one her aunt and cousin left the room, and she was left alone with him. He had taken up a newspaper as a refuge in his wrath, for in truth he did not like the manner in which his allusions to his own country were generally treated at the parsonage. There are Englishmen who think that every man differing with them is bound to bet with them on any point in dispute. "Then you decline to back your opinion," such men say when the bet is refused. The feeling of an American is the same as to those

who are unwilling to argue with him. He considers
that every intelligent being is bound to argue whenever
matter of argument is offered to him; nor can he
understand that any subject may be too sacred for argument. Frederic F. Frew, on the present occasion, was
as a dog from whose very mouth a bone had been
taken. He had given one or two loud, open growls,
and now sat with his newspaper, showing his teeth as
far as the spirit of the thing went. And it was in this
humour that Nora found herself called upon to attack
him on the question of her own proposed charity. She
knew well that he could bark, even at her, if things
went wrong with him. "But then he never bites," she
said to herself. He had told her that she might come
to her wedding in an old cloak if she pleased, but she
had understood that there was nothing serious in this
permission. Now, at this very moment, it was incumbent on her to open his eyes to the reality of her
intention.

"Fred," she said, "are you reading that newspaper
because you are angry with me?"

"I am reading the newspaper because I want to know
what there is in it."

"You know all that now, just as well as if you had
written it. Put it down, Sir!" And she put her hand

on to the top of the sheet. "If we are to be married in three weeks' time, I expect that you will be a little attentive to me now. You'll read as many papers as you like after that, no doubt."

"Upon my word, Nora, I think your uncle is the most unfair man I ever met in my life."

"Perhaps he thinks the same of you, and that will make it equal."

"He can't think the same of me. I defy him to think that I'm unfair. There's nothing so unfair as hitting a blow, and then running away when the time comes for receiving a counterblow. It's what your Lord Chatham did, and he never ought to have been listened to in parliament again."

"That's a long time ago," said Nora, who probably felt that her lover should not talk to her about Lord Chatham just three weeks before their marriage.

"I don't know that the time makes any difference."

"Ah! but I have got something else that I want to speak about. And, Fred, you mustn't turn up your nose at what we are all doing here,—as to giving away things I mean."

"I don't turn up my nose at it. Haven't I been begging of every American in Liverpool till I'm ashamed of myself?"

"I know you have been very good, and now you must be more good still,—good to me specially, I mean. That isn't being good. That's only being foolish." What little ceremony had led to this last assertion I need not perhaps explain. "Fred, I'm an Englishwoman to-day, but in a month's time I shall be an American."

"I hope so, Nora,—heart and soul."

"Yes; that is what I mean. Whatever is my husband's country must be mine. And you know how well I love your country; do you not? I never run away when you talk to me about Philadelphia,—do I? And you know how I admire all your institutions,—my institutions, as they will be."

"Now I know you're going to ask some very great favour."

"Yes, I am; and I don't mean to be refused, Master Fred. I'm to be an American almost to-morrow, but as yet I am an Englishwoman, and I am bound to do what little I can before I leave my country. Don't you think so?"

"I don't quite understand."

"Well, it's about my wedding-clothes. It does seem stupid talking about them, I know. But I want you to let me do without them altogether. Now you've got the plain truth. I want to give Uncle Robert the money for his soup-kitchen, and to be married just as I am now. I do not care one straw what any other creature in the world may say about it, so long as I do not displease you."

"I think it's nonsense, Nora."

"Oh, Fred, don't say so. I have set my heart upon it. I'll do anything for you afterwards. Indeed, for the matter of that, I'd do anything on earth for you, whether you agree or whether you do not. You know that."

"But, Nora, you wouldn't wish to make yourself appear foolish? How much money will you save?"

"Very nearly twenty pounds altogether."

"Let me give you twenty pounds, so that you may leave it with your uncle by way of your two mites, as you call it."

"No, no, certainly not. I might just as well send you the milliner's bill, might I not?"

"I don't see why you shouldn't do that."

"Ah, but I do. You wouldn't wish me to be guilty of the pretence of giving a thing away, and then doing it out of your pocket. I have no doubt that what you were saying about the evil of promiscuous charity is quite true." And then, as she flattered him with this wicked

flattery, she looked up with her bright eyes into his face.
" But now, as the things are, we must be charitable, or
the people will die. I feel almost like a rat leaving a
falling house, in going away at this time; and if you
would postpone it——"

" Nora ! "

" Then I must be like a rat , but I won't be a rat in a
white silk gown. Come now, say that you agree. I never
asked you for anything before."

" Everybody will think that you're mad, and that I'm
mad, and that we are all mad together."

" Because I go to church in a merino dress ? Well ;
if that makes madness, let us be mad. Oh, Fred, do
not refuse me the first thing I've asked you ! What
difference will it make ? Nobody will know it over in
Philadelphia ! "

" Then you are ashamed of it ? "

" No, not ashamed. Why should I be ashamed ?
But one does not wish to have that sort of thing talked
about by everybody."

" And you are so strong-minded, Nora, that you do
not care about finery yourself ? "

" Fred, that's ill-natured. You know very well what
my feelings are. You are sharp enough to understand
them without any further explanation. I do like finery,

quite well enough, as you'll find out to your cost some day. And if ever you scold me for extravagance, I shall tell you about this."

"It's downright Quixotism."

"Quixotism leads to nothing, but this will lead to twenty pounds' worth of soup,—and to something else too."

When he pressed her to explain what that something else was, she declined to speak further on the subject. She could not tell him that the satisfaction she desired was that of giving up something,—of having made a sacrifice,—of having thrown into the treasury her two mites,—two mites off her own back, as she had said to her aunt, and out of her own mouth. He had taxed her with indifference to a woman's usual delight in gay plumage, and had taxed her most unjustly. "He ought to know," she said to herself, "that I should not take all this trouble about it, unless I did care for it." But, in truth, he did understand her motive thoroughly, and half approved them. He approved the spirit of self-abandonment, but disapproved the false political economy by which, according to his light, that spirit was accompanied. "After all," said he, "the widow would have done better to have invested her small capital in some useful trade."

"Oh, Fred;—but never mind now. I have your consent, and now I've only got to talk over my aunt."

So saying, she left her lover to turn over in his mind the first principles of that large question of charity.

"The giving of pence and halfpence, of scraps of bread and sups of soup, is, after all, but the charity of a barbarous, half-civilised race. A dog would let another dog starve before he gave him a bone, and would see his starved fellow-dog die without a pang. We have just got beyond that, only beyond that, as long as we dole out sups of soup. But charity, when it shall have made itself perfect, will have destroyed this little trade of giving, which makes the giver vain and the receiver humble. The charity of the large-hearted is that which opens to every man the profit of his own industry; to every man and to every woman." Then having gratified himself with the enunciation of this fine theory, he allowed his mind to run away to a smaller subject, and began to think of his own wedding garments. If Nora insisted on carrying out this project of hers, in what guise must he appear on the occasion? He also had ordered new clothes. "It's just the sort of thing that they'll make a story of in Chestnut Street." Chest-

nut Street, as we all know, is the West End of Philadelphia.

When the morning came of the twelfth of January,—
the morning that was to make Nora Field a married
woman, she had carried her point; but she was not
allowed to feel that she had carried it triumph-
antly.

Her uncle had not forbidden her scheme, but had
never encouraged it. Her lover had hardly spoken to
her on the subject since the day on which she had explained to him her intention.

"After all, it's a mere bagatelle," he had said; "I am
not going to marry your clothes."

One of her cousins, Bob, had approved; but he had
coupled his approval with an intimation that something
should be done to prevent any other woman from wear-
ing bridal wreaths for the next three months. Charley
had condemned her altogether, pointing out that it was
bad policy to feed the cotton-spinners at the expense of
the milliners. But the strongest opposition had come
from her aunt and the Miss Fosters. Mrs. Granger,
though her heart was in the battle which her husband
was fighting, could not endure to think that all the
time-honoured ceremonies of her life should be abandoned. In spite of all that was going on around her,

she had insisted on having mince-pies on the table on
Christmas Day. True, there were not many of them,
and they were small and flavourless. But the mince-
pies were there, with whisky to burn with them instead
of brandy, if any of the party chose to go through the
ceremony. And to her the idea of a wedding without
wedding-clothes was very grievous. It was she who had
told Nora that she was a widow with two mites, or
might make herself one, if she chose to encounter self-
sacrifice. But in so saying she had by no means anticipated such a widowhood as this.

"I really think, Nora, you might have one of
those thinner silks, and you might do without a
wreath; but you should have a veil; — indeed you
should."

But Nora was obstinate. Having overcome her future
lord, and quieted her uncle, she was not at all prepared
to yield to the mild remonstrances of her aunt. The
two Miss Fosters were very much shocked, and for
three days there was a disagreeable coolness between
them and the Plumstock family. A friend's bridal is
always an occasion for a new dress, and the Miss
Fosters naturally felt that they were being robbed of
their rights.

'Sensible girl," said old Foster, when he heard of it.

"When you're married, if ever you are, I hope you'll do the same."

"Indeed we won't, papa," said the two Miss Fosters. But the coolness gradually subsided, and the two Miss Fosters consented to attend in their ordinary Sunday bonnets.

It had been decided that they should be married early, at eight o'clock; that they should then go to the parsonage for breakfast, and that the married couple should start for London immediately afterwards. They were to remain there for a week, and then return to Liverpool for one other remaining week before their final departure for America.

"I should only have had them on for about an hour if I'd got them, and then it would have been almost dark," she said to her aunt.

"Perhaps it won't signify very much," her aunt replied. Then when the morning came, it seemed that the sacrifice had dwindled down to a very little thing. The two Miss Fosters had come to the parsonage over night, and as they sat up with the bride over a bed-room fire, had been good-natured enough to declare that they thought it would be very good fun.

"You won't have to get up in tne cold to dress me,"

said Nora, " because I can do it all myself; that will be
one comfort."

" Oh, we shouldn't have minded that ; and as it is, of
course, we'll turn you out nice.   You'll wear one of your
other new dresses ; won't you ? "

" Oh, I don't know ; just what I'm to travel in.   It
isn't very old.   Do you know, after all, I'm not sure that
it isn't a great deal better."

"I suppose it will be the same thing in the end," said
the younger Miss Foster.

" Of course it will," said the elder.

"And there won't be all that bother of changing my
dress," said Nora.

Frederic F. Frew came out to Plumstock by an early
train from Liverpool, bringing with him a countryman of
his own as his friend on the occasion.   It had been explained to the friend that he was to come in his usual
habiliments.

" Oh, nonsense ! " said the friend, " I guess I'll see
you turned off in a new waistcoat."   But Frederic
F. Frew had made it understood that an old waistcoat
was imperative.

" It's something about the cotton, you know.   They're
all beside themselves here, as though there was never
going to be a bit more in the country to eat.   That's

England all over. Never mind; do you come just as if you were going into your counting-house. Brown cotton gloves, with a hole in the thumbs, will be the thing, I should say."

There were candles on the table when they were all assembled in the parsonage drawing-room previous to the marriage. The two gentlemen were there first. Then came Mrs. Granger, who rather frightened Mr. Frew by kissing him, and telling him that she should always regard him as a son-in-law.

" Nora has always been like one of ourselves, you know," she said, apologisingly.

" And let me tell you, Master Frew,' said the parson, " that you're a very lucky fellow to get her."

" I say, isn't it cold ? " said Bob, coming in—" where are the girls ? "

" Here are the girls," said Miss Foster, heading the procession of three which now entered the room, Nora, of course, being the last. Then Nora was kissed by everybody, including the strange American gentleman, who seemed to have made some mistake as to his privilege in the matter. But it all passed off very well, and I doubt if Nora knew who kissed her. It was very cold, and they were all wrapped close in their brown shawls and greatcoats, and the women looked very snug and comfortable in their ordinary winter bonnets.

"Come," said the parson, "we mustn't wait for Charley; he'll follow us to church." So the uncle took his niece on his arm, and the two Americans took the two bridesmaids, and Bob took his mother, and went along the beaten path over the snow to the church, and, as they got to the door, Charley rushed after them quite out of breath.

"I haven't even got a pair of gloves at all," he whispered to his mother.

"It doesn't matter; nobody's to know," said Mrs. Granger.

Nora by this time had forgotten the subject of her dress altogether, and it may be doubted if even the Misses Foster were as keenly alive to it as they thought they would have been. For myself, I think they all looked more comfortable on that cold winter morning without the finery which would have been customary than they could have done with it. It had seemed to them all beforehand that a marriage without veils and wreaths, without white gloves and new gay dresses, would be but a triste affair; but the idea passed away altogether when the occasion came. Mr. Granger and his wife and the two lads clustered around Nora as they made themselves ready for the ceremony, uttering words of warm love, and it seemed as though even the clerk and the servants took nothing amiss. Frederic F. Frew had met with a rebuff in the hall of the parsonage, in being forbidden to take his own bride under his own arm; but when the time for action came, he bore no malice, but went through his work manfully. On the whole, it was a pleasant wedding, homely, affectionate, full of much loving greeting; but not without many sobs on the part of the bride and of Mrs. Granger, and some slight suspicion of an eagerly-removed tear in the parson's eye; but this, at any rate, was certain, that the wedding-clothes were not missed. When they all sat down to their breakfast in the parsonage dining-room, that little matter had come to be clean forgotten. No one knew, not even the Misses Foster, that there was anything extraordinary in their garb. Indeed, as to all gay apparel, we may say that we only miss it by comparison. It is very sad to be the wearer of the only frock-coat in company, to carry the one solitary black silk handerchief at a dinner-party. But I do not know but that a dozen men so arrayed do not seem to be as well dressed as though they had obeyed the latest rules of fashion as to their garments. One thing, however, had been made secure. That sum of twenty pounds, saved from the milliners, had been duly paid over into Mr. Granger's hands. "It has been all very nice," said Mrs. Granger, still sobbing, when Nora went up stairs to tie on her bonnet before she started. "Only you are going!"

"Yes, I'm going now, aunt. Dear aunt! But aunt, I have failed in one thing—absolutely failed."

"Failed in what, my darling?"

"There has been no widow's mite. It is not easy to be a widow with two mites."

"What you have given will be blessed to you, and blessed to those who will receive it."

"I hope it may; but I almost feel that I have been wrong in thinking of it so much. It has cost me nothing. I tell you, aunt, that it is not easy to be a widow with two mites."

When Mrs. Granger was alone with her husband after this, the two Miss Fosters having returned to Liverpool under the discreet protection of the two young Grangers, for they had positively refused to travel with no other companion than the strange American,—she told him all that Nora had said.

"And who can tell us," he replied, "that it was not the same with the widow herself? She threw in all that she had, but who can say that she suffered aught in consequence? It is my belief that all that is given in a right spirit comes back instantly, in this world, with interest."

"I wish my coals would come back," said Mrs. Granger.

"Perhaps you have not given them in a right spirit, my dear."

THE LAST AUSTRIAN
WHO LEFT VENICE.

THE LAST AUSTRIAN WHO LEFT VENICE.

IN the spring and early summer of the year last past, — the year 1866, — the hatred felt by Venetians towards the Austrian soldiers who held their city in thraldom, had reached its culminating point. For years this hatred had been very strong; how strong can hardly be understood by those who never recognise the fact that there had been, so to say, no mingling of the conquered and the conquerors, no process of assimilation between the Italian vassals and their German masters.

Venice as a city was as purely Italian as though its barracks were filled with no Hungarian long-legged soldiers, and its cafés crowded with no white-coated Austrian officers. And the regiments which held the town, lived as completely after their own fashion as though they were quartered in Pesth, or Prague, or Vienna,—with this exception, that in Venice they were enabled, and, indeed, from circumstances were compelled,—to exercise a palpable ascendency which belonged to them nowhere else. They were masters, daily visible as such to the eye of every one who merely walked the narrow ways of the city or strolled through the open squares; and, as masters, they were as separate as the gaoler is separate from the prisoner.

The Austrian officers sat together in the chief theatre, —having the best part of it to themselves. Few among them spoke Italian. None of the common soldiers did so. The Venetians seldom spoke German; and could hold no intercourse whatever with the Croats, Hungarians, and Bohemians, of whom the garrison was chiefly composed. It could not be otherwise than that there should be intense hatred in a city so ruled. But the hatred which had been intense for years had reached its boiling point in the May preceding the outbreak of the war.

Whatever other nations might desire to do, Italy, at any rate, was at this time resolved to fight. It was not that the King and the Government were so resolved. What was the purpose just then of the powers of the state, if any purpose had then been definitely formed by them, no one now knows. History, perhaps, may some day tell us. But the nation was determined to fight. Hitherto all had been done for the Italians by outside allies, and now the time had come in which Italians would do something for themselves.

The people hated the French aid by which they had been allowed to live, and burned with a desire to prove that they could do something great without aid. There was an enormous army, and that army should be utilised for the enfranchisement of Venetia and to the great glory of Italy. The King and the ministers appreciated the fact that the fervour of the people was too strong to be repressed, and were probably guided to such resolutions as they did make by that appreciation.

The feeling was as strong in Venice as it was in Florence or in Milan; but in Venice only,—or rather in Venetia only—all outward signs of such feeling were repressible, and were repressed. All through Lombardy and Tuscany any young man who pleased might volunteer with Garibaldi; but to volunteer with Garibaldi was not, at first, so easy for young men in Verona or in Venice. The more complete was this repression, the greater was this difficulty, the stronger, of course, arose the hatred of the Venetians for the Austrian soldiery. I have never heard that the Austrians were cruel in what they did; but they were determined; and, as long as they had any intention of holding the province, it was necessary that they should be so.

During the past winter there had been living in Venice a certain Captain von Vincke,—Hubert von Vincke,—an Austrian officer of artillery, who had spent the last four or five years among the fortifications of Verona, and who had come to Venice, originally, on account of ill health. Some military employment had kept him in Venice, and he remained there till the outbreak of the war; going backwards and forwards, occasionally, to Verona, but still having Venice as his head-quarters.

Now Captain von Vincke had shown so much consideration for the country which he assisted in holding under subjection as to learn its language, and to study its manners; and had, by these means, found his way, more or less, into Italian society. He was a thorough soldier, good-looking, perhaps eight-and-twenty or thirty years of age, well educated, ambitious, very free from the common vice of thinking that the class of mankind to which he belonged was the only class in which it would be worth a man's while to live; but nevertheless imbued with a strong feeling that Austria ought to hold her own, that an Austrian army was indomitable, and that the quadri lateral fortresses, bound together as they were now bound by Austrian strategy, were impregnable. So much Captain von Vincke thought and believed on the part of his country; but in thinking and believing this, he was still desirous that much should be done to relieve Austrian-Italy from the grief of foreign rule. That Italy should think of succeeding in repelling Austria from Venice was to him an absurdity.

He had become intimate at the house of a widow lady, who lived in the Campo San Luca, one Signora Pepé, whose son had first become acquainted with Captain von Vincke at Verona.

Carlo Pepé was a young advocate, living and earning his bread at Venice, but business had taken him for a time to Verona; and when leaving that city he had asked his Austrian friend to come and see him in his mother's house.

Both Madame Pepé and her daughter Nina, Carlo's only sister, had somewhat found fault with the young advocate's rashness in thus seeking the close intimacy of home-life with one whom, whatever might be his own peculiar virtues, they could not but recognise as an enemy of their country.

"That would be all very fine if it were put into a book," said the Signora to her son, who had been striving to show that an Austrian, if good in himself, might be as worthy a friend as an Italian; "but it is always well to live on the safe side of the wall. It is not convenient that the sheep and the wolves should drink at the same stream."

This she said with all that caution which everywhere forms so marked a trait in the Italian character. "Who goes softly goes soundly." Half of the Italian nature is told in that proverb, though it is not the half which was becoming most apparent in the doings of the nation in these days. And the Signorina was quite of one mind with her mother.

"Carlo," she said, "how is it that one never sees one of these Austrians in the house of any friend? Why is it that I have never yet found myself in a room with one of them?"

"Because men and women are generally so pig-headed and unreasonable," Carlo had replied. "How am I, for instance, ever to learn what a German is at the core, or a Frenchman, or an Englishman, if I refuse to speak to one?"

It ended by Captain von Vincke being brought to the house in the Campo San Luca, and there becoming as intimate with the Signora and the Signorina as he was with the advocate.

Our story must be necessarily too short to permit us to

see how the affair grew in all its soft and delicate growth; but by the beginning of April Nina Pepé had confessed her love to Hubert von Vincke, and both the captain and Nina had had a few words with the Signora on the subject of their projected marriage.

"Carlo will never allow it," the old lady had said, trembling as she thought of the danger that was coming upon the family.

"He should not have brought Captain von Vincke to the house, unless he was prepared to regard such a thing as possible," said Nina proudly.

"I think he is too good a fellow to object to anything that you will ask him," said the captain, holding by the hand the lady whom he hoped to call his mother-in-law.

Throughout January and February Captain von Vincke had been an invalid. In March he had been hardly more than convalescent, and had then had time and all that opportunity which convalescence gives for the sweet business of love-making.

During this time, through March and in the first weeks of April, Carlo Pepé had been backwards and forwards to Verona, and had in truth had more business on hand than that which simply belonged to him as a lawyer. Those were the days in which the Italians were beginning to prepare for the great attack which was to be made, and in which correspondence was busily carried on between Italy and Venetia as to the enrolment of Venetian volunteers.

It will be understood that no Venetian was allowed to go into Italy without an Austrian passport, and that at this time the Austrians were becoming doubly strict in seeing that the order was not evaded. Of course it was evaded daily, and twice in that April did young Pepé travel between Verona and Bologna in spite of all that Austria could say to the contrary.

When at Venice he and Von Vincke discussed very freely the position of the country, nothing of course being said as to those journeys to Bologna. Indeed, of them no one in the Campo San Luca knew aught. They were such journeys that a man says nothing of them to his mother or his sister, or even to his wife, unless he has as much confidence in her courage as he has in her love. But of politics he would talk freely, as would also the German ; and though each of them would speak of the cause as though they two were simply philosophical lookers-on, and were not and could not become actors, and though each had in his mind a settled resolve to bear with the political opinion of the other, yet it came to pass that they now and again were on the verge of quarrelling.

The fault, I think, was wholly with Carlo Pepé, whose enthusiasm of course was growing as those journeys to Bologna were made successfully, and who was beginning to feel assured that Italy at last would certainly do something for herself. But there had not come any open quarrel,—not as yet, when Nina, in her lover's presence, was arguing as to the impropriety of bringing Captain von Vincke to the house, if Captain von Vincke was to be regarded as altogether unfit for matrimonial purposes. At that moment Carlo was absent at Verona, but was to return on the following morning. It was decided at this conference between the two ladies and the lover, that Carlo should be told on his return of Captain von Vincke's intentions. Captain von Vincke himself would tell him.

There is a certain hotel or coffee-house, or place of general public entertainment in Venice, kept by a German, and called the Hotel Bauer, probably from the name of the German who keeps it. It stands near the church of St. Moses, behind the grand piazza, between that and the great canal, in a narrow intricate throng of little streets, and is approached by a close dark water-way which robs it of any attempt at hotel grandeur. Nevertheless it is a large and commodious house, at which good dinners may be eaten at prices somewhat lower than are compatible with the grandeur of the Grand Canal. It used to be much affected by Germans, and had, perhaps, acquired among Venetians a character of being attached to Austrian interests.

There was not much in this, or Carlo Pepé would not have frequented the house, even in company with his friend Von Vincke. He did so frequent it, and now, on this occasion of his return home, Von Vincke left word for him that he would breakfast at the hotel at eleven o'clock. Pepé by that time would have gone home after his journey, and would have visited his office. Von Vincke also would have done the greatest part of his day's work. Each understood the habits of the other, and they met at Bauer's for breakfast.

It was the end of April, and Carlo Pepé had returned to Venice full of schemes for that revolution which he now regarded as imminent. The alliance between Italy and Prussia was already discussed. Those Italians who were most eager said that it was a thing done, and no Italian was more eager than Carlo Pepé. And it was believed at this time, and more thoroughly believed in Italy than elsewhere, that Austria and Prussia would certainly go to war. Now, if ever, Italy must do something for herself.

Carlo Pepé was in this mood, full of these things,

when he sat down to breakfast at Bauer's with his friend Captain von Vincke.

"Von Vincke," he said, "in three months time you will be out of Venice."

"Shall I?" said the other; "and where shall I be?"

"In Vienna, as I hope; or at Berlin if you can get there. But you will not be here, or in the Quadrilatere, unless you are left behind as a prisoner."

The captain went on for awhile cutting his meat and drinking his wine, before he made any reply to this. And Pepé said more of the same kind, expressing strongly his opinion that the empire of the Austrians in Venice was at an end. Then the captain wiped his moustaches carefully with his napkin, and did speak.

"Carlo, my friend," he said, "you are rash to say all this."

"Why rash?" said Carlo; "you and I understand each other."

"Just so, my friend; but we do not know how far that long-eared waiter may understand either of us."

"The waiter has heard nothing, and I do not care if he did."

"And beyond that," continued the captain, 'you make a difficulty for me. What am I to say when you tell me these things? That you should have one political opinion and I another is natural. The question between us, in an abstract point of view, I can discuss with you willingly. The possibility of Venice contending with Austria I could discuss, if no such rebellion were imminent. But when you tell me that it is imminent, that it is already here, I cannot discuss it."

" It is imminent," said Carlo.

" So be it," said Von Vincke.

And then they finished their breakfast in silence. All this was very unfortunate for our friend the captain, who had come to Bauer's with the intention of speaking on quite another subject. His friend Pepé had evidently taken what he had said in a bad spirit, and was angry with him. Nevertheless, as he had told Nina and her mother that he would declare his purpose to Carlo on this morning, he must do it. He was not a man to be frightened out of his purpose by his friend's ill-humour.

" Will you come into the piazza, and smoke a cigar?" said Von Vincke, feeling that he could begin upon the other subject better as soon as the scene should be changed.

" Why not let me have my cigar and coffee here?" said Carlo.

"Because I have something to say which I can say better walking than sitting. Come along."

Then they paid the bill and left the house, and walked in silence through the narrow ways to the piazza. Von Vincke said no word till he found himself in the broad passage leading into the great square. Then he put his hand through the other's arm and told his tale at once.

"Carlo," said he, "I love your sister, and would have her for my wife. Will you consent?"

"By the body of Bacchus, what is this you say?" said the other, drawing his arm away, and looking up into the German's face.

"Simply that she has consented and your mother. Are you willing that I should be your brother?"

"This is madness," said Carlo Pepé.

"On their part, you mean?"

"Yes, and on yours. Were there nothing else to prevent it, how could there be marriage between us when this war is coming?"

"I do not believe in the war; that is, I do not believe in war between us and Italy. No war can affect you here in Venice. If there is to be a war in which I shall be concerned, I'm quite willing to wait till it be over."

"You understand nothing about it," said Carlo, after a pause; "nothing! You are in the dark altogether. How should it not be so, when those who are over you never tell you anything? No, I will not consent. It is a thing out of the question."

"Do you think that I am personally unfit to be your sister's husband?"

"Not personally, but politically and nationally. You are not one of us; and now, at this moment, any attempt at close union between an Austrian and a Venetian must be ruinous. Von Vincke, I am heartily sorry for this. I blame the women, and not you."

Then Carlo Pepé went home, and there was a rough scene between him and his mother, and a scene still rougher between him and his sister.

And in these interviews he told something, though not the whole of the truth as to the engagements into which he had entered. That he was to be the officer second in command in a regiment of Venetian volunteers, of those volunteers whom it was hoped that Garibaldi would lead to victory in the coming war, he did not tell them; but he did make them understand that when the struggle came he would be away from Venice, and would take a part in it.

"And how am I to do this," he said, "if you here are

joined hand and heart to an Austrian? A house divided against itself must fall."

Let the reader understand that Nina Pepé, in spite of her love and of her lover, was as good an Italian as her brother, and that their mother was equally firm in her political desires and national antipathies. Where would you have found the Venetian, man or woman, who did not detest Austrian rule, and look forward to the good day coming when Venice should be a city of Italia?

The Signora and Nina had indeed, some six months before this, been much stronger in their hatred of all things German, than had the son and brother. It had been his liberal feeling, his declaration that even a German might be good, which had induced them to allow this Austrian to come among them.

Then the man and the soldier had been two; and Von Vincke had himself shown tendencies so strongly at variance with those of his comrades that he had disarmed their fears. He had read Italian, and condescended to speak it; he knew the old history of their once great city, and would listen to them when they talked of their old doges. He loved their churches, and their palaces, and their pictures. Gradually he had come to love Nina Pepé with all his heart, and Nina loved him too with all her heart.

But when her brother spoke to her and to her mother with more than his customary vehemence of what was due from them to their country, of the debt which certainly should be paid by him, of obligations to him from which they could not free themselves; and told them also, that by that time six months not an Austrian would be found in Venice, they trembled and believed him, and Nina felt that her love would not run smooth.

"You must be with us or against us," said Carlo.

"Why then did you bring him here?" Nina replied.

"Am I to suppose that you cannot see a man without falling in love with him?"

"Carlo, that is unkind, almost unbrotherly. Was he not your friend, and were not you the first to tell us how good he is? And he is good; no man can be better."

"He is an honest young man," said the Signora.

"He is Austrian to the backbone," said Carlo.

"Of course he is," said Nina. "What should he be?"

"And will you be Austrian?" her brother asked.

"Not if I must be an enemy of Italy," Nina said. "If an Austrian may be a friend to Italy, then I will be an Austrian. I wish to be Hubert's wife. Of course I shall be an Austrian if he is my husband."

"Then I trust that you may never be his wife," said Carlo.

By the middle of May Carlo Pepé and Captain von Vincke had absolutely quarrelled. They did not speak, and Von Vincke had been ordered by the brother not to show himself at the house in the Campo San Luca.

Every German in Venice had now become more Austrian than before, and every Venetian more Italian. Even our friend the captain had come to believe in the war.

Not only Venice but Italy was in earnest, and Captain von Vincke foresaw, or thought that he foresaw, that a time of wretched misery was coming upon that devoted town. He would never give up Nina, but perhaps it might be well that he should cease to press his suit till he might be enabled to do so with something of the éclat of Austrian success.

And now at last it became necessary that the two women should be told of Carlo's plans, for Carlo was going to leave Venice till the war should be over and he could re-enter the city as an Italian should enter a city of his own.

"Oh! my son, my son," said the mother; "why should it be you?"

" Many must go, mother. Why not I as well as another ? "

" In other houses there are fathers ; and in othe
families more sons than one."

"The time has come, mother, in which no woman
should grudge either husband or son to the cause. But
the thing is settled. I am already second colonel in a
regiment which will serve with Garibaldi. You would
not ask me to desert my colours ? "

There was nothing further to be said. The Signora
threw herself on her son's neck and wept, and both
mother and sister felt that their Carlo was already a
second Garibaldi. When a man is a hero to women,
they will always obey him. What could Nina do at
such a time, but promise that she would not see Hubert
von Vincke during his absence. Then there was a com-
pact made between the brother and sister.

During three weeks past, that is, since the breakfast at
Bauer's, Nina had seen Hubert von Vincke but once,
and had then seen him in the presence of her mother
and brother. He had come in one evening in the old
way, before the quarrel, to take his coffee, and had been
received, as heretofore, as a friend, Nina sitting very
silent during the evening, but with a gracious silence ;
and after that the mother had signified to the lover that

he had better come no more for the present. He therefore came no more.

I think it is the fact that love, though no doubt it
may run as strong with an Italian or with an Austrian as
it does with us English, is not allowed to run with so un-
controllable a stream. Young lovers, and especially
young women, are more subject to control, and are less
inclined to imagine that all things should go as they
would have them. Nina, when she was made to understand that the war was come, that her brother was
leaving her and her mother and Venice, that he might
fight for them, that an Austrain soldier must for the time
be regarded as an enemy in that house, resolved with a
slow, melancholy firmness that she would accept the circumstances of her destiny.

"If I fall," said Carlo, "you must then manage for
yourself. I would not wish to bind you after my death."

"Do not talk like that, Carlo."

"Nay, my child, but I must talk like that; and it is at
least well that we should understand each other. I know
that you will keep your promise to me."

"Yes," said Nina; "I will keep my promise."

"Till I come back, or till I be dead, you will not
again see Captain von Vincke; or till the cause be
gained."

"I will not see him, Carlo, till you come back, or till the cause be gained."

"Or till I be dead. Say it after me."

"Or till you be dead, if I must say it."

But there was a clause in the contract that she was to see her lover once before her brother left them. She had acknowledged the propriety of her brother's be-hests, backed as they came to be at last by their mother; but she declared through it all that she had done no wrong, and that she would not be treated as though she were an offender. She would see her lover and tell him what she pleased. She would obey her brother, but she would see her lover first. Indeed, she would make no promise of obedience at all, would promise disobedience instead, unless she were allowed to see him. She would herself write to him and bid him come.

This privilege was at last acceded to her, and Captain von Vincke was summoned to the Campo San Luca. The morning sitting-room of the Signora Pepé was up two pairs of stairs, and the stairs were not paved as are the stairs of the palaces in Venice. But the room was large and lofty, and seemed to be larger than its size from the very small amount of furniture which it con-tained. The floor was of hard, polished cement, which looked like variegated marble, and the amount of carpet upon it was about four yards long, and was extended simply beneath the two chairs in which sat habitually the Signora and her daughter. There were two large mirrors and a large gold clock, and a large table and a small table, a small sofa and six chairs, and that was all. In England the room would have received ten times as much furniture, or it would not have been furnished at all. And there were in it no more than two small books, belonging both to Nina, for the Signora read but little. In England, in such a sitting-room, tables, various tables, would have been strewed with books; but then, perhaps, Nina Pepé's eye required the comfort of no other volumes than those she was actually using.

Nina was alone in the room when her lover came to her. There had been a question whether her mother should or should not be present; but Nina had been imperative, and she received him alone.

"It is to bid you good-bye, Hubert," she said, as she got up and touched his hand,—just touched his hand.

"Not for long, my Nina."

"Who can say for how long, now that the war is upon us? As far as I can see, it will be for very long. It is better that you should know it all. For myself, I think, I fear that it will be for ever."

"For ever! why for ever?"

"Because I cannot marry an enemy of Italy. I do not think that we can ever succeed."

"You can never succeed."

"Then I can never be your wife. It is so, Hubert; I see that it must be so. The loss is to me, not to you."

"No, no—no. The loss is to me,—to me."

"You have your profession. You are a soldier. I am nothing."

"You are all in all to me."

"I can be nothing, I shall be nothing, unless I am your wife. Think how I must long for that which you say is so impossible. I do long for it; I shall long for it. Oh, Hubert! go and lose your cause: let our men have their Venice. Then come to me, and your country shall be my country, and your people my people."

As she said this she gently laid her hand upon his arm, and the touch of her fingers thrilled through his whole frame. He put out his arms as though to grasp her in his embrace.

"No, Hubert—no; that must not be till Venice is our own."

"I wish it were," he said; "but it will never be so. You may make me a traitor in heart, but that will not drive out fifty thousand troops from the fortresses."

"I do not understand these things, Hubert, and I have felt your country's power to be so strong, that I cannot now doubt it."

"It is absurd to doubt it."

"But yet they say that we shall succeed."

"It is impossible. Even though Prussia should be able to stand against us, we should not leave Venetia. We shall never leave the fortresses."

"Then, my love, we may say farewell for ever. I will not forget you. I will never be false to you. But we must part."

He stood there arguing with her, and she argued with him, but they always came round to the same point. There was to be the war, and she would not become the wife of her brother's enemy. She had sworn, she said, and she would keep her word. When his arguments became stronger than hers, she threw herself back upon her plighted word.

"I have said it, and I must not depart from it. I have told him that my love for you should be eternal, and I tell you the same. I told him that I would see you no more, and I can only tell you so also."

He could ask her no questions as to the cause of her resolution, because he could not make enquiries as to her brother's purpose. He knew that Carlo was at work for the Venetian cause; or, at least, he thought that he knew it. But it was essential for his comfort that he should really know as little of this as might be possible. That Carlo Pepé was coming and going in the service of the cause he could not but surmise; but should authenticated information reach him as to whither Carlo went, and how he came, it might become his duty to put a stop to Carlo's comings and Carlo's goings. On this matter, therefore, he said nothing, but merely shook his head, and smiled with a melancholy smile when she spoke of the future struggle. "And now, Hubert, you must go. I was determined that I would see you, that I might tell you that I would be true to you."

"What good will be such truth?"

"Nay: it is for you to say that. I ask you for no pledge."

"I shall love no other woman. I would if I could. I would if I could—to-morrow."

"Let us have our own, and then come and love me. Or you need not come. I will go to you, though it be to the furthest end of Galicia. Do not look like that at me. You should be proud when I tell you that I love you. No, you shall not kiss me. No man shall ever kiss me till Venice is our own. There, I have sworn it. Should that time come, and should a certain Austrian gentleman care for Italian kisses then, he will know where to seek for them. God bless you now, and go."

She made her way to the door and opened it, and there was nothing for him but that he must go. He touched her hand once more as he went, but there was no other word spoken between them.

"Mother," she said, when she found herself again with the Signora, "my little dream of life is over. It has been very short."

"Nay, my child, life is long for you yet. There will be many dreams, and much of reality."

"I do not complain of Carlo," Nina continued. "He is sacrificing much, perhaps everything, for Venice. And why should his sacrifice be greater than mine? But I feel it to be severe,—very severe. Why did he bring him here if he felt thus?"

June came, that month of June that was to be so fatal to Italian glory, and so fraught with success for the Italian cause, and Carlo Pepé was again away.

Those who knew nothing of his doings, knew only that he had gone to Verona—on matters of law. Those who were really acquainted with the circumstances of his present life were aware that he had made his way out of Verona, and that he was already with his volunteers near the lakes, waiting for Garibaldi, who was then expected from Caprera. For some weeks to come, for some months probably, during the war, perhaps, the two women in the Campo San Luca would know nothing of the whereabouts or of the fate of him whom they loved. He had gone to risk all for the cause, and they too must be content to risk all in remaining desolate at home without the comfort of his presence ;—and she also, without the sweeter comfort of that other presence.

It is thus that women fight their battles. In these days men by hundreds were making their way out of Venice, and by thousands out of the province of Venetia, and the Austrians were endeavouring in vain to stop the emigration. Some few were caught, and kept in prison ; and many Austrian threats were uttered against those who should prove themselves to be insubordinate. But it is difficult for a garrison to watch a whole people, and very difficult indeed when there is a war on hand.

It at last became a fact, that any man from the province could go and become a volunteer under Garibaldi if he pleased, and very many did go. History will say that they were successful,—but their success certainly was not glorious.

It was in the month of June that all the battles of that short war were fought. Nothing will ever be said or sung in story to the honour of the volunteers who served in that campaign with Garibaldi, amidst the mountains of the Southern Tyrol; but nowhere, probably, during the war, was there so much continued fighting, or an equal amount endured of the hardships of military life.

The task they had before them, of driving the Austrians from the fortresses amidst their own mountains, was an impossible one, impossible even had Garibaldi been supplied with ordinary military equipments,—but ridiculously impossible for him in all the nakedness in which he was sent. Nothing was done to enable him to succeed. That he should be successful was neither intended nor desired. He was, in fact, then, as he has been always, since the days in which he gave Naples to Italy,—simply a stumbling-block in the way of the king, of the king's ministers, and of the king's generals. "There is that Garibaldi again, — with volunteers flocking to him by thousands : — what shall we do to rid ourselves of Garibaldi and his volunteers? How shall we dispose of them?" That has been the feeling of those in power in Italy,—and not unnaturally their feeling,—with regard to Garibaldi. A man so honest, so brave, so patriotic, so popular, and so impracticable, cannot but have been a trouble to them. And here he was with twenty-five thousand volunteers, all armed after a fashion, all supplied, at least, with a red shirt. What should be done with

Garibaldi and his army? So they sent him away up into the mountains, where his game of play might at any rate detain him for some weeks; and in the meantime everything might get itself arranged by the benevolent and omnipotent interference of the emperor.

Things did get themselves arranged while Garibaldi was up among the mountains, kicking with unarmed toes against Austrian pricks—with sad detriment to his feet. Things did get themselves arranged very much to the advantage of Venetia, but not exactly by the interference of the emperor.

The facts of the war became known more slowly in Venice than they did in Florence, in Paris, or in London. That the battle of Custozza had been fought and lost by the Italian troops was known. And then it was known that the battle of Lissa also had been fought and lost by Italian ships. But it was not known, till the autumn was near at hand, that Venetia had, in fact, been surrendered. There were rumours, but men in Venice doubted these rumours; and women, who knew that their husbands had been beaten, could not believe that success was to be the result of such calamities.

There were weeks in which came no news from Carlo Pepé to the women in the Campo San Luca, and then came simply tidings that he had been wounded.

"I shall see my son never again," said the widow in her ecstasy of misery.

And Nina was able to talk to her mother only of Carlo. Of Hubert von Vincke she spoke not then a word. But she repeated to herself over and over again the last promise she had given him. She had sent him away from her, and now she knew nothing of his whereabouts. That he would be fighting she presumed. She had heard that most of the soldiers from Venice had gone to the fortresses. He, too, might be wounded,—might be dead. If alive at the end of the war, he would hardly return to her after what had passed between them. But if he did not come back no lover should ever take a kiss from her lips.

Then there was the long truce, and a letter from Carlo reached Venice. His wound had been slight, but he had been very hungry. He wrote in great anger, abusing, not the Austrians, but the Italians. There had been treachery, and the Italian general-in-chief had been the head of the traitors. The king was a traitor! The emperor was a traitor! All concerned were traitors, but yet Venetia was to be surrendered to Italy.

I think that the two ladies in the Campo San Luca never really believed that this would be so until they received that angry letter from Carlo.

"When I may get home, I cannot tell," he said. "I hardly care to return, and I shall remain with the General as long as he may wish to have anyone remaining with him. But you may be sure that I shall never go soldiering again. Venetia, may, perhaps, prosper, and become a part of Italy; but there will be no glory for us. Italy has been allowed to do nothing for herself." The mother and sister endeavoured to feel some sympathy for the young soldier who spoke so sadly of his own career, but they could hardly be unhappy because his fighting was over and the cause was won.

The cause was won. Gradually there came to be no doubt about that.

It was now September, and as yet it had not come to pass that shop-windows were filled with wonderful portraits of Victor Emmanuel and Garibaldi, cheek by jowl —they being the two men who at that moment were perhaps, in all Italy, the most antagonistic to each other; nor were there as yet fifty different new journals cried day and night under the arcades of the Grand Piazza, all advocating the cause of Italy, one and indivisible, as there came to be a month afterwards; but still it was known that Austria was to cede Venetia, and that Venice would henceforth be a city of Italy. This was known; and it was also known in the Campo San Luca that Carlo Pepé, though very hungry up among the mountains, was still safe.

Then Nina thought that the time had come in which it would become her to speak of her lover. "Mother," she said, "I must know something of Hubert."

"But how, Nina? how will you learn? Will you not wait till Carlo comes back?"

"No," she said. "I cannot wait longer. I have kept my promise. Venice is no longer Austrian, and I will seek him. I have kept my word to Carlo, and now I will keep my word to Hubert."

But how to seek him? The widow, urged by her daughter, went out and asked at barrack doors; but new regiments had come and gone, and everything was in confusion. It was supposed that any officer of artillery who had been in Venice and had left it during the war must be in one of the four fortresses.

"Mother," she said, "I shall go to Verona."

And to Verona she went, all alone, in search of her lover. At that time the Austrians still maintained a sort of rule in the province; and there were still current orders against private travelling, orders that passports should be investigated, orders that the communication with the four fortresses should be specially guarded; but there was an intense desire on the part of the Austrians themselves that the orders should be regarded as little as possible. They had to go, and the more quietly they went the better. Why should they care now who passed hither and thither? It must be confessed on their behalf that in their surrender of Venetia they gave as little trouble as it was possible in them to cause.

The chief obstruction to Nina's journey she experienced in the Campo San Luca itself. But in spite of her mother, in spite of the not yet defunct Austrian mandates, she did make her way to Verona. "As I was true in giving him up," she said to herself, "so will I be true in clinging to him."

Even in Verona her task was not easy, but she did at last find all that she sought. Captain von Vincke had been in command of a battery at Custozza, and was now lying wounded in an Austrian hospital. Nina contrived to see an old gray-haired surgeon before she saw Hubert himself. Captain von Vincke had been terribly mauled; so the surgeon told her; his left arm had been amputated, and—and—and——

It seemed as though wounds had been showered on him. The surgeon did not think that his patient would die; but he did think that he must be left in Verona when the Austrians were marched out of the fortress. "Can he not be taken to Venice?" said Nina Pepé.

At last she found herself by her lover's bedside ; but with her there were two hospital attendants, both of them worn-out Austrian soldiers, — and there was also there the gray-haired surgeon. How was she to tell her love, all that she had in her heart, before such witnesses ? The surgeon was the first to speak. " Here is your friend, captain," he said ; but as he spoke in German Nina did not understand him.

" Is it really you, Nina ? " said her lover. " I could hardly believe that you should be in Verona."

" Of course it is I. Who could have so much business to be in Verona as I have ? Of course I am here."

" But,—but—what has brought you here, Nina ? "

" If you do not know I cannot tell you."

" And Carlo ? "

" Carlo is still with the general ; but he is well."

" And the Signora ? "

" She also is well ; well, but not easy in mind while I am here."

" And when do you return ? "

" Nay ; I cannot tell you that. It may be to-day. It may be to-morrow. It depends not on myself at all."

He spoke not a word of love to her then, nor she to

him, unless there was love in such greeting as has been here repeated. Indeed, it was not till after that first interview that he fully understood that she had made her journey to Verona, solely in quest of him. The words between them for the first day or two were very tame, as though neither had full confidence in the other ; and she had taken her place as nurse by his side, as a sister might have done by a brother, and was established in her work,—nay, had nearly completed her work, before there came to be any full understanding between them. More than once she had told herself that she would go back to Venice and let there be an end of it. "The great work of the war," she said to herself, "has so filled his mind, that the idleness of his days in Venice and all that he did then, are forgotten. If so, my presence here is surely a sore burden to him, and I will go." But she could not now leave him without a word of farewell. "Hubert," she said, for she had called him Hubert when she first came to his bedside, as though she had been his sister, "I think I must return now to Venice. My mother will be lonely without me."

At that moment it appeared almost miraculous to her that she should be sitting there by his bedside, that she should have loved him, that she should have had the courage to leave her home and seek him after the war, that she should have found him, and that she should now be about to leave him, almost without a word between them.

"She must be very lonely," said the wounded man.

"And you, I think, are stronger than you were?"

"For me, I am strong enough. I have lost my arm, and I shall carry this gaping scar athwart my face to the grave, as my cross of honour won in the Italian war; but otherwise I shall soon be well."

"It is a fair cross of honour."

"Yes; they cannot rob us of our wounds when our service is over. And so you will go, Signorina?"

"Yes; I will go. Why should I remain here? I will go, and Carlo will return, and I will tend upon him. Carlo also was wounded."

"But you have told me that he is well again."

"Nevertheless, he will value the comfort of a woman's care after his sufferings. May I say farewell to you now, my friend?" And she put her hand down upon the bed so that he might reach it. She had been with him for days, and there had been no word of love. It had seemed as though he had understood nothing of what she had done in coming to him; that he had failed altogether in feeling that she had come as a wife goes to a husband. She had made a mistake in this journey, and must now rectify her error with as much of dignity as might be left to her.

He took her hand in his, and held it for a moment before he answered her. "Nina," he said, "why did you come hither?"

"Why did I come?"

"Why are you here in Verona, while your mother is alone in Venice?"

"I had business here; a matter of some moment. It is finished now, and I shall return."

"Was it other business than to sit at my bedside?"

She paused a moment before she answered him.

"Yes," she said; "it was other business than that."

"And you have succeeded?"

"No; I have failed."

He still held her hand; and she, though she was thus fencing with him, answering him with equivoques, felt that at last there was coming from him some word which would at least leave her no longer in doubt.

"And I too, have I failed?" he said. "When I left Venice I told myself heartily that I had failed."

"You told yourself, then," said she, "that Venetia never would be ceded. You know that I would not triumph over you, now that your cause has been lost. We Italians have not much cause for triumphing."

"You will admit always that the fortresses have not been taken from us," said the sore-hearted soldier.

"Certainly we shall admit that."

"And my own fortress,—the stronghold that I thought I had made altogether mine,—is that, too, lost for ever to the poor German?"

"You speak in riddles, Captain von Vincke," she said.

She had now taken back her hand; but she was sitting quietly by his bedside, and made no sign of leaving him.

"Nina," he said, "Nina,—my own Nina. In losing a single share of Venice,—one soldier's share of the province,—shall I have gained all the world for myself? Nina, tell me truly, what brought you to Verona?"

She knelt slowly down by his bedside, and again taking his one hand in hers, pressed it first to her lips and then to her bosom. "It was an unmaidenly purpose," she said. "I came to find the man I loved."

"But you said you had failed?"

"And I now say that I have succeeded. Do you not know that success in great matters always trembles in the balance before it turns the beam, thinking, fearing, all but knowing that failure has weighed down the scale?"

" But now—— ? "

" Now I am sure that—Venice has been won."

It was three months after this, and half of December had passed away, and all Venetia had in truth been ceded, and Victor Emmanuel had made his entry into Venice and exit out of it, with as little of real triumph as ever attended a king's progress through a new province, and the Austrian army had moved itself off very quietly, and the city had become as thoroughly Italian as Florence itself, and was in a way to be equally discontented, when a party of four, two ladies and two gentlemen, sat down to breakfast in the Hôtel Bauer.

The ladies were the Signora Pepé and her daughter, and the men were Carlo Pepé and his brother-in-law, Hubert von Vincke. It was but a poor fête, this family breakfast at an obscure inn, but it was intended as a gala feast to mark the last day of Nina's Italian life.

To-morrow, very early in the morning, she was to leave Venice for Trieste,—so early that it would be necessary that she should be on board this very night.

My child," said the Signora, " do not say so ; you will never cease to be Italian. Surely, Hubert, she may still call herself Venetian ? "

" Mother," she said, " I love a losing cause. I will be Austrian now. I told him that he could not have both. If he kept his Venice, he could not have me; but as he has lost his province, he shall have his wife entirely."

"I told him that it was fated that he should lose Venetia," said Carlo, "but he would never believe me."

"Because I knew how true were our soldiers," said Hubert, "and could not understand how false were our statesmen."

"See how he regrets it," said Nina; "what he has lost, and what he has won, will, together, break his heart for him."

"Nina," he said, "I learned this morning in the city, that I shall be the last Austrian soldier to leave Venice, and I hold that of all who have entered it, and all who have left it, I am the most successful and the most triumphant."

MISS OPHELIA GLEDD.

MISS OPHELIA GLEDD.

HO can say what is a lady? My intelligent and well-bred reader of either sex will at once declare that he and she knows very well who is a lady. So, I hope, do I. But the present question goes further than that. What is it, and whence does it come? Education does not give it, nor intelligence, nor birth, not even the highest. The thing, which in its presence or absence is so well known and understood, may be wanting to the most polished manners, to the sweetest disposition, to the truest heart. There are thousands among us who know it at a glance, and recognise its presence from the sound of a dozen words, but there is not one among us who can tell us what it is.

Miss Ophelia Gledd was a young lady of Boston, Massachusetts, and I should be glad to know whether in the estimation of my countrymen and countrywomen she is to be esteemed a lady.

An Englishman, even of the best class, is often at a loss to judge of the "ladyship" of a foreigner, unless he has really lived in foreign cities and foreign society; but I do not know that he is ever so much puzzled in this matter by any nationality as he is by the American.

American women speak his own language, read his own literature, and in many respects think his own thoughts; but there have crept into American society so many little social ways at variance with our social ways, there have been wafted thither so many social atoms which there fit into their places, but which with us would clog the wheels, that the words, and habits, and social carriage, of an American woman of the best class, too often offend the taste of an Englishman; as do, quite as strongly, those of the Englishwoman offend the American.

There are those who declare that there are no American ladies; but these are people who would probably declare the same of the French and the Italians, if the languages of France and Italy were as familiar to their ears as is the language of the States. They mean that American women do not grow up to be English ladies,—

not bethinking themselves that such a growth was hardly to be expected. Now I will tell my story, and ask my readers to answer this question, — Was Miss Ophelia Gledd a lady?

When I knew her she was at any rate great in the society of Boston, Massachusetts, in which city she had been as well known for the last four or five years as the yellow dome of the State House. She was as pure and perfect a specimen of a Yankee girl as ever it was my fortune to know.

Standing about five feet eight, she seemed to be very tall, because she always carried herself at her full height. She was thin too, and rather narrower at the shoulders than the strictest rules of symmetry would have made her. Her waist was very slight; so much so, that to the eye it would seem that some unjust and injurious force had created its slender compass; but I have fair ground for stating my belief that no such force had been employed. But yet, though she was slight and thin, and even narrow, there was a vivacity and quickness about all her movements, and an easiness in her mode of moving which made it impossible to deny to her the merit of a pleasing figure.

No man would, I think, at first sight, declare her to be pretty, and certainly no woman would do so; and yet

I have seldom known a face in the close presence of which it was more gratifying to sit, and talk, and listen. Her brown hair was always brushed close off from her forehead. Her brow was high, and her face narrow and thin; but that face was ever bright with motion, and her clear, deep, gray eyes, full of life and light, were always ready for some combat or some enterprise. Her nose and mouth were the best features in her face, and her teeth were perfect,—miracles of perfection; but her lips were too thin for feminine beauty; and indeed such personal charms as she had were not the charms which men love most,—sweet changing colour, soft full flowing lines of grace, and womanly gentleness in every movement. Ophelia Gledd had none of these. She was hard and sharp in shape, of a good brown steady colour, hard and sharp also in her gait; with no full flowing lines, with no softness; but she was bright as burnished steel.

And yet she was the belle of Boston. I do not know that any man of Boston,—or any stranger knowing Boston, would have ever declared that she was the prettiest girl in the city; but this was certain almost to all,—that she received more of that admiration which is generally given to beauty than did any other lady there; and that the upper social world of Boston had become so used to her appearance, such as it was, that no one ever seemed to question the fact of her being a beauty. She had been passed as a beauty by examiners whose certificate in that matter was held to be good, and had received high rank as a beauty in the drawing-rooms at Boston.

The fact was never questioned now, unless by some passing stranger who would be told in flat terms that he was wrong.

"Yes, Sir; you'll find you're wrong; you'll find you aire, if you'll bide here awhile."

I did bide there awhile, and did find that I was wrong. Before I left I was prepared to allow that Miss Ophelia Gledd was a beauty. And moreover, which was more singular, all the women allowed it.

Ophelia Gledd, though the belle of Boston, was not hated by the other belles. The female feeling with regard to her was, I think, this, that the time had arrived in which she should choose her husband and settle down, so as to leave room for others less attractive than herself.

When I knew her she was very fond of men's society; but I doubt if anyone could fairly say that Miss Gledd ever flirted. In the proper sense of the word she certainly never flirted. Interesting conversations with interesting young men at which none but themselves were present she had by the dozen. It was as common for her to walk up and down Beacon Street,—the parade of Boston,

—with young Jones, or Smith, or more probably with young Mr. Optimus M. Opie, or young Mr. Hannibal H. Hoskins, as it is for our young Joneses, and young Smiths, and young Hoskinses, to saunter out together.

That is the way of the country, and no one took wider advantage of the ways of her own country than did Miss Ophelia Gledd. She told young men also when to call upon her, if she liked them; and in seeking or in avoiding their society, did very much as she pleased.

But these practices are right or wrong, not in accordance with a fixed rule of morality prevailing over all the earth,—such a rule, for instance, as that which orders men not to steal; but they are right or wrong according to the usages of the country in which they are practised.

In Boston it is right that Miss Ophelia Gledd should walk up Beacon Street with Hannibal Hoskins the morning after she has met him at a ball, and that she should invite him to call upon her at twelve o'clock on the following day.

She had certainly a nasal twang in speaking. Before my intercourse with her was over, her voice had become pleasant in my ears, and it may be that that nasal twang which had at first been so detestable to me, had recommended itself to my sense of hearing. At different periods of my life I have learned to love an Irish brogue and a northern burr.

Be that as it may, I must acknowledge that Miss Ophelia Gledd spoke with a certain nasal twang. But then such is the manner of speech at Boston; and she only did that which the Joneses and Smiths, the Opies and Hoskinses, were doing around her.

Ophelia Gledd's mother was, for a living being, the nearest thing to a nonentity that I ever met. Whether within her own house in Chesnut Street she exerted herself in her domestic duties and held authority over her maidens I cannot say, but neither in her dining parlour nor in her drawing-room did she hold any authority. Indeed, throughout the house, Ophelia was paramount, and it seemed as though her mother could not venture on a hint in opposition to her daughter's behests.

Mrs. Gledd never went out, but her daughter frequented all balls, dinners, and assemblies, which she chose to honour. To all these she went alone, and had done since she was eighteen years of age. She went also to lectures, to meetings of wise men, for which the Western Athens is much noted, to political debates, and wherever her enterprising heart and enquiring head chose to carry her. But her mother never went anywhere; and it always seemed to me that Mrs. Gledd's intercourse with her domestics must have been nearer, closer, and almost dearer to her, than any that she could have with her daughter.

Mr. Gledd had been a merchant all his life. When Ophelia Gledd first came before the Boston world he had been a rich merchant; and as she was an only child she had opened her campaign with all the advantages which attach to an heiress. But now, in these days, Mr. Gledd was known to be a merchant without riches. He still kept the same house, and lived apparently as he had always lived; but the world knew that he had been a broken merchant and was now again struggling. That Miss Gledd felt the disadvantage of this no one can, I suppose, doubt. But she never showed that she felt it. She spoke openly of her father's poverty as of a thing that was known, and of her own. Where she had been exigeant before, she was exigeant now. Those she disliked when rich she disliked now that she was poor. Where she had been patronising before, she patronised now. Where she had loved, she still loved. In former days she had a carriage, and now she had none. Where she had worn silk, she now wore cotton. In her gloves, her laces, her little belongings, there was all the difference which money makes or the want of money; but in her manner there was none.

Nor was there any difference in the manner of others to her. The loss of wealth seemed to entail on Miss Gledd no other discomfort than the actual want of those things which hard money buys. To go in a coach might have been a luxury to her, and that she had lost; but she had lost none of her ascendency, none of her position, none of her sovereignty.

I remember well where, when, and how, I first met Miss Gledd. At that time her father's fortune was probably already gone, but if so, she did not then know that it was gone.

It was in winter,—towards the end of winter,—when the passion for sleighing became ecstatic. I expect all my readers to know that sleighing is the grand winter amusement of Boston. And indeed it is not bad fun. There is the fashionable course for sleighing, — the Brighton Road,—and along that you drive, seated among furs, with a young lady beside you if you can get one to trust you; your horse or horses carry little bells, which add to the charms; the motion is rapid and pleasant, and, which is the great thing, you see and are seen by everybody. Of course it is expedient that the frost should be sound and perfect, so that the sleigh should run over a dry, smooth surface. But as the season draws to an end, and when sleighing intimacies have become close and warm, the horses are made to travel through slush and wet, and the scene becomes one of peril and discomfort, though one also of excitement, and not unfrequently of love.

Sleighing was fairly over at the time of which I now speak, so that the Brighton Road was deserted in its slush and sloppiness. Nevertheless, there was a possibility of sleighing; and as I was a stranger newly arrived, a young friend of mine took me, or rather allowed me to take him out, so that the glory of the charioteer might be mine.

"I guess we're not alone," said he, after we had passed the bridge out of the town. "There's young Hoskins with Pheely Gledd just ahead of us."

That was the first I had ever heard of Ophelia, and then as I pushed along after her, instigated by a foolish Briton's ambition to pass the Yankee whip, I did hear a good deal about her; and in addition to what has already been told, I then heard that this Mr. Hannibal Hoskins, to pass whom on the road was now my only earthly desire, was Miss Gledd's professed admirer; in point of fact, that it was known to all Boston that he had offered his hand to her more than once already

"She has accepted him now, at any rate," said I, looking at their close contiguity on the sleigh before me. But my friend explained to me that such was by no means probable; that Miss Gledd had twenty hangers-on of the same description, with any one of whom she might be seen sleighing, walking, or dancing; but that no argument as to any further purpose on her part was to be deduced from any such practice. "Our girls," said my friend, "don't go about tied to their mothers' aprons, as girls do in the old country. Our free institutions," &c., &c. I confessed my blunder, and acknowledged that a wide and perhaps salutary latitude was allowed to the feminine creation on his side of the Atlantic. But, do what I would, I couldn't pass Hannibal Hoskins. Whether he guessed that I was an ambitious Englishman, or whether he had a general dislike to be passed on the road, I don't know; but he raised his whip to his horses and went away from us suddenly and very quickly through the slush. The snow was half gone, and hard ridges of it remained across the road, so that his sleigh was bumped about most uncomfortably. I soon saw that his horses were running away, and that Hannibal Hoskins was in a fix. He was standing up, pulling at them with all his strength and weight, and the carriage was yawing about and across the road in a manner that made us fear it would go to pieces. Miss Ophelia Gledd, however, kept her seat, and there was no shrieking. In about five minutes they were well planted into a ditch, and we were alongside of them.

"You fixed that pretty straight, Hoskins," said my friend.

"Darn them for horses," said Hoskins, as he wiped the perspiration from his brow and looked down upon the fiercest of the quadrupeds, sprawling up to his withers in the snow. Then he turned to Miss Gledd, who was endeavouring to unroll herself from her furs.

"Oh, Miss Gledd, I am so sorry. What am I to say?"

"You'd better say that the horses ran away, I think," said Miss Gledd. Then she stepped carefully out, on to a buffalo-robe, and moved across from that, quite dry-footed, on to our sleigh. As my friend and Hoskins were very intimate, and could, as I thought, get on very well by themselves with the débris in the ditch, I offered to drive Miss Gledd back to town. She looked at me with eyes which gave me, as I thought, no peculiar thanks, and then remarked that she had come out with Mr. Hoskins, and that she would go back with him.

"Oh, don't mind me," said Hoskins, who was at that time up to his middle in snow.

"Ah, but I do mind you," said Ophelia. "Don't you think we could go back and send some people to help these gentlemen?"

It was the coolest proposition that I had ever heard, but in two minutes Miss Gledd was putting it into execution. Hannibal Hoskins was driving her back in the sleigh which I had hired, and I was left with my friend to extricate those other two brutes from the ditch.

"That's so like Pheely Gledd," said my friend. "She always has her own way."

Then it was that I questioned Miss Gledd's beauty, and was told that before long I should find myself to be wrong. I had almost acknowledged myself to be wrong before that night was over.

I was at a tea-party that same evening at which Miss Gledd was present;—it was called a tea-party, though I saw no tea. I did, however, see a large hot supper, and a very large assortment of long-necked bottles. I was standing rather listlessly near the door, being short of acquaintance, when a young Yankee dandy, with a very stiff neck, informed me that Miss Gledd wanted to speak to me. Having given me this intimation he took himself off, with an air of disgust, among the long-necked bottles.

"Mr. Green," she said,—I had just been introduced to her as she was being whisked away by Hoskins in my sleigh—"Mr. Green, I believe I owe you an apology. When I took your sleigh from you I didn't know you were a Britisher,—I didn't, indeed."

I was a little nettled, and endeavoured to explain to her that an Englishman would be just as ready to give up his carriage to a lady as any American.

"Oh, dear, yes; of course," she said. "I didn't mean that; and now I've put my foot into it worse than ever; I thought you were at home here, and knew our ways, and if so you wouldn't mind being left with a broken sleigh."

I told her that I didn't mind it. That what I had minded was the being robbed of the privilege of driving her home, which I had thought to be justly mine.

"Yes," said she, "and I was to leave my friend in the ditch! That's what I never do. You didn't suffer any disgrace by remaining there till the men came."

"I didn't remain there till any men came. I got it out and drove it home."

"What a wonderful man! But then you're English. However, you can understand that if I had left my driver he would have been disgraced. If ever I go out anywhere with you, Mr. Green, I'll come home with you. At any rate it sha'n't be my fault if I don't." After that I couldn't be angry with her, and so we became great friends.

Shortly afterwards the crash came; but Miss Gledd seemed to disregard the crash altogether, and held her own in Boston. As far as I could see there were just as many men desirous of marrying her as ever, and among the number Hannibal H. Hoskins was certainly no defaulter.

My acquaintance with Boston had become intimate; but, after awhile, I went away for twelve months, and when I returned, Miss Gledd was still Miss Gledd. "And what of Hoskins?" I said to my friend,—the same friend who had been with me in the sleighing expedition.

"He's just on the old tack. I believe he proposes once a-year regularly. But they say now that she's going to marry an Englishman."

It was not long before I had an opportunity of renewing my friendship with Miss Gledd,—for our acquaintance had latterly amounted to a friendship,—and of seeing the Englishman with her. As it happened, he also was a friend of my own,—an old friend, and the last man in the world whom I should have picked out as a husband for Ophelia. He was a literary man of some mark, fifteen years her senior, very sedate in his habits, not much given to love-making, and possessed of a small fortune sufficient for his own wants, but not sufficient to enable him to marry with what he would consider comfort. Such was Mr. Pryor, and I was given to understand that Mr

Pryor was a suppliant at the feet of Ophelia. He was a suppliant, too, with so much hope, that Hannibal Hoskins and the other suitors were up in arms against him. I saw them together at some evening assembly, and on the next morning I chanced to be in Miss Gledd's drawing-room. On my entrance there were others there, but the first moment that we were alone, she turned round sharp upon me with a question,—

"You know your countryman, Mr. Pryor; what sort of a man is he?"

"But you know him also," I answered. "If the rumours in Boston are true, he is already a favourite in Chesnut Street."

"Well, then, for once in a way the rumours in Boston are true, for he is a favourite. But that is no reason you shouldn't tell me what sort of a man he is. You've known him these ten years."

"Pretty nearly twenty," I said. I had known him ten or twelve.

"Ah," said she, "you want to make him out to be older than he is. I knew his age to-day."

"And does he know yours?"

"He may if he wishes it. Everybody in Boston knows it,—including yourself. Now tell me; what sort of man is Mr. Pryor?"

"He is a man highly esteemed in his own country."

"So much I knew before; and he is highly esteemed here also. But I hardly understand what high estimation means in your country."

"It is much the same thing in all countries, as I take it," said I.

"There you are absolutely wrong. Here in the States, if a man be highly esteemed it amounts almost to everything; such estimation will carry him everywhere,—and will carry his wife everywhere too, so as to give her a chance of making standing ground for herself."

"But Mr. Pryor has not got a wife."

"Don't be stupid. Of course he hasn't got a wife, and of course you know what I mean.

But I did not know what she meant. I knew that she was meditating whether or no it would be good for her to become Mrs. Pryor, and that she was endeavouring to get from me some information which might assist her in coming to a decision on that matter; but I did not understand the exact gist and point of her enquiry.

"You have so many prejudices of which we know nothing," she continued. "Now don't put your back up and fight for that blessed old country of yours, as though I were attacking it."

"It is a blessed old country," said I, patriotically.

"Quite so; very blessed, and very old,—and very nice too, I'm sure. But you must admit that you have prejudices. You are very much the better, perhaps, for having them. I often wish that we had a few." Then she stopped her tongue, and asked no further question about Mr. Pryor; but it seemed to me that she wanted me to go on with the conversation.

"I hate discussing the relative merits of the two countries," said I; "and I especially hate to discuss them with you. You always begin as though you meant to be fair, and end by an amount of unfairness, that— that——"

"Which would be insolent if I were not a woman, and which is pert as I am one. That is what you mean."

"Something like it."

"And yet I love your country so dearly, that I would sooner live there than in any other land in the world, if only I thought that I could be accepted. You English people," she continued, "are certainly wanting in intelligence, or you would read in the anxiety of all we say about England how much we all think of you. What will England say of us? what will England think of us? what will England do in this or that matter as it concerns us? that is our first thought as to every matter that is of importance to us. We abuse you, and admire you. You

abuse us, and despise us. That is the difference. So
you won't tell me anything about Mr. Pryor? Well, I
sha'n't ask you again. I never again ask a favour that
has been refused." Then she turned away to some old
gentleman that was talking to her mother, and the conversation was at an end.

I must confess, that as I walked away from Chesnut
Street into Beacon Street, and across the common, my
anxiety was more keen with regard to Mr. Pryor than as
concerned Miss Gledd. He was an Englishman and an
old friend, and being also a man not much younger than
myself, he was one regarding whom I might, perhaps,
form some correct judgment as to what would and what
would not suit him. Would he do well in taking Ophelia
Gledd home to England with him as his wife? Would
she be accepted there, as she herself had phrased it,—
accepted in such fashion as to make him contented?
She was intelligent,—so intelligent that few women whom
she would meet in her proposed new country could beat
her there; she was pleasant, good-humoured, true, as I
believed; but would she be accepted in London? There
was a freedom and easiness about her, a readiness to say
anything that came into her mind, an absence of all
reticence, which would go very hard with her in London.
But I never had heard her say anything that she should

not have said. Perhaps, after all, we have got our prejudices in England. When next I met Pryor, I spoke
to him about Miss Gledd.

"The long and the short of it is," I said, "that people
say that you are going to marry her."

"What sort of people?"

"They were backing you against Hannibal Hoskins
the other night at the club, and it seemed clear that you
were the favourite."

"The vulgarity of these people surpasses anything that
I ever dreamed of," said Pryor. "That is, of some of
them. It's all very well for you to talk, but could such
a bet as that be proposed in the open room of any club
in London?"

"The clubs in London are too big, but I dare say it
might down in the country. It would be just the thing
for Little Pedlington."

"But Boston is not Little Pedlington. Boston assumes
to be the Athens of the States. I shall go home by the
first boat next month." He had said nothing to me
about Miss Gledd, but it was clear that if he went home
by the first boat next month, he would go home without
a wife; and as I certainly thought that the suggested
marriage was undesirable, I said nothing to persuade him
to remain at Boston.

It was again sleighing time, and some few days after my meeting with Pryor I was out upon the Brighton Road in the thick of the crowd. Presently I saw the hat and back of Hannibal Hoskins, and by his side was Ophelia Gledd. Now, it must be understood that Hannibal Hoskins, though he was in many respects most unlike an English gentleman, was neither a fool nor a bad fellow. A fool he certainly was not. He had read much. He could speak glibly, as is the case with all Americans. He was scientific, classical, and poetical,— probably not to any great depth. And he knew how to earn a large income with the full approbation of his fellow-citizens. I had always hated him since the day on which he had driven Miss Gledd home; but I had generally attributed my hatred to the manner in which he wore his hat on one side. I confess I had often felt amazed that Miss Gledd should have so far encouraged him. I think I may at any rate declare that he would not have been accepted in London,—not accepted for much! And yet Hannibal Hoskins was not a bad fellow. His true devotion to Ophelia Gledd proved that.

"Miss Gledd," said I, speaking to her from my sleigh, "do you remember your calamity? There is the very ditch not a hundred yards ahead of you."

"And here is the very knight that took me home in your sleigh," said she, laughing.

Hoskins sat bolt upright and took off his hat. Why he took off his hat I don't know, unless that thereby he got an opportunity of putting it on again a little more on one side.

"Mr. Hoskins would not have the goodness to upset you again, I suppose?" said I.

"No, Sir," said Hoskins; and he raised the reins and squared up his elbows, meaning to look like a knowing charioteer. "I guess we'll go back; eh, Miss Gledd?"

"I guess we will," said she. "But, Mr. Green, don't you remember that I once told you if you'd take me out, I'd be sure to come home with you? You never tried me, and I take it bad of you." So encouraged I made an engagement with her, and in two or three days' time from that I had her beside me in my sleigh on the same road.

By this time I had quite become a convert to the general opinion, and was ready to confess in any presence, that Miss Gledd was a beauty. As I started with her out of the city warmly enveloped in buffalo furs, I could not but think how nice it would be to drive on and on, so that nobody should ever catch us. There was a sense of companionship about her in which no woman that I have ever known excelled her. She had a way of adapting herself to the friend of the moment which was beyond anything winning. Her voice was decidedly very pleasant; and as to that nasal twang I am not sure that I was ever right about it. I wasn't in love with her myself, and didn't want to fall in love with her. But I felt that I should have liked to cross the Rocky Mountains with her, over to the Pacific, and to have come home round by California, Peru, and the Pampas. And for such a journey I should not at all have desired to hamper the party with the society either of Hannibal Hoskins or of Mr. Pryor! "I hope you feel that you're having your revenge," said she.

"But I don't mean to upset you."

"I almost wish you would, so as to make it even. And my poor friend Mr. Hoskins would feel himself so satisfied. He says you Englishmen are conceited about your driving."

"No doubt, he thinks we are conceited about everything."

"So you are, and so you should be. Poor Hannibal! He is wild with despair because——"

"Because what?"

"Oh, never mind. He is an excellent fellow, but I know you hate him."

"Indeed, I don't."

"Yes, you do; and so does Mr. Pryor. But he is so good! You can't either understand or appreciate the kind of goodness which our young men have. Because he pulls his hat about, and can't wear his gloves without looking stiff, you won't remember that out of his hard earnings he gives his mother and sisters everything that they want."

"I didn't know anything of his mother and sisters."

"No, of course you didn't. But you know a great deal about his hat and gloves. You are too hard, and polished, and well-mannered in England to know anything about anybody's mother or sisters, or indeed to know anything about anybody's anything. It is nothing to you whether a man be moral, or affectionate, or industrious, or good-tempered. As long as he can wear his hat properly, and speak as though nothing on the earth, or over the earth, or under the earth, could ever move him, that is sufficient."

"And yet I thought you were so fond of England?"

"So I am. I too like, — nay, love that ease of manner which you all possess and which I cannot reach."

Then there was silence between us for perhaps half a mile, and yet I was driving slow, as I did not wish to bring our journey to an end. I had fully made up my mind that it would be in every way better for my friend Pryor that he should give up all thoughts of this Western Aspasia, and yet I was anxious to talk to her about him as though such a marriage were still on the cards. It had seemed that lately she had thrown herself much into an intimacy with myself, and that she was anxious to speak openly to me if I would only allow it. But she had already declared, on a former occasion, that she would ask me no further question about Mr. Pryor. At last I plucked up courage, and put to her a direct proposition about the future tenor of her life. "After all that you have said about Mr. Hoskins, I suppose I may expect to hear that you have at last accepted him?" I could not have asked such a question of any English girl that I ever knew,—not even of my own sister in these plain terms. And yet she took it not only without anger, but even without surprise. And she answered it, as though I had asked her the most ordinary question in the world.

"I wish I had," she said. "That is, I think I wish I had. It is certainly what I ought to do."

"Then why do you not do it?"

"Ah! why do I not? Why do we not all do just what we ought to do? But why am I to be cross-questioned by you? You would not answer me a question when I asked you the other day."

"You tell me that you wish you had accepted Mr. Hoskins. Why do you not do so?" said I, continuing my cross-examination.

"Because I have a vain ambition,—a foolish ambition,—a silly, moth-like ambition,—by which, if I indulge it, I shall only burn my wings. Because I am such an utter ass that I would fain make myself an Englishwoman."

"I don't see that you need burn your wings!"

"Yes; should I go there I shall find myself to be nobody, whereas here I am in good repute. Here I could make my husband a man of mark by dint of my own power. There I doubt whether even his esteem would so shield and cover me as to make me endurable. Do you think that I do not know the difference; that I am not aware of what makes social excellence there? And yet, though I know it all, and covet it, I despise it. Social distinction with us is given on sounder terms than it is with you, and is more frequently the deserved reward of merit. Tell me; if I go to London they will ask who was my grandfather?"

"Indeed, no; they will not ask even of your father unless you speak of him."

"No; their manners are too good. But they will speak of their fathers, and how shall I talk with them? Not but what my grandfather was a good man; and you are not to suppose that I am ashamed of him because he stood in a store and sold leather with his own hands. Or rather, I am ashamed of it. I should tell my husband's old friends and my new acquaintances that it was so because I am not a coward; and yet, as I told them, I should be ashamed. His brother is what you call a baronet."

"Just so!"

"And what would the baronet's wife say to me with all my sharp Boston notions? Can't you see her looking at me over the length of the drawing-room? And can't you fancy how pert I should be, and what snappish words I should say to the she baronet? Upon the whole, don't you think I should do better with Mr. Hoskins?"

Again I sat silent for some time. She had now asked me a question to which I was bound to give her a true answer,—an answer that should be true as to herself without reference to Pryor. She was sitting back in the sleigh, tamed as it were by her own thoughts, and she had looked at me as though she had really wanted counsel. "If I am to answer you in truth——"

"You are to answer me in truth."

"Then," said I, "I can only bid you take him of the two whom you love; that is, if it be the case that you love either."

"Love!" she said.

"And if it be the case," I continued, "that you love neither, then leave them both as they are."

"I am not then to think of the man's happiness?"

"Certainly not by marrying him without affection."

"Ah! but I may regret him,—with affection."

"And for which of them do you feel affection?" I asked. And as I asked, we were already within the streets of Boston.

She again remained silent, almost till I had placed her at her own door; then she looked at me with eyes full, not only of meaning, but of love also;—with that in her eyes for which I had not hitherto given her credit.

"You know the two men," she said, "and do you ask me that?" When these words were spoken, she jumped from the sleigh, and hurried up the steps to her father's door. In very truth, the hat and gloves of Hannibal Hoskins had influenced her as they had influenced me, and they had done so although she knew how devoted he was as a son and a brother.

For a full month after that I had no further conversation with Miss Gledd or with Mr. Pryor on the subject. At this time I was living in habits of daily intimacy with Pryor, but as he did not speak to me about Ophelia, I did not often mention her name to him. I was aware that he was often with her,—or at any rate often in her company. But I did not believe that he had any daily habit of going to the house, as he would have done had he been her accepted suitor. And indeed I believed him to be a man who would be very persevering in offering his love ; but who, if persistently refused, would not probably tender it again. He still talked of returning to England, though he had fixed no day. I myself purposed doing so early in May, and used such influence as I had in endeavouring to keep him at Boston till that time. Miss Gledd, also, I constantly saw. Indeed, one could not live in the society of Boston without seeing her almost daily, and I was aware that Mr. Hoskins was frequently with her. But, as regarded her, this betokened nothing, as I have before endeavoured to explain. She never deserted a friend, and had no idea of being reserved in her manners with a man because it was reported that such man was her lover. She would be very gracious to Hannibal in Mr. Pryor's presence ; and yet it was evident, at any rate to me, that in doing so, she had no thought of grieving her English admirer.

I was one day seated in my room at the hotel when a servant brought me up a card. " Misther Hoskins; he's a waiting below, and wants to see yer honour very partickler," said the raw Irishman. Mr. Hoskins had never done me the honour of calling on me before, nor had I ever become intimate with him even at the club; but, nevertheless, as he had come to me, of course I was willing to see him, and so he was shown up into my room. When he entered, his hat was, I suppose, in his hand; but it looked as though it had been on one side of his head ·the moment before, and as though it would be on one side again the moment he left me.

"I beg your pardon, Mr. Green," said he. "Perhaps I ought not to intrude upon you here."

"No intrusion at all. Won't you take a chair, and put your hat down?" He did take a chair, but he wouldn't put his hat down. I confess that I had been actuated by a foolish desire to see it placed for a few minutes in a properly perpendicular position.

"I've just come,—I'll tell you why I've come. There are some things, Mr. Green, in which a man doesn't like to be interfered with." I could not but agree with this, but in doing so I expressed a hope that Mr. Hoskins had not been interfered with to any very disagreeable extent. "Well!" I scorn to say that the Boston dandy said "wa'all," but if this story were written by any Englishman less conscientious than myself, that latter form of letters is the one which he would adopt in his endeavour to convey the sound as uttered by Mr. Hoskins. "Well, I don't quite know about that. Now, Mr. Green, I'm not a quarrelsome man. I don't go about with six-shooters in my pocket, and I don't want to fight, nohow, if I can help it."

In answer to this I was obliged to tell him that I sincerely hoped that he would not have to fight; but that if fighting became necessary to him, I trusted that his fighting propensities would not be directed against any friend of mine.

"We don't do much in that way on our side of the water," said I.

"I am well aware of that," said he. "I don't want any one to teach me what are usages of genteel life in England. I was there the whole fall, two years ago."

"As regards myself," said I, "I don't think much good was ever done by duelling."

"That depends, Sir, on how things eventuate. But, Mr. Green, satisfaction of that description is not what I desiderate on the present occasion. I wish to know whether Mr. Pryor is, or is not, engaged to marry Miss Ophelia Gledd."

"If he is, Mr. Hoskins, I don't know it."

"But, Sir, you are his friend."

This I admitted, but again assured Mr. Hoskins that I knew nothing of any such engagement. He pleaded also that I was her friend as well as his. This, too, I admitted, but again declared that from neither side had I been made aware of the fact of any such engagement.

"Then, Mr. Green," said he, "may I ask you for your own private opinion?"

Upon the whole I was inclined to think that he might not, and so I told him in what most courteous words I could find for the occasion. His bust at first grew very long and stiff, and his hat became more and still more sloped as he held it. I began to fear, that though he might not have a six-shooter in his pocket, he had nevertheless some kind of pistol in his thoughts. At last he started up on his feet and confronted me, as I thought, with a look of great anger. But his words when they came were no longer angry.

"Mr. Green," said he, "if you knew all that I've done to get that girl!"

My heart was instantly softened to him.

"For aught that I know," said I, "you may have her this moment for asking."

"No," said he, "no." His voice was very melancholy, and as he spoke he looked into his sloping hat. "No; I've just come from Chesnut Street, and I think she's rather more turned against me than ever."

He was a tall man, good-looking after a fashion, dark, with thick black shiny hair, and huge bold moustachios. I myself do not like his style of appearance, but he certainly had a manly bearing. And in the society of Boston generally he was regarded as a stout fellow, well able to hold his own; as a man, by no means soft, or green, or feminine. And yet now, in the presence of me, a stranger to him, he was almost crying about his lady love. In England no man tells another that he has been rejected; but then in England so few men tell to others anything of their real feeling. As Ophelia had said to me, we are hard and polished, and nobody knows anything about anybody's anything. What could I say to him? I did say something. I went so far as to assure him that I had heard Miss Gledd speak of him in the highest language; and at last perhaps I hinted,—though I don't think I did quite hint it,—that

if Pryor were out of the way, Hoskins might find the
lady more kind. He soon became quite confidential, as
though I were his bosom friend. He perceived, I think,
that I was not anxious that Pryor should carry off the
prize, and he wished me to teach Pryor that the prize
was not such a prize as would suit him.

"She's the very girl for Boston," he said, in his
energy; "but, I put it to you, Mr. Green, she hasn't
the gait of going that would suit London."

Whether her gait of going would or would not suit
our metropolis, I did not undertake to say in the presence of Mr. Hoskins, but I did at last say that I would
speak to Pryor, so that the field might be left open for
others if he had no intention of running for the cup
himself.

I could not but be taken, and indeed charmed, by the
honest strength of affection which Hannibal Hoskins felt
for the object of his adoration. He had come into my
room determined to display himself as a man of will, of
courage, and of fashion. But he had broken down in all
that, under his extreme desire to obtain assistance in
getting the one thing which he wanted. When he
parted with me he shook hands almost boisterously,
while he offered me most exuberant thanks. And yet I
had not suggested that I could do anything for him. I

did think that Ophelia Gledd would accept his offer as soon as Pryor was gone; but I had not told him that I thought so.

About two days afterwards I had a very long and a very serious conversation with Pryor, and at that time I do not think that he had made up his mind as to what he intended to do. He was the very opposite to Hoskins in all his ways and all his moods. There was not only no swagger with him, but a propriety and quiescence of demeanour the very opposite to swagger. In conversation his most violent opposition was conveyed by a smile. He displayed no other energy than what might be shown in the slight curl of his upper lip. If he reproved you he did it by silence. There could be no greater contrast than that between him and Hoskins, and there could be no doubt which man would recommend himself most to our English world by his gait and demeanour. But I think there may be a doubt as to which was the best man, and a doubt also as to which would make the best husband. That my friend was not then engaged to Miss Gledd I did learn,—but I learned nothing further,—except this, that he would take his departure with me the first week in May, unless anything special occurred to keep him in Boston.

It was some time early in April that I got a note from Miss Gledd, asking me to call on her.

"Come at once," she said, "as I want your advice above all things." And she signed herself, "Yours in all truth, O. G."

I had had many notes from her, but none written in this strain; and therefore, feeling that there was some circumstance to justify such instant notice, I got up and went to her then, at ten o'clock in the morning. She jumped up to meet me, giving me both her hands.

"Oh, Mr. Green," she said to me, "I'm so glad you have come to me. It is all over."

"What is over?" said I.

"My chance of escape from the she baronet. I gave in last night. Pray tell me that I was right. Yet I want you to tell me the truth. And yet, above all things, you must not tell me that I have been wrong."

"Then you have accepted Mr. Pryor?"

"I could not help it," she said. "The temptation was too much for me. I love the very cut of his coat, the turn of his lip, the tone of his voice. The very sound which he makes as he closes the door behind him is too much for me. I believe that I ought to have let him go, —but I could not do it."

"And what will Mr. Hoskins do?"

"I wrote to him immediately and told him everything. Of course I had John's leave for doing so."

This calling of my sedate friend by the name of John was, to my feeling, a most wonderful breaking down of all proprieties.

"I told him the exact truth. This morning I got an answer from him saying that he should visit Russia. I am so sorry because of his mother and sisters."

"And when is it to be?"

"Oh, at once, immediately. So John says. When we resolve on doing these things here, on taking the plunge, we never stand shilly-shallying on the brink as your girls do in England. And that is one reason why I have sent for you. You must promise to go over with us. Do you know I am half afraid of him,—much more afraid of him than I am of you."

They were to be married very early in May, and of course I promised to put off my return for a week or two to suit them.

"And then for the she baronet," she said, "and for all the terrible grandeur of London!"

When I endeavoured to explain to her that she would encounter no great grandeur, she very quickly corrected me.

"It is not grandeur of that sort, but the grandeur of

coldness that I mean. I fear that I shall not do for them. But, Mr. Green, I must tell you one thing. I have not cut off from myself all means of retreat."

"Why, what do you mean? You have resolved to marry him."

"Yes, I have promised to do so; but I did not promise till he had said that if I could not be made to suit his people in Old England, he would return here with me and teach himself to suit my people in New England. The task will be very much easier."

They were married in Boston, not without some considerable splendour of ceremony, as far as the splendour of Boston went. She was so unusual a favourite that everyone wished to be at her wedding, and she had no idea of giving herself airs and denying her friends a favour. She was married with much *éclat*, and, as far as I could judge, seemed to enjoy the marriage herself.

Now comes the question; will she or will she not be received in London as a lady,—as such a lady as my friend Pryor might have been expected to take for his wife?

THE JOURNEY TO
PANAMA.

THE JOURNEY TO PANAMA.

HERE is perhaps no form of life in which
men and women of the present day frequently
find themselves for a time existing, so unlike
their customary conventional life, as that experienced on
board the large ocean steamers. On the voyages so
made, separate friendships are formed and separate
enmities are endured. Certain lines of temporary politics
are originated by the energetic, and intrigues, generally
innocent in their conclusions, are carried on with the
keenest spirit by those to whom excitement is necessary;
whereas the idle and torpid sink into insignificance and
general contempt,—as it is their lot to do on board ship
as in other places. But the enjoyments and activity of
such a life do not display themselves till the third or
fourth day of the voyage. The men and women at first

regard each with distrust and illconcealed dislike. They by no means anticipate the strong feelings which are to arise, and look forward to ten, fifteen, or twenty days of gloom or sea-sickness. Sea-sickness disappears, as a general condition, on the evening of the second day, and the gloom about noon on the fourth. Then the men begin to think that the women are not so ugly, vulgar, and insipid; and the women drop their monosyllables, discontinue the close adherence to their own niches, which they first observed, and become affable, perhaps even beyond their wont on shore. And alliances spring up among the men themselves. On their first entrance to this new world, they generally regard each other with marked aversion, each thinking that those nearest to him are low fellows, or perhaps worse; but by the fourth day, if not sooner, every man has his two or three intimate friends with whom he talks and smokes, and to whom he communicates those peculiar politics, and perhaps intrigues, of his own voyage. The female friendships are slower in their growth, for the suspicion of women is perhaps stronger than that of men; but when grown they also are stronger, and exhibit themselves sometimes in instances of feminine affection.

But the most remarkable alliances are those made between gentlemen and ladies. This is a matter of course on board ship quite as much as on shore, and it is of such an alliance that the present tale purports to tell the story. Such friendships, though they may be very dear, can seldom be very lasting. Though they may be full of sweet romance,—for people become very romantic among the discomforts of a sea-voyage—such romance is generally short-lived and delusive, and occasionally is dangerous.

There are several of these great ocean routes, of which by the common consent, as it seems, of the world, England is the centre. There is the Great Eastern line, running from Southampton across the Bay of Biscay and up the Mediterranean. It crosses the Isthmus of Suez, and branches away to Australia, to India, to Ceylon, and to China. There is the great American line, traversing the Atlantic to New York and Boston with the regularity of clockwork. The voyage here is so much a matter of everyday routine, that romance has become scarce upon the route. There are one or two other North American lines, perhaps open to the same objection. Then there is the line of packets to the African coast,—very romantic as I am given to understand; and there is the great West-Indian route, to which the present little history is attached,—great, not on account of our poor West Indian Islands, which cannot at the present moment make any-

:hing great, but because it spreads itself out from thence to Mexico and Cuba, to Guiana and the republics of Grenada and Venezuela, to Central America, the Isthmus of Panama, and from thence to California, Vancouver's Island, Peru and Chili.

It may be imagined how various are the tribes which leave the shores of Great Britain by this route. There are Frenchmen for the French sugar islands, as a rule not very romantic; there are old Spaniards, Spaniards of Spain, seeking to renew their fortunes amidst the ruins of their former empire; and new Spaniards—Spaniards, that is, of the American republics, who speak Spanish, but are unlike the Don both in manners and physiognomy,—men and women with a touch perhaps of Indian blood, very keen after dollars, and not much given to the graces of life. There are Dutchmen too, and Danes, going out to their own islands. There are citizens of the stars and stripes, who find their way everywhere— and, alas! perhaps, now also citizens of the new Southern flag, with the palmetto leaf. And there are Englishmen of every shade and class, and Englishwomen also.

It is constantly the case that women are doomed to make the long voyage alone. Some are going out to join their husbands, some to find a husband, some few peradventure to leave a husband. Girls who have been

educated at home in England, return to their distant
homes across the Atlantic, and others follow their relatives who have gone before them as pioneers into a
strange land. It must not be supposed that these
females absolutely embark in solitude, putting their feet
upon the deck without the aid of any friendly arm. They
are generally consigned to some prudent elder, and
appear as they first show themselves on the ship to
belong to a party. But as often as not their real loneliness shows itself after awhile. The prudent elder is not,
perhaps, congenial; and by the evening of the fourth day a
new friendship is created.

Not a long time since such a friendship was formed
under the circumstances which I am now about to tell.
A young man—not very young, for he had turned his
thirtieth year, but still a young man—left Southampton
by one of the large West Indian steam-boats, purposing
to pass over the Isthmus of Panama, and thence up to
California and Vancouver's Island. It would be too long
to tell the cause which led to these distant voyagings.
Suffice to say, it was not the accursed hunger after gold
—*auri sacra fames*—which so took him; nor had he any
purpose of permanently settling himself in those distant
colonies of Great Britain. He was at the time a widower,
and perhaps his home was bitter to him without the

young wife whom he had early lost. As he stepped on
board he was accompanied by a gentleman some fifteen
years his senior, who was to be the companion of his
sleeping apartment as far as St. Thomas. The two had
been introduced to each other, and therefore appeared
as friends on board the "Serrapiqui;" but their acquaintance had commenced in Southampton, and my hero,
Ralph Forrest by name, was alone in the world as he
stood looking over the side of the ship at the retreating
shores of Hampshire.

"I say, old fellow, we'd better see about our places,"
said his new friend, slapping him on his back. Mr.
Matthew Morris was an old traveller, and knew how to
become intimate with his temporary allies at a very short
notice. A long course of travelling had knocked all
bashfulness out of him, and when he had a mind to do
so he could make any man his brother in half an hour,
and any woman his sister in ten minutes.

"Places? what places?" said Forrest.

"A pretty fellow you are to go to California. If you
don't look sharper than that you'll get little to drink
and nothing to eat till you come back again. Don't
you know the ship's as full as ever she can hold?"

Forrest acknowledged that she was full.

"There are places at table for about a hundred, and

we have a hundred and thirty on board. As a matter of course those who don't look sharp will have to scramble. However, I've put cards on the plates and taken the seats. We had better go down and see that none of these Spanish fellows oust us." So Forrest descended after his friend, and found that the long tables were already nearly full of expectant dinner-eaters. When he took his place a future neighbour informed him, not in the most gracious voice, that he was encroaching on a lady's seat; and when he immediately attempted to leave that which he held, Mr. Matthew Morris forbade him to do so. Thus a little contest arose, which, however, happily was brought to a close without bloodshed. The lady was not present at the moment, and the grumpy gentleman agreed to secure for himself a vacant seat on the other side.

For the first three days the lady did not show herself. The grumpy gentleman, who, as Forrest afterwards understood, was the owner of stores in Bridge-town, Barbadoes, had other ladies with him also. First came forth his daughter, creeping down to dinner on the second day, declaring that she would be unable to eat a morsel, and prophesying that she would be forced to retire in five minutes. On this occasion, however, she agreeably surprised herself and her friends. Then came the grumpy gentleman's wife, and the grumpy gentleman's wife's brother — on whose constitution the sea seemed to have an effect quite as violent as on that of the ladies; and lastly, at breakfast on the fourth day, appeared Miss Viner, and took her place as Mr. Forrest's neighbour at his right hand.

He had seen her before on deck, as she lay on one of the benches, vainly endeavouring to make herself comfortable, and had remarked to his companion that she was very unattractive and almost ugly. Dear young ladies, it is thus that men always speak of you when they first see you on board ship! She was disconsolate, sick at heart, and ill at ease in body also. She did not like the sea. She did not in the least like the grumpy gentleman in whose hands she was placed; she did not, especially, like the grumpy gentleman's wife; and she altogether hated the grumpy gentleman's daughter, who was the partner of her berth. That young lady had been very sick and very selfish; and Miss Viner had been very sick also, and perhaps equally selfish. They might have been angels, and yet have hated each other under such circumstances. It was no wonder that Mr. Forrest thought her ugly as she twisted herself about on the broad bench, vainly striving to be comfortable.

"She'll brighten up wonderfully before we're in the tropics," said Mr. Morris. "And you won't find her so bad then. It's she that is to sit next you."

"Heaven forbid!" said Forrest. But, nevertheless, he was very civil to her when she did come down on the fourth morning. On board the West Indian Packets, the world goes down to its meals. In crossing between Liverpool and the States, the world goes up to them.

Miss Viner was by no means a very young lady. She also was nearly thirty. In guessing her age on board the ship the ladies said that she was thirty-six, but the ladies were wrong. She was an Irish woman, and when seen on shore, in her natural state, and with all her wits about her, was by no means without attraction. She was bright-eyed, with a clear dark skin, and good teeth; her hair was of a dark brown and glossy, and there was a touch of feeling and also of humour about her mouth, which would have saved her from Mr. Forrest's ill-considered criticism, had he first met her under more favourable circumstances.

"You'll see a good deal of her," Mr. Morris said to him, as they began to prepare themselves for luncheon, by a cigar immediately after breakfast. "She's going across the isthmus and down to Peru."

" How on earth do you know ? "

" I pretty well know where they're all going by this time. Old Grumpy told me so. He has her in tow as far as St. Thomas, but knows nothing about her. He gives her up there to the captain. You'll have a chance of making yourself very agreeable as you run across with her to the Spanish main."

Mr. Forrest replied that he did not suppose he should know her much better than he did now; but he made no further remark as to her ugliness. She had spoken a word or two to him at table, and he had seen that her eyes were bright, and had found that her tone was sweet.

" I also am going to Panama," he said to her, on the morning of the fifth day. The weather at that time was very fine, and the October sun as it shone on them, while hour by hour they made more towards the South, was pleasant and genial. The big ship lay almost without motion on the bosom of the Atlantic, as she was driven through the waters at the rate of twelve miles per hour. All was as pleasant now as things can be on board a ship, and Forrest had forgotten that Miss Viner had seemed so ugly to him when he first saw her. At this moment, as he spoke to her, they were running through the Azores, and he had been assisting her with his field-glass to look for orange-groves on their slop-ing shores, orange-groves they had not succeeded in seeing, but their failure had not disturbed their peace.

"I also am going to Panama."

"Are you, indeed?" said she. "Then I shall not feel so terribly alone and disconsolate. I have been looking forward with such fear to that journey on from St. Thomas."

"You shall not be disconsolate, if I can help it," he said. "I am not much of a traveller myself, but what I can do I will."

"Oh, thank, you!"

"It is a pity Mr. Morris is not going on with you. He's at home everywhere, and knows the way across the isthmus as well as he does down Regent Street."

"Your friend, you mean!"

"My friend, if you call him so; and indeed I hope he is, for I like him. But I don't know more of him than I do of you. I also am as much alone as you are. Per-haps more so."

"But," she said, "a man never suffers in being alone."

"Oh! does he not? Don't think me uncivil, Miss Viner, if I say that you may be mistaken in that. You feel your own shoe when it pinches, but do not realise the tight boot of your neighbour."

"Perhaps not," said she. And then there was a pause, during which she pretended to look again for the orange-groves. "But there are worse things, Mr. Forrest, than being alone in the world. It is often a woman's lot to wish that she were let alone." Then she left him and retreated to the side of the grumpy gentleman's wife, feeling perhaps that it might be prudent to discontinue a conversation, which, seeing that Mr. Forrest was quite a stranger to her, was becoming particular.

"You're getting on famously, my dear," said the lady from Barbadoes.

"Pretty well, thank you, Ma'am," said Miss Viner.

"Mr. Forrest seems to be making himself quite agreeable. I tell Amelia,"—Amelia was the young lady to whom in their joint cabin Miss Viner could not reconcile herself,—"I tell Amelia that she is wrong not to receive attentions from gentlemen on board ship. If it is not carried too far," and she put great emphasis on the "too far,"—"I see no harm in it."

"Nor I, either," said Miss Viner.

"But then Amelia is so particular."

"The best way is to take such things as they come," said Miss Viner, — perhaps meaning that such things never did come in the way of Amelia. "If a lady knows what she is about she need not fear a gentleman's attentions."

" That's just what I tell Amelia; but then, my dear, she has not had so much experience as you and I."

Such being the amenities which passed between Miss Viner and the prudent lady who had her in charge, it was not wonderful that the former should feel ill at ease with her own " party," as the family of the Grumpy Barbadian was generally considered to be by those on board.

" You're getting along like a house on fire with Miss Viner," said Matthew Morris, to his young friend.

' Not much fire I can assure you," said Forrest.

"She aint so ugly as you thought her ? "

" Ugly !—no ! she's not ugly. I don't think I ever said she was. But she is nothing particular as regards beauty."

" No ; she won't be lovely for the next three days to come, I dare say. By the time you reach Panama, she'll be all that is perfect in woman. I know how these things go."

" Those sort of things don't go at all quickly with me," said Forrest, gravely. " Miss Viner is a very interesting young woman, and as it seems that her route and mine will be together for some time, it is well that we should be civil to each other. And the more so, seeing that the people she is with are not congenial to her.

"No; they are not. There is no young man with them. I generally observe that on board ship no one is congenial to unmarried ladies except unmarried men. It is a recognised nautical rule. Uncommon hot, isn't it? We are beginning to feel the tropical air. I shall go and cool myself with a cigar in the fiddle." The "fiddle" is a certain part of the ship devoted to smoking, and thither Mr. Morris betook himself. Forrest, however, did not accompany him, but going forward into the bow of the vessel, threw himself along upon the sail, and meditated on the loneliness of his life.

On board the Serrapiqui, the upper tier of cabins opened on to a long gallery, which ran round that part of the ship, immediately over the saloon, so that from thence a pleasant inspection could be made of the viands as they were being placed on the tables. The custom on board these ships is for two bells to ring preparatory to dinner, at an interval of half an hour. At the sound of the first, ladies would go to their cabins to adjust their toilets; but as dressing for dinner is not carried to an extreme at sea, these operations are generally over before the second bell, and the lady passengers would generally assemble

in the balcony for some fifteen minutes before dinner.
At first they would stand here alone, but by degrees they
were joined by some of the more enterprising of the men,
and so at last a kind of little drawing-room was formed.
The cabins of Miss Viner's party opened to one side of
this gallery, and that of Mr. Morris and Forrest on the
other. Hitherto Forrest had been contented to remain
on his own side, occasionally throwing a word across to
the ladies on the other; but on this day he boldly went
over as soon as he had washed his hands and took his
place between Amelia and Miss Viner.

"We are dreadfully crowded here, Ma'am," said
Amelia.

"Yes, my dear, we are," said her mother. "But what
can one do?"

"There's plenty of room in the ladies' cabin," said Miss
Viner. Now if there be one place on board a ship more
distasteful to ladies than another, it is the ladies' cabin.
Mr. Forrest stood his ground, but it may be doubted
whether he would have done so had he fully understood
all that Amelia had intended.

Then the last bell rang. Mr. Grumpy gave his arm
to Miss Grumpy. The brother-in-law gave his arm to
Amelia, and Forrest did the same to Miss Viner. She
hesitated for a moment, and then took it, and by so

doing transferred herself mentally and bodily from the charge of the prudent and married Mr. Grumpy to that of the perhaps imprudent, and certainly unmarried Mr. Forrest. She was wrong. A kind-hearted, motherly old lady from Jamaica, who had seen it all, knew that she was wrong, and wished that she could tell her so. But there are things of this sort which kind-hearted old ladies cannot find it in their hearts to say. After all, it was only for the voyage. Perhaps Miss Viner was imprudent, but who in Peru would be the wiser? Perhaps, indeed, it was the world that was wrong, and not Miss Viner. "*Honi soit qui mal y pense*," she said to herself, as she took his arm, and leaning on it, felt that she was no longer so lonely as she had been. On that day she allowed him to give her a glass of wine out of his decanter. "Hadn't you better take mine, Miss Viner?" asked Mr. Grumpy, in a loud voice, but before he could be answered, the deed had been done.

"Don't go too fast, old fellow," Morris said to our hero that night, as they were walking the deck together before they turned in. "One gets into a hobble in such matters before one knows where one is."

"I don't think I have anything particular to fear," said Forrest.

I dare say not, only keep your eyes open. Such

haridans as Mrs. Grumpy allow any latitude to their tongues out in these diggings. You'll find that unpleasant tidings will be put on board the ship going down to Panama, and everybody's eye will be upon you." So warned, Mr. Forrest did put himself on his guard, and the next day and a half his intimacy with Miss Viner progressed but little. These were, probably, the dullest hours that he had on the whole voyage.

Miss Viner saw this and drew back. On the afternoon of that second day she walked a turn or two on deck with the weak brother-in-law, and when Mr. Forrest came near her, she applied herself to her book. She meant no harm; but if she were not afraid of what people might say, why should he be so? So she turned her shoulder towards him at dinner, and would not drink of his cup.

"Have some of mine, Miss Viner," said Mr. Grumpy, very loudly. But on that day Miss Viner drank no wine.

The sun sets quickly as one draws near to the tropics, and the day was already gone, and the dusk had come on, when Mr. Forrest walked out upon the deck that evening a little after six. But the night was beautiful and mild, and there was a hum of many voices from the benches. He was already uncomfortable, and sore with a sense of being deserted. There was but one person on board the ship that he liked, and why should he avoid her and be avoided? He soon perceived where she was standing. The Grumpy family had a bench to themselves, and she was opposite to it, on her feet, leaning against the side of the vessel. "Will you walk this evening, Miss Viner?" he asked.

"I think not," she answered.

"Then I shall persevere in asking till you are sure. It will do you good, for I have not seen you walking all day."

"Have you not? Then I will take a turn. Oh, Mr. Forrest, if you knew what it was to have to live with such people as those." And then, out of that, on that evening, there grew up between them something like the confidence of real friendship. Things were told such as none but friends do tell to one another, and warm answering words were spoken such as the sympathy of friendship produces. Alas, they were both foolish; for friendship and sympathy should have deeper roots.

She told him all her story. She was going out to Peru to be married to a man who was nearly twenty years her senior. It was a long engagement, of ten years standing. When first made, it was made as being contingent on certain circumstances. An option of escaping from it had then been given to her, but now there was no longer an option. He was rich and she was penniless. He had even paid her passage-money and her outfit. She had not at last given way and taken these irrevocable steps till her only means of support in England had been taken from her. She had lived the last two years with a relative who was now dead. "And he also is my cousin, —a distant cousin,—you understand that."

"And do you love him ? "

"Love him! What; as you loved her whom you have lost?—as she loved you when she clung to you before she went? No; certainly not. I shall never know anything of that love."

"And is he good? "

He is a hard man. Men become hard when they deal in money as he has done. He was home five years since, and I swore to myself that I would not marry him. But his letters to me are kind."

Forrest sat silent for a minute or two, for they were up in the bow again, seated on the sail that was bound round the bowsprit, and then he answered her, "A woman should never marry a man unless she loves him."

"Ah," says she, "of course you will condemn me. That is the way in which women are always treated.

They have no choice given them, and are then scolded for choosing wrongly."

" But you might have refused him."

" No ; I could not. I cannot make you understand the whole,—how it first came about that the marriage was proposed, and agreed to by me under certain conditions. Those conditions have come about, and I am now bound to him. I have taken his money and have no escape. It is easy to say that a woman should not marry without love, as easy as it is to say that a man should not starve. But there are men who starve,—starve although they work hard."

" I did not mean to judge you, Miss Viner."

" But I judge myself, and condemn myself so often. Where should I be in half-an-hour from this if I were to throw myself forward into the sea ? I often long to do it. Don t you feel tempted sometimes to put an end to it all ? "

" The waters look cool and sweet, but I own I am afraid of the bourne beyond."

" So am I, and that fear will keep me from it."

" We are bound to bear our burden of sorrow. Mine, I know, is heavy enough."

" Yours, Mr. Forrest ! Have you not all the pleasures of memory to fall back on, and every hope for the future? What can I remember, or what can I hope? But, however, it is near eight o'clock, and they have all been at tea this hour past. What will my Cerberus say to me? I do not mind the male mouth, if only the two feminine mouths could be stopped." Then she rose and went back to the stern of the vessel; but as she slid into a seat, she saw that Mrs. Grumpy was standing over her.

From thence to St. Thomas the voyage went on in the customary manner. The sun became very powerful, and the passengers in the lower part of the ship complained loudly of having their port-holes closed. The Spaniards sat gambling in the cabin all day, and the ladies prepared for the general move which was to be made at St. Thomas. The alliance between Forrest and Miss Viner went on much the same as ever, and Mrs. Grumpy said very ill-natured things. On one occasion she ventured to lecture Miss Viner; but that lady knew how to take her own part, and Mrs. Grumpy did not get the best of it. The dangerous alliance, I have said, went on the same as ever; but it must not be supposed that either person in any way committed aught that was wrong. They sat together and talked together, each now knowing the other's circumstances; but had it not been for the prudish caution of some of the ladies there would have been nothing amiss. As it was there was not much amiss. Few of the passengers really cared whether or no Miss Viner had found an admirer. Those who were going down to Panama were mostly Spaniards, and as the great separation became nearer, people had somewhat else of which to think.

And then the separation came. They rode into that pretty harbour of St. Thomas early in the morning, and were ignorant, the most of them, that they were lying in the very worst centre of yellow fever among all those plague-spotted islands. St. Thomas is very pretty as seen from the ships ; and when that has been said, all has been said that can be said in its favour. There was a busy, bustling time of it then. One vessel after another was brought up alongside of the big ship that had come from England, and each took its separate freight of passengers and luggage. First started the boat that ran down the Leeward Islands to Demerara, taking with her Mr. Grumpy and all his family.

"Good-bye, Miss Viner," said Mrs. Grumpy. "I hope you'll get quite safely to the end of your voyage ; but do take care."

"I'm sure I hope everything will be right," said Amelia, as she absolutely kissed her enemy. It is astonishing how well young women can hate each other, and yet kiss at parting.

"As to everything being right," said Miss Viner, "that is too much to hope. But I do not know that anything is going especially wrong.—Good-bye, Sir," and then she put out her hand to Mr. Grumpy. He was at the moment leaving the ship laden with umbrellas, sticks, and coats, and was forced to put them down in order to free his hand.

"Well, good-bye," he said. "I hope you'll do, till you meet your friends at the isthmus."

"I hope I shall, Sir," she replied; and so they parted. Then the Jamaica packet started.

"I dare say we shall never see each other again," said Morris, as he shook his friend's hand heartily. "One never does. Don't interfere with the rights of that gentleman in Peru, or he might run a knife into you."

"I feel no inclination to injure him on that point."

"That's well; and now good-bye." And thus they also were parted. On the following morning the branch ship was despatched to Mexico; and then, on the afternoon of the third day, that for Colon—as we Englishmen call the town on this side of the Isthmus of Panama. Into that vessel Miss Viner and Mr. Forrest moved themselves and their effects; and now that the three-headed Cerberus was gone, she had no longer hesitated in allowing him to do for her all those little things which it is well that men should do for women when they are travelling. A woman without assistance under such circumstances is very forlorn, very apt to go to the wall, very ill able to assert her rights as to accommodation; and I think that few can blame Miss Viner for putting herself and her belongings under the care of the only person who was disposed to be kind to her.

Late in the evening the vessel steamed out of St. Thomas' harbour, and as she went Ralph Forrest and Emily Viner were standing together at the stern of the boat looking at the retreating lights of the Danish town. If there be a place on the earth's surface odious to me, it is that little Danish isle to which so many of our young seamen are sent to die,—there being no good cause whatever for such sending. But the question is one which cannot well be argued here.

"I have five more days of self and liberty left me," said Miss Viner. "That is my life's allowance."

"For Heaven's sake do not say words that are so horrible."

"But am I to lie for Heaven's sake, and say words that are false; or shall I be silent for Heaven's sake, and say nothing during these last hours that are allowed to me for speaking? It is so. To you I can say that it is so, and why should you begrudge me thé speech?"

"I would begrudge you nothing that I could do for you."

"No, you should not. Now that my incubus has gone to Barbadoes, let me be free for a day or two. What chance is there, I wonder, that the ship's machinery should all go wrong, and that we should be tossed about in the seas here for the next six months? I suppose it would be very wicked to wish it?"

"We should all be starved; that's all."

"What, with a cow on board, and a dozen live sheep, and thousands of cocks and hens! But we are to touch at Santa Martha and Cartagena. What would happen to me if I were to run away at Santa Martha?"

"I suppose I should be bound to run with you."

"Oh, of course. And therefore, as I would not wish to destroy you, I won't do it. But it would not hurt you much to be shipwrecked, and wait for the next packet."

"Miss Viner," he said after a pause,—and in the meantime he had drawn nearer to her, too near to her considering all things—"in the name of all that is good, and true, and womanly, go back to England. With your feelings, if I may judge of them by words which are spoken half in jest——"

"Mr. Forrest, there is no jest."

"With your feelings a poorhouse in England would be better than a palace in Peru."

"An English workhouse would be better, but an English poorhouse is not open to me. You do not know what it is to have friends—no, not friends, but people belonging to you—just so near as to make your respectability a matter of interest to them, but not so near that they should care for your happiness. Emily Viner married to Mr. Gorloch in Peru is put out of the way respectably. She will cause no further trouble, but her name may be mentioned in family circles without annoyance. The fact is, Mr. Forrest, that there are people who have no business to live at all."

"I would go back to England," he added, after another pause. "When you talk to me with such bitterness of five more days of living liberty you scare my very soul. Return, Miss Viner, and brave the worst. He is to meet you at Panama. Remain on this side of the isthmus, and send him word that you must return. I will be the bearer of the message."

"And shall I walk back to England?" said Miss Viner.

"I had not quite forgotten all that," he replied, very gently. "There are moments when a man may venture to propose that which under ordinary circumstances would be a liberty. Money, in a small moderate way, is not greatly an object to me. As a return for my valiant defence of you against your West Indian Cerberus, you shall allow me to arrange that with the agent at Colon."

"I do so love plain English, Mr. Forrest. You are proposing I think, to give me something about fifty guineas."

"Well, call it so if you will," said he, "if you will have plain English that is what I mean."

"So that by my journey out here, I should rob and deceive the man I do know, and also rob the man I don't know. I am afraid of that bourne beyond the waters of which we spoke; but I would rather face that than act as you suggest."

"Of the feelings between him and you, I can of course be no judge."

"No, no; you cannot. But what a beast I am not to thank you! I do thank you. That which it would be mean in me to take, it is noble, very noble, in you to offer. It is a pleasure to me—I cannot tell why—but it is a pleasure to me to have had the offer. But think of me as a sister, and you will feel that it would not be accepted ;—could not be accepted, I mean, even if I could bring myself to betray that other man."

Thus they ran across the Carribbean Sea, renewing very often such conversations as that just given. They touched at Santa Martha and Cartagena on the coast of the Spanish main, and at both places he went with her on shore. He found that she was fairly well educated, and anxious to see and to learn all that might be seen and learned in the course of her travels. On the last day, as they neared the isthmus, she became more tranquil and quiet in the expression of her feelings than before, and spoke with less of gloom than she had done.

"After all ought I not to love him ?" she said. "He is coming all the way up from Callao merely to meet me. What man would go from London to Moscow to pick up a wife ?"

"I would—and thence round the world to Moscow again—if she were the wife I wanted."

"Yes; but a wife who has never said that she loved you! It is purely a matter of convenience. Well; I have locked my big box, and I shall give the key to him before it is ever again unlocked. He has a right to it, for he has paid for nearly all that it holds."

"You look at things from such a mundane point of view."

"A woman should, or she will always be getting into difficulty. Mind, I shall introduce you to him, and tell him all that you have done for me. How you braved Cerberus and the rest of it."

"I shall certainly be glad to meet him."

"But I shall not tell him of your offer;—not yet at least. If he be good and gentle with me, I shall tell him that too after a time. I am very bad at keeping secrets, — as no doubt you have perceived. We go across the isthmus at once; do we not?"

"So the captain says."

"Look!"—and she handed him back his own field-glass. "I can see the men on the wooden platform. Yes; and I can see the smoke of an engine." And then, in little more than an hour from that time the ship had swung round on her anchor.

Colon, or Aspinwall as it should be called, is a place in itself as detestable as St. Thomas. It is not so odious to an Englishman, for it is not used by Englishmen more than is necessary. We have no great dépôt of traffic there, which we might with advantage move else-where.

Taken, however, on its own merits, Aspinwall is not a

detestable place. Luckily, however, travellers across the isthmus to the Pacific are never doomed to remain there long. If they arrive early in the day, the railway thence to Panama takes them on at once. If it be not so, they remain on board ship till the next morning. Of course it will be understood that the transit line chiefly affects Americans, as it is the highroad from New York to California.

In less than an hour from their landing, their baggage had been examined by the Custom House officers of New Grenada, and they were on the railway cars, crossing the isthmus. The officials in those out-of-the-way places always seem like apes imitating the doings of men. The officers at Aspinwall open and look at the trunks just as monkeys might do, having clearly no idea of any duty to be performed, nor any conception that goods of this or that class should not be allowed to pass. It is the thing in Europe to examine luggage going into a new country; and why should not they be as good as Europeans?

"I wonder whether he will be at the station?" she said, when the three hours of the journey had nearly passed. Forrest could perceive that her voice trembled as she spoke, and that she was becoming nervous.

"If he has already reached Panama, he will be there.

As far as I could learn the arrival up from Peru had not been telegraphed."

"Then I have another day,—perhaps two. We cannot say how many. I wish he were there. Nothing is so intolerable as suspense."

"And the box must be opened again."

When they reached the station at Panama they found that the vessel from the South American coast was in the roads, but that the passengers were not yet on shore. Forrest, therefore, took Miss Viner down to the hotel, and there remained with her, sitting next to her in the common drawing-room of the house, when she had come back from her own bed-room. It would be necessary that they should remain there four or five days, and Forrest had been quick in securing a room for her. He had assisted in taking up her luggage, had helped her in placing her big box, and had thus been recognised by the crowd in the hotel as her friend. Then came the tidings that the passengers were landing, and he became nervous as she was. "I will go down and meet him," said he, "and tell him that you are here. I shall soon find him by his name." And so he went out.

Everybody knows the scrambling manner in which passengers arrive at an hotel out of a big ship. First came two or three energetic, heated men, who, by dint of screeching and bullying, have gotten themselves first disposed. They always get the worst rooms at the inns, the housekeepers having a notion that the richest people, those with the most luggage, must be more tardy in their movements. Four or five of this nature passed by Forrest in the hall, but he was not tempted to ask questions of them. One, from his age, might have been Mr. Gorloch, but he instantly declared himself to be Count Sapparello. Then came an elderly man alone, with a small bag in his hand. He was one of those who pride themselves on going from pole to pole without encumbrance, and who will be behoved to no one for the carriage of their luggage. To him, as he was alone in the street, Forrest addressed himself. "Gorloch," said he. "Gorloch: are you a friend of his?"

"A friend of mine is so," said Forrest.

"Ah, indeed; yes," said the other. And then he hesitated. "Sir," he then said, "Mr. Gorloch died at Callao, just seven days before the ship sailed. You had better see Mr. Cox." And then the elderly man passed in with his little bag.

Mr. Gorloch was dead. "Dead!" said Forrest, to himself, as he leaned back against the wall of the hotel still standing on the street pavement. "She has come out here; and now he is gone!" And then a thousand

thoughts crowded on him. Who should tell her? And
how would she bear it? Would it in truth be a relief to
her to find that that liberty for which she had sighed had
come to her? Or now that the testing of her feelings
had come to her, would she regret the loss of home and
wealth, and such position as life in Peru would give her?
And above all would this sudden death of one who was
to have been so near to her, strike her to the heart?

But what was he to do? How was he now to show
his friendship? He was returning slowly in at the hotel
door, where crowds of men and women were now throng-
ing, when he was addressed by a middle-aged, good-
looking gentleman, who asked him whether his name was
Forrest. "I am told," said the gentleman, when Forrest
had answered him, "that you are a friend of Miss Viner's.
Have you heard the sad tidings from Callao?" It then
appeared that this gentleman had been a stranger to Mr.
Gorloch, but had undertaken to bring a letter up to Miss
Viner. This letter was handed to Mr. Forrest, and he
found himself burdened with the task of breaking the
news to his poor friend. Whatever he did do, he must
do at once, for all those who had come up by the Pacific
steamer knew the story, and it was incumbent on him
that Miss Viner should not hear the tidings in a sudden
manner and from a stranger's mouth.

He went up into the drawing-room, and found Miss Viner seated there in the midst of a crew of women. He went up to her, and taking her hand, asked her in a whisper whether she would come out with him for a moment.

"Where is he?" said she. "I know that something is the matter. What is it?"

"There is such a crowd here. Step out for a moment." And he led her away to her own room.

"Where is he?" said she. "What is the matter? He has sent to say that he no longer wants me. Tell me; am I free from him?"

"Miss Viner, you are free."

Though she had asked the question herself, she was astounded by the answer; but, nevertheless, no idea of the truth had yet come upon her. "It is so," she said. "Well, what else? Has he written? He has bought me, as he would a beast of burden, and has, I suppose, a right to treat me as he pleases."

"I have a letter; but, dear Miss Viner——"

"Well, tell me all,—out at once. Tell me everything."

"You are free, Miss Viner; but you will be cut to the heart when you learn the meaning of your freedom."

"He has lost everything in trade. He is ruined."

"Miss Viner, he is dead!"

She stood staring at him for a moment or two, as though she could not realise the information which he gave her. Then gradually she retreated to the bed, and sat upon it. "Dead, Mr. Forrest!" she said. He did not answer her, but handed her the letter, which she took and read as though it were mechanically. The letter was from Mr. Gorloch's partner, and told her everything which it was necessary that she should know.

"Shall I leave you now?" he said, when he saw that she had finished reading it.

"Leave me; yes,—no. But you had better leave me, and let me think about it. Alas me, that I should have so spoken of him!"

"But you have said nothing unkind."

"Yes; much that was unkind. But spoken words cannot be recalled. Let me be alone now, but come to me soon. There is no one else here that I can speak to."

He went out, and finding that the hotel dinner was ready, he went in and dined. Then he strolled into the town, among the hot, narrow, dilapidated streets; and then, after two hours' absence, returned to Miss Viner's room. When he knocked, she came and opened the door, and he found that the floor was strewed with clothes. "I am preparing, you see, for my return. The vessel starts back for St. Thomas the day after to-morrow "

"You are quite right to go,—to go at once. Oh, Miss Viner! Emily, now at least you must let me help you."

He had been thinking of her most during those last two hours, and her voice had become pleasant to his ears, and her eyes very bright to his sight.

"You shall help me," she said. "Are you not helping me when at such a time you come to speak to me?"

"And you will let me think that I have a right to act as your protector?"

"My protector! I do know that I want such aid as that. During the days that we are here together you shall be my friend."

"You shall not return alone. My journeys are nothing to me. Emily, I will return with you to England."

Then she rose up from her seat and spoke to him.

"Not for the world," she said. "Putting out of question the folly of your forgetting your own objects, do you think it possible that I should go with you, now that he is dead? To you I have spoken of him harshly; and now that it is my duty to mourn for him, could I do so heartily if you were with me? While he lived, it seemed to me that in those last days I had a right to speak my thoughts plainly. You and I were to part and meet no more, and I regarded us both as people apart, who for a while might drop the common usages of the world. It is so no longer. Instead of going with you farther, I must ask you to forget that we were ever together."

"Emily, I shall never forget you."

"Let your tongue forget me. I have given you no cause to speak good of me, and you will be too kind to speak evil."

After that she explained to him all that the letter had contained. The arrangements for her journey had all been made; money also had been sent to her? and Mr. Gorloch in his will had provided for her, not liberally, seeing that he was rich, but still sufficiently.

And so they parted at Panama. She would not allow him even to cross the isthmus with her, but pressed his hand warmly as he left her at the station. "God bless you!" he said. "And may God bless you, my friend!" she answered.

Thus alone she took her departure for England, and he went on his way to California.

THE END.

READ MORE IN PENGUIN

In every corner of the world, on every subject under the sun, Penguin represents quality and variety – the very best in publishing today.

For complete information about books available from Penguin – including Puffins, Penguin Classics and Arkana – and how to order them, write to us at the appropriate address below. Please note that for copyright reasons the selection of books varies from country to country.

In the United Kingdom: Please write to *Dept. JC, Penguin Books Ltd, FREEPOST, West Drayton, Middlesex UB7 OBR*

If you have any difficulty in obtaining a title, please send your order with the correct money, plus ten per cent for postage and packaging, to *PO Box No. 11, West Drayton, Middlesex UB7 OBR*

In the United States: Please write to *Penguin USA Inc., 375 Hudson Street, New York, NY 10014*

In Canada: Please write to *Penguin Books Canada Ltd, 10 Alcorn Avenue, Suite 300, Toronto, Ontario M4V 3B2*

In Australia: Please write to *Penguin Books Australia Ltd, 487 Maroondah Highway, Ringwood, Victoria 3134*

In New Zealand: Please write to *Penguin Books (NZ) Ltd,182–190 Wairau Road, Private Bag, Takapuna, Auckland 9*

In India: Please write to *Penguin Books India Pvt Ltd, 706 Eros Apartments, 56 Nehru Place, New Delhi 110 019*

In the Netherlands: Please write to *Penguin Books Netherlands B.V., Keizersgracht 231 NL–1016 DV Amsterdam*

In Germany: Please write to *Penguin Books Deutschland GmbH, Friedrichstrasse 10–12, W–6000 Frankfurt/Main 1*

In Spain: Please write to *Penguin Books S. A., C. San Bernardo 117–6° E–28015 Madrid*

In Italy: Please write to *Penguin Italia s.r.l., Via Felice Casati 20, I–20124 Milano*

In France: Please write to *Penguin France S. A., 17 rue Lejeune, F–31000 Toulouse*

In Japan: Please write to *Penguin Books Japan, Ishikiribashi Building, 2–5–4, Suido, Tokyo 112*

In Greece: Please write to *Penguin Hellas Ltd, Dimocritou 3, GR–106 71 Athens*

In South Africa: Please write to *Longman Penguin Southern Africa (Pty) Ltd, Private Bag X08, Bertsham 2013*

READ MORE IN PENGUIN

THOMAS HARDY – A SELECTION

Tess of the D'Urbervilles
Introduced by A. Alvarez and Edited by David Skilton

Tess is Hardy's most striking and tragic heroine and the character who meant most to him. In a novel full of poetry and mysterious luminous settings, he unfolds the story of his beautiful, suffering Tess with unforgettable tenderness and intensity.

The Return of the Native
Edited by George Woodcock

The Return of the Native is set in Egdon Heath whose lowering, titanic presence dominates the men and women who live on it, and whose menace and beauty Hardy so surely and superbly evokes.

Far from the Madding Crowd
Edited by Ronald Blythe

Far from the Madding Crowd, perhaps the best-known and most humorous of Hardy's novels is the product of his intimate and first-hand knowledge of the attitudes, habits, inconsistencies and idiosyncrasies of rural men and women.

Jude the Obscure
Edited by C. H. Sisson

A haunting love story, *Jude* is the most outspoken, the most powerful and the most despairing of Thomas Hardy's creations. It is also a rich source of social history, accurately reflecting the encroachment of the modern world on the rural traditions of England.

READ MORE IN PENGUIN

GEORGE ELIOT – A SELECTION

Adam Bede
Edited by Stephen Gill

The story of a beautiful country girl's seduction by the local squire and its bitter, tragic sequel is an old and familiar one which George Eliot invests with peculiar and haunting power. As Stephen Gill comments: 'Reading the novel is a process of learning simultaneously about the world of Adam Bede and the world of *Adam Bede.*'

Felix Holt
Edited with an Introduction by Peter Coveney

By contrasting the lives of two women – Mrs Transome unbending and bloodless, a woman who embodies the worst elements of the past; and Esther, who fights free of her Transome connection in order to face the future with Felix, whose politics and attitudes embody a vital, creative future – she achieves both a personal drama and political debate in a novel that is an imaginative *tour de force.*

Daniel Deronda
Edited by Barbara Hardy

With her hero, Daniel Deronda, George Eliot set out to come to terms with the position of English Jews in society. With her heroine, Gwendolen Harleth, who marries for power rather than love, she uncovered a vein in human relations that could lead, through the best intentions, only to despair.

Silas Marner
Edited by Q. D. Leavis

Marner's spiritual death and his resurrection through the child Eppie and the neighbourliness of the village community have, as Mrs Leavis points out, 'a multiple typicality'; through his case are examined the dire effects of the Industrial Revolution and the rich human possibilities of a way of life that, even in George Eliot's lifetime, was passing away.

READ MORE IN PENGUIN

CHARLES DICKENS – A SELECTION

The Old Curiosity Shop
Edited by Angus Easson with an Introduction by Malcolm Andrews

Described as a 'tragedy of sorrows', *The Old Curiosity Shop* tells of 'Little Nell' uprooted from a secure and innocent childhood and cast into a world where evil takes many shapes, the most fascinating of which is the stunted, lecherous Quilp. He is Nell's tormentor and destroyer, and it is his demonic energy that dominates the book.

Nicholas Nickleby
Edited with an Introduction by Michael Slater

The work of a young man at the height of his powers, *Nicholas Nickleby* will remain one of the touchstones of the English comic novel. Around his central story of Nicholas Nickleby and the misfortunes of his family, Dickens weaves a great gallery of comic types.

David Copperfield
Edited by Trevor Blount

Written in the form of an autobiography, it tells the story of David Copperfield, growing to maturity in the affairs of the world and the affairs of the heart – his success as an artist arising out of his sufferings and out of the lessons he derives from life.

Oliver Twist
Edited by Peter Fairclough with an Introduction by Angus Wilson

Scathing in its exposure of contemporary cruelties, always exciting, and clothed in an unforgettable atmosphere of mystery and pervasive evil, Dickens's second novel was a huge popular success, its major characters – Fagin, Bill Sykes, and the Artful Dodger – now creatures of myth.

READ MORE IN PENGUIN

JANE AUSTEN – A SELECTION

Sense and Sensibility
Edited with an Introduction by Tony Tanner

Sense and Sensibility has as its heroines two strikingly different sisters, Elinor and Marianne Dashwood. Elinor is reserved, tactful, self-controlled, Marianne impulsively emotional and demonstrative; but Jane Austen goes beyond this simple antithesis to explore with subtle precision the tension that exists in every community between the needs of the individual and the demands of society.

Pride and Prejudice
Edited with an Introduction by Tony Tanner

Much has been said of the light and sparkling side of *Pride and Prejudice* – the delicious social comedy, the unerring dialogue, the satisfying love stories and its enchanting and spirited heroine. Nonetheless, the novel is also about deeper issues in which Jane Austen demonstrates her belief that the truly civilized being maintains a proper balance between reason and energy.

Persuasion
Edited with an Introduction by D. W. Harding

Persuasion is a tale of love and marriage told with the irony, insight and just evaluation of human conduct which sets Jane Austen's novels apart. Anne Elliott and Captain Wentworth have met and separated years before. Their reunion forces a recognition of the false values that drove them apart.

Lady Susan/The Watsons/Sanditon
Edited with an Introduction by Margaret Drabble

Lady Susan is a sparkling melodrama which takes its tone from the outspoken and robust eighteenth century. *The Watsons* is a tantalizing and highly delightful story whose vitality and optimism centres on the marital prospects of the Watson sisters in a small provinicial town. *Sanditon* is set in a seaside town and its themes concern the new speculative consumer society and foreshadow the great social upheavals of the Industrial Revolution.

THE PENGUIN TROLLOPE

THE PENGUIN TROLLOPE